olicka bolicka

& Pink Bluebells

olicka bolicka

& Pink Bluebells

Best wishes

Sheila Morgan.

Oct. 09.

Sheila Morgan

y Lolfa

For my husband and daughters,
with my love and grateful thanks for all their
help, patience and encouragement.

First impression: 2009

Cover design: Alan Thomas
Cover image: Llewellyn Street, Pontygwaith by Elwyn Thomas

ISBN: 978 1 84771 095 6

Printed on acid-free and partly recycled paper
and published and bound in Wales by
Y Lolfa Cyf., Talybont, Ceredigion SY24 5AP
e-mail ylolfa@ylolfa.com
website www.ylolfa.com
tel 01970 832 304
fax 832 782

Chapter 1

The House

The girls followed excitedly behind their mother and grandmother as their father led the way from room to room of their newly rented house. They squeezed past boxes of china, stepped over rolled-up mats and lino, and bumped into various items of furniture dumped at random by the now departed van men. The sounds of their voices and footsteps ricocheted from the bare flagstoned floors to the empty corners and unadorned walls of the rooms, returning distorted and unreal to their ears.

The mother, saying nothing but looking books, swept a critical eye over everything as she went. She had given up a brand new council house on the outskirts of a South Wales town near the sea to come here to the mountains, to the back of beyond, to a house with no bathroom, no hot water, no blood-red tiles on the kitchen floor – no draining board even! Not that she was a stranger to such living conditions – she had been born and brought up in the valleys. But when you've had a taste of such luxuries, you can't help but be loath to give them up again. It's comparison that makes for dissatisfaction. It's only natural.

The Edwards family: Jim, Ivy and their two girls, Pauline and Liz, moved to Crymceynon on the second Saturday of October, 1939. It was not the best of days to move house and Ivy was not in the best of moods to cope with it all. To put it bluntly, she'd had a gutsful of moving. Jim was a collier, and colliers being traditionally and of necessity a mobile workforce, Ivy had expected and accepted, when she had married him, that they would have to move house occasionally. But this latest move was the last straw. She was convinced now that there must be gipsy blood in her husband from somewhere way back. This would make it the seventh place his 'caravan' had rested in the nine years of their married life. She was giddy, never mind their poor girls!

Chasing after work or better conditions wasn't the reason for this latest upheaval though. Oh no – it was the war. The war? Huh! Nothing had happened. Chamberlain had announced over the wireless at 11.15 on 3 September that Britain was at war with Nazi Germany; but since then? Absolutely nothing. No massed German bombers, no devastation, no roads choked with wandering refugees. Everyone, it seemed, was taking things quite calmly. Except Jim.

"Better to be safe than sorry, gel," he told her. "We're sitting targets here, see – between the docks and the munitions factory."

He always called her 'gel' when he was trying to get round her – as if she didn't know! She didn't accept there was a risk. Not yet, anyway. They could have delayed the decision a bit at least, to see how things went, instead of rushing like a bull at a gate. But it was too late now. Her beautiful little palace had already been allocated to someone else and it would be years now before they'd get another one. It was all so pointless. This war was going to fizzle out by Christmas; everybody said so. Well, nearly everybody. There were a few pessimists who said that what started with a whimper might well go out with a bang – but you always had people like that.

It was her own parents she blamed. They had fully agreed

with Jim from the start. It was her father, Albert, who had got him a job at Crymceynon Colliery and it was her mother who had got them the house by putting in a timely word with the rent man. Three working against one. She hadn't stood a snowball's chance in Hell!

Jim, looking at her now, could see by her expression – that thin line of her lips – what she was thinking about. As he mounted the creaking staircase he kept up a running commentary over his shoulder, extolling the possible virtues of the new place. He had been the first to arrive, travelling with the van while the girls and Ivy had come by train, so he'd had a few hours to pick out the more favourable aspects of the house; to prepare his defence, as it were.

"We'll be much better off up here in the mountains, gel, you'll see. Germany won't waste their bombs on places like this."

That hadn't come out the way Jim had intended and Ivy nodded grim agreement with a "Hmph!" No, she couldn't see Hitler bothering to send his aeroplanes on a special mission to wipe this place off the map either!

Jim tried a different approach: "It'll be company for you, having your mam and dad at the bottom of the next street, eh? Once Pauline starts school, you, Mam and Liz can go shopping together, take a trip into town. Right, Mam?"

"Oh, she'll soon settle down, don't worry!" said Carrie, with a dismissive wave of her hand. "You've made the right decision, Jim." She turned to Ivy. "Your father fought in the last war, don't forget. It's the men that know best at times like these. And anyway, it's not such a bad place. There's many worse, God knows!"

Carrie spoke from experience – Albert was a collier, too. She turned to the girls, took their hands and squeezed them tightly. She was obviously delighted at the prospect of her grandchildren living so close by.

"Whenever you are feeling a bit fed up, see Ivy, I can have these two pickles for you to give you a break," she said.

"Hmph!" said Ivy again. This time, the look on her face said 'chance would be a fine thing!' She knew, only too well, that as long as her mother had nine pence in her purse, she would be off out of an evening at the pictures. Carrie Thomas was a hopeless addict, hooked irrevocably on the fantasies of the film world, totally believing all that happened up there on the silver screen. Once, so carried away had she been by the plight of an actor wrongfully arrested for the murder of his wife, that she had shouted out in the dark and silence of the cinema: "But he didn't do it! He didn't do it!" Ivy, who had been with her at the time, was mortified. No, much as she loved her mother, despite her faults, she would prefer to be back in that perfect little council house on the estate with her own friends of her own age for company, thank you very much!

They were in the smaller of the two back bedrooms now, its window overlooking the flagstoned backyard and part of the garden.

"See?" said Jim, forcing enthusiasm. "There's a nice little garden here. You can't see half of it from by here mind, and it's in a bit of a mess right now, but I'll soon whip it into shape."

Ivy was looking straight ahead at the mountain facing them, bare and bleak and shrouded in thick autumn mist. Jim, following her gaze, added, "Summer will soon be here. You'll have your sweet peas and kidney beans again by then. You wait!"

Ivy didn't want to wait. She wanted to run. She walked

back onto the landing and looked down into the stairwell once more. Drab brown paint was everywhere: on the doors, skirting boards, banisters – even the three foot wide leatherette along the bottom of the passage walls was covered in it. All the paintwork had been white in her council house. Pure white.

Jim took her elbow and ushered her into the larger of the two front bedrooms.

"Plenty of room here, see, isn't there? One more room than the last house anyway," he said. At last, something in its favour! "The girls can have a room each by and by, when we can afford to get another bed and we'll still have one spare for visitors." He smiled and raised his eyebrows, before adding, "Or something!"

Ivy threw him a look but still said nothing. She looked pointedly at the peeling wallpaper, more brown paintwork and the bare floorboards, punctured with pinholes where woodworm had copiously dined. She would have woodworm in her one and only bedroom suite. Sighing, she looked out of the window at the houses opposite. It was drizzling heavily now, soaking the grey slates and grey stonework, darkening them. The rain seemed to soak up the colour till the very air took on a greyness.

I don't like it here, thought Ivy, very near to tears. I'm not going to like it and I never wanted to come here in the first place.

CHAPTER 2

The Lie of the Land

WHEN IVY AND the girls had got off the train at Crymceynon, her first impression of the place had not been favourable. Two pitheads, their huge wheels of winding gear dominating the skyline, stood about a mile and a half apart: one down the valley behind them, the other not far from the station itself. The railway sidings were choc-a-bloc with full and empty coal trucks. Varying degrees of the ubiquitous coal dust contaminated the earth beneath them, the nearby river and the roofs of the countless terrace houses.

The walk from the railway station to the house was a long and steady, though not steep, upward climb. To begin with, the road ran parallel to the river: a pitch black, boulder-strewn flow that drew the girls' eyes hypnotically downward to its surface, nine feet below them. Only tall lance-like iron railings, looking rather fragile and inadequate, stood between them and it. They gripped their mother's hands tighter. On the opposite bank rose a huge, smooth, concrete wall, interspersed with numerous oblong windows, magnifying the drop and adding to their dizziness.

"Look!" whispered Pauline to Liz in a sinister tone. "Those windows are staring at us. Like eyes. Dark, blind, staring eyes!"

Liz shivered involuntarily. She was four and seven months and lived a bit in awe of her big and clever sister, who seemed to know everything. Pauline was seven and a bit and a good reader. She would read anything and everything, from sauce-bottle labels to her mother's library books, given half a chance. She had recently read one about a haunted house. The wall was, in fact, the back of a pop factory.

The road turned at right angles to form a wide bridge over the river. They walked on, passed a wrought-iron urinal – a necessity, built as it was halfway between the Station Hotel, the Miners' Arms and the long streets of houses up ahead. There was no provision for women. Women weren't supposed to go drinking.

At the end of the bridge the road turned again, this time to the left where Toni Morelli's two shops, a fish and chip shop and a café, formed the corner. Both shops did well, especially when the crowds came out from the pictures and walked home.

"A fistful of business is worth a field full of work," Carrie had said, "and trust a foreigner to fill both fists!"

Who could resist the smell of hot, vinegary fish and chips emanating from one side of the corner, only to be bombarded by aromas of strong coffee and steam-heated pies from the other? Toni Morelli had been there for donkey's years. He was part of the scenery now.

They entered the main street. Several of the houses on both sides had shops in their front parlours, with some of their wares spilling out onto the pavements or hanging from the windows and doorways. Nearly everything could be bought here, from fly papers to zinc baths. It was busy with people to-ing and fro-ing, picking and prodding, meeting and chatting.

Halfway up the hill, Ivy called in to Powell's the paper shop and bought two comics: the *Film Fun* and the *Beano*. She wasn't keen on comics, but they would keep the girls quiet for a bit that evening. Then she crossed the road and popped into the baker's for a fresh loaf, just in case her mother had forgotten.

At a junction further along the street sat the impressive, three-storied Workmen's Hall, dominating all it surveyed. Its basement was leased to a Mr and Mrs Martin, proprietors of the ironmonger's, grocer's and post office housed there. All three establishments were known simply as 'Martin's'.

The main street carried on, just houses now, until another junction led down a hill to the left. At the bottom lay the schools, the park and the playing fields. But Ivy had had instructions from her mother to turn right at Martin's. They did so – slowing their pace to climb a short but very steep hill. At the top was the main entrance to the hall where dances and dramas were held, snooker and billiards were played, liquid refreshments were supplied for members only, and library books were borrowed. The top storey was taken over by insurance offices.

They now passed two or three individual houses, a small church and a large vicarage, before taking another left turn into a long but not-so-steep street. *Nefoedd*! thought Ivy, panting for breath. How much further? She was thinking of the weekly shopping treks. The council estate had been on a bus route and shopping had been a pure pleasure for a tuppenny ticket. But no buses ran through these streets.

A flat, horizontal terrace topped the long street and groups of children were playing whip-and-top or scotch across it, despite the cold and damp. Behind the terrace, the ground climbed upward again, but they were almost there now. On the left-hand side was the bottom of Stephen's Street and on the right, the bottom of Duke Street, where Ivy's parents lived. A narrow, black-earthed gulley separated the two rows of back gardens.

They saw Carrie at her front door, watching and waiting for them. She was like a hen on hot bricks as she set about dishing up a hot dinner for the three weary walkers.

"I hope you lot are hungry," she said. "I've enough left by here for a regiment of soldiers! Jim and me have already had ours. He's just this minute gone back over to get started."

"Mm," said Pauline, rubbing her tummy as Carrie took a big tin out of the oven. "Faggots! I love faggots and I'm starving!"

"And me," said Liz, climbing into a chair.

Carrie smiled. She wasn't worried about the girls. They would eat anything she put in front of them. But Ivy, that was different. Ivy had left home when she was fourteen to go into service in London. She had ended up being the cook in a great big house there, doing dinner parties for professional people and cooking whole salmons and pheasants and soufflés and God knows what! Carrie now had a bit of an inferiority complex as far as Ivy and cooking were concerned. She pottered about, filling the kettle and washing up the pots and pans, while keeping a surreptitious eye on her daughter and waiting for the verdict.

Ivy picked at her food, eating mechanically, her mind on other matters, till Carrie could contain herself no longer.

"Well? How is it?" she asked.

Ivy looked up absently and was momentarily puzzled by the concern on her mother's face. Then the penny dropped. She may have been preoccupied but she was not insensitive. Pretending to be cross, she said, "Oh come on, Mam! Stop fishing for compliments. You know nobody makes faggots like you do!"

Carrie beamed, completely satisfied with that.

"Yes, well, I may not go in for anything fancy, but plain cooking, well, I'll take some beating yet!"

Ivy smiled to herself. She had started her mother off now. Wait for it...

"I've told you the secret before. All they need is a cooking apple. A nice big Bramley's the best. One of those instead of those ol' lights. *Uch a fi*! I could never stomach them with lights in."

Liz looked up. Lights? How could you put lights in faggots? Her mind conjured up a picture of a daft old woman stirring tiny torch bulbs into a mucky mixture. Grown-ups talked double-dutch sometimes.

Ivy carried on with her dinner, not in the least hungry. She had lived on anxiety ever since she had started packing. But the dinner was delicious and fair play, Mam had gone to a lot of trouble making it. Now that they all had a good meal inside them, it was one less problem for her to have to deal with. She waited until her mother paused for breath in her monologue of the virtues of simple but nourishing meals, then held up her plate.

"Any chance of seconds?" she said.

CHAPTER 3

Reluctant Acceptance

HAVING FINISHED HER inspection of the upstairs of the 'new' house, Ivy now stood in the centre of the back kitchen, looking again at the big, old grate with its high wooden mantelpiece. Back to black-lead again then, she thought, and rising ashes every day. And all that brass paraphernalia Jim's mother had given them that had been stored in their new garden shed for the last six months would have to be unpacked and polished up: the stand, the fender, the ash-pan, the plate, the rod and the candle sticks. She felt exhausted at the very thought of it all. Oh! for her cast iron stove, with its all-night burner and steel hotplate. A wipe with a damp cloth was all it ever needed. The longing to go back there came and went in almost unbearable waves.

"Oh well," she sighed at last, knowing it was never any good crying over spilt milk. "We had better get started, I suppose."

She hung up her coat in the cwtch under the stairs, took a wrap-around pinny from a brown paper carrier bag and rolled up her sleeves. She wasn't a stranger to hard work, it was just that she had been on more friendly terms with it recently.

"We'll have to get the oilcloth down first: in here, the middle room, the parlour and two of the bedrooms," she said. "None of it will be big enough but it will have to do."

There was resignation on Ivy's face, swiftly followed by relief on Jim's and slight alarm on her mother's.

"I'll take the girls back over out of your way, Ivy," Carrie said, shooing them into the passage. "And I'll send your father over to give you a hand with the beds. He's been nights all this week but he should be up by now." She caught up with the girls and whispered conspiratorially to them, "We'll leave them to it and have a bit of fun over our house. Besides, two women into one kitchen don't go. Remember that when you do your sums, Pauline!"

Chuckling together, they closed the door to No. 26 Stephen's Street behind them.

CHAPTER 4

In Rooms

IVY'S PARENTS HAD also had their fill of 'picking up their beds and walking' – as Carrie rather inappropriately put it – having moved twice in the last eighteen months within Crymceynon. Mind, before that, they'd had a good spell of sitting still in one place – eight years nearly. But the colliery there had closed and they'd had to move. It had been hard at first; the only place available for rent had been an almost derelict cottage about half a mile away from where they now lived. There had been no electric light, no mains drainage, one room and a slope-to downstairs and two tiny bedrooms. But they had stuck it out for nearly a year and were glad to get it. 'Any port in a storm' as they say. Pauline and Liz had loved visiting the cottage, and had run around its wilderness of a garden like young pups during August 1938.

It was at this time that Jim, Ivy and the girls were living in rooms with a Miss Hardacre in a village not far from the sea – their fifth move since their marriage. Sharing a house and having a young family increased their chances of getting one of the new council houses that were springing up in the area.

On receiving a letter from her daughter one day which said that Jim had cracked some ribs in an underground fall, Carrie had grabbed her hat and coat and set off to find the place, her main purpose being to collect the girls. Ivy would have enough on her hands with Jim. Carrie left a note and the letter on the kitchen table for Albert and his dinner on the hob. Never having been to the area before, she headed for the main bus stop in front of the pop factory to make enquiries and was soon on her way. The bus conductor was very helpful, even getting off the bus at her stop to walk a short way with her and point out the street. She had shaken his hand and thanked him very much. What a nice man!

She found the house and knocked on the door, which was almost immediately opened by a thin, scrawny woman, about her own age, dressed in a drab dress and an overlarge cardigan, her grey hair scraped back off her face into a tight bun at the nape of her neck. She did not look welcoming. And no wonder! It didn't take Carrie long to find out just what an old cow she was. A good man and a couple of strapping kids would have done her the world of good.

"Yes?" the woman asked, bluntly.

Carrie explained who she was and why she had come.

"Mm. This way."

Carrie followed her down the short passage, through the middle room to the kitchen door, which was obviously Ivy's room. With a perfunctory tap, the woman opened it and entered, and to Carrie's amazement, promptly sat herself down on the nearest chair.

"Visitor for you, Mrs Edwards."

"Mam! What on earth are you doing here?"

Before Carrie could answer, Miss Hardacre butted in. Seeing the airing rods loaded with wet clothes, she remarked in an accusing voice, "Washing again, Mrs Edwards? All these damp clothes hanging around – they're not doing my chest any good you know!"

There didn't seem to be much wrong with her chest

to Carrie. What did she expect Ivy to do with all the dirty clothes from two kids and a collier? Put salt on them? And in these restricted circumstances washing had to be done little and often, to keep it down. The woman didn't have a clue.

Carrie, still standing by the door behind Miss Hardacre's back, caught Ivy's eye and gave her a questioning look, jerking her head to the occupied chair. Ivy mouthed back, "I know! She won't go yet. You wait!" The woman had definitely dropped anchor; there was no sign of her budging.

Ivy reached for a packet of cigarettes from the mantelpiece and shook it till one of them protruded. She offered the packet to Miss Hardacre, watching her mother's reaction as she lit a match for her. Ahh, thought Carrie, so that's her routine, is it? They made small, unimportant conversation as the cigarette burned down to a length difficult to hold without burning her fingers. She would go now, surely, Carrie thought. But she didn't.

Ivy winked at her mother, whose eyes and mouth opened wide in amazement as she watched the spinster remove a hairpin from her bun, fix the cigarette end into its loop and continue to extract several more puffs from it before depositing what little was left in an ashtray. She stood up to leave with the words: "Well, I must get on. I can't sit here chatting all day!"

"Well, don't let us keep you!" said Carrie quickly, but adding with a smile, "It's been nice meeting you!" You don't meet many like that in a month of Sundays, she thought.

"Right, Mam, that's over," Ivy said with relief. "Let's have a nice cuppa, eh? You need one, I can see. And a bit of toasted tea cake, is it? It's lovely to see you. It's what I needed right now. Everything is driving me up the wall."

"Where are the kids then Ivy? And Jim?"

"Oh, their adopted granny from next door has taken the girls to the swings for me to have a break. She's a kind woman and the kids love her. Jim is in bed, having a bit of quiet. He's aching all over after that 'bump'." She buttered the teacake and passed some to Carrie. "So I'm going to enjoy this little visit and have you all to myself. Get things off my chest."

Carrie tutted. "You look after yourself, my girl. Things can't go on like this."

"You don't know the half of it, Mam. She," Ivy nodded in Miss Hardacre's direction, "is a right old cow!"

"Yes, that's the impression I got," said Carrie. "Great minds think alike."

"Tight?" said Ivy. "She's as tight as a gnat's arse."

Carrie realised that things were getting to her daughter. She never swore. Well, rarely.

Ivy mimicked the woman's whining voice: "'You'll burn the back out of my grate with that big fire!' she says, but she's not above borrowing, for keeps, endless buckets of our coal for her own fire. 'Do try and keep the children quiet today, Mrs Edwards. I've got an awful headache.' Not as bad as the ones she gives me!" Ivy sighed.

She looked worn out, Carrie thought.

"I'm at my wits' end 'trying' Mam. She would try the patience of a saint, that one. Honestly, she's driving me mad!"

The more Ivy talked, the more concerned Carrie became about her daughter and the more determined that she would not take 'no' for an answer about taking the girls back with her. She didn't say anything on that score yet. Let Ivy get it all out of her system first, then she would have more chance of winning the argument about it, because argument there would be, she knew.

"We haven't been here five minutes, Mam, and already I don't know how much longer I can stick it. Jim says if we want that council house, then we've got to for a few more months. We stand a much better chance of qualifying for one if we've got a family and are living in rooms. So I'm going to have to stick it, aren't I?" She paused and stared into the distance. "I want that so much, Mam. The estate is only about five miles from the seaside. Imagine that for my kids. And it would be mostly young families. They would have loads of kids to play with. There's no-one for them round here and I'm afraid to let them out by themselves." She sipped her tea and sighed again. "A nice modern house of my own! A brand new house. A bathroom, running hot water, as much as you want, an indoor toilet and a grate that almost looks after itself. Heaven!" She focused again. "Ah well. A day at a time, eh Mam? That's what Dad always says, isn't it? 'A day at a time and we'll get there'."

So Carrie insisted on taking the girls back with her to the cottage for two weeks and met with little opposition. She wouldn't answer for Ivy's state of mind otherwise – or Miss Hardacre's state of health!

CHAPTER 5

The Holiday

THERE HAD BEEN little house work done that fortnight with her young grandchildren for company. Carrie didn't believe in re-arranging dust every day, anyway. Albert had been on nights regularly then, so every morning, after they'd had a quick swill and a bit of breakfast, she had shooed the girls out to play, "for Gramps to have a bit of quiet."

During those two weeks, Carrie became very adept at stretching the time it took to fill a bucket of coal, peg a few bits on the line or walk to the cesspit in the field behind the garden to empty the slops. Any excuse to look busy and unconcerned while she watched and eavesdropped on those two young 'uns playing.

The cottage was one of a row of four, with no other houses nearby. There were no children living in any of the other cottages, but the girls hadn't needed company. There was more than enough to amuse and occupy their inquisitive young minds in the garden alone. It had been carefully tended once, but Albert hadn't bothered much with it because they kept hoping they would be moving before long. He had dug a bit over by the house and had grown kidney beans, a bit of parsley, lettuce and jibbons, but there was no point in him slogging his guts out only for someone else to reap the benefit.

At the beginning of the girls' stay, Carrie had been a bit apprehensive as she watched them run wild. Freedom, when you're not used to it, can be a hard thing to handle. But she wanted them to find that out for themselves, to learn from their mistakes, so she deliberately left them to it – up to a point. Every day had been an expedition of discovery for them and they soon learned what to avoid, as she knew they would. Nettles 'burned' your skin and brought up a cluster of little red bumps that tingled and took ages to subside; strawberry and buttercup runners brought you down with winding suddenness if you ran without watching where you put your feet; and thorns ripped nasty little cuts just deep enough to allow droplets of blood to trickle out. But they derived some pleasure even from these hazards. All children get a certain amount of satisfaction from scratching at black and brittle dried blood, easing off a scab with a persistent fingernail or spitting onto hot skin to cool it. Never once did they run back inside in tears, though there were many in those first few days. They kissed and comforted each other then resumed their adventures.

It always surprised Carrie how quickly children learned to cope and become self-reliant. She could practically see their confidence grow from hour to hour and the rewards for their perseverance were legion. Blackberries – big, mauve-black and squashy with sweet juice – grew in abundance in the perimeter hedge. Their fingers and faces were bruise-stained every day. They climbed precariously up a small, gnarled old apple tree after pippins and filled the skirts of their dresses to carry them in for Gran, looking all noble like two of the three kings bearing gifts.

"Oo, lovely!" said Carrie, wondering what on earth to do with them all and thinking, thank God they can't climb the greengage tree! "Grampa can take one to work tonight in his tommy-box. He likes an apple with a bit of cheese." Come to think of it, he could take a bagful of them and feed them to those poor pit ponies.

The scores of black and orange butterflies that couldn't resist 'calling by passing' to the michaelmas daisies had fascinated the girls, and Carrie, ensconced in the slope-to, washing the same cup over and over, had watched and listened to their whoops and shrieks, sharing their delight as they tried their level best to catch them. The butterflies were safe enough though, even with one of Carrie's hairnets looped on wire and tied to a stick coming at them from all angles.

Now and again, the girls presented her with little posies of pansies, survivors from the garden's better days. Drowsy from hot, tight little hands, the blooms drank their fill from jam jars of water and in no time their heads hung blotto over the rims. They collected roses too, passed their best but still drenched in perfume like past-their-prime floosies. They didn't take long to shed their apparel, either. Pink, white and lemon satin petals left a trail from the tap to every windowsill. Still, it was worth it, just to catch a whiff of that gorgeous scent as she went about her work.

Sometimes, Carrie had sat out in the backyard in the sunshine on an old kitchen chair, crocheting while they played. She meditated there, thinking about how funny life was, while hooking the cotton in and out. When her own children were that age, she never had time to enjoy them like this, and yet the days went by quicker now than they had ever done. They had all gone years ago, except her youngest. The two boys had emigrated as soon as they were old enough, looking for a better deal in life. She would probably never see them again. And the north of England may as well be abroad for all she ever saw or heard of from Doris. Twenty-eight and still not married! She didn't know what was to become of her.

She had always had a wilful streak in her, had Doris. Carrie didn't know where she got it from.

Where had all the years gone? It seemed only yesterday the children had all been before her, one after the other going through exactly the same stages as Liz and Pauline were now. Damn, her eyes were watering again. Another bloody sign of old age creeping up. She put her crochet in her lap and fished in her pocket for her hanky.

"Grannie! Grannie! Look what we've found!"

She couldn't dwell on things for long with these two around. Putting her lace and hanky in her pocket, she wondered what it was this time. It was another of the scraps of pretty china they had been collecting. They had filled the windowsill in their bedroom with the 'luckies' they had found. Ivy would not be best pleased when they carted them all home. Pauline spat on it and was about to wipe it on the hem of her dress when Carrie lifted a warning finger.

"Uh-uh! Go and wash it under the tap."

The pattern turned out to be blue cornflowers on a white background, which Pauline would try to draw and colour in.

Carrie fully understood the pleasure they got from saving these broken little bits. She derived exactly the same sort of thrill buying, when she could afford it, a bargain china cup and saucer from the market. It was held 'over-the-other-side' of the village – its lower half – beyond the railway station and across the river where the council offices, the Odeon and Palace cinemas and 'proper' shops (rather than converted houses) were located. There was even a Woolworth's there. Most of the *crachach* (posh) lived over there. Carrie had taken the girls a couple of times, once to the market and once to the pictures to see Laurel and Hardy, but it was a long walk for their little legs and Liz was getting too heavy for her to carry for long. They had gone straight to bed after these outings, without their 'good wash'. Ah well, Carrie reasoned philosophically, flowers grow in dirt!

Waiting for Pauline to come back with the now clean piece of china, Liz had suddenly plonked her podgy elbows on Carrie's knees, cupped her chubby cheeks in her hands, looked straight into her eyes and said with a contented sigh, "Gran, I like having holidays!"

You and me both, love, thought Carrie.

CHAPTER 6

Grampa

"ALBERT!" CARRIE SHOUTED up the stairs, as she and the girls returned to Duke Street. "Are you awake?"

If he hadn't been, he was now.

"Ivy and Jim want you to give them a hand with the beds. Your dinner's ready for you on a saucepan."

Liz and Pauline hadn't seen Grampa 'Ralbert' since their holiday the previous year. They loved him every bit as much as Gran but were always a little more subdued in his presence. Grampa had a more sober personality. He always seemed to look neat and clean even in his working clothes, and he never put his boots on without brushing them, including the arches underneath. He was a bit taller than Gran and much thinner, but they both had blue eyes and grey hair.

"Aye-aye," said Grampa from the kitchen doorway, looking tidy even now in his braces and with his short crinkly hair all tousled from bed. "You're with us again then, are you?"

There was a scowl on his face that others might have taken for real, but twinkling eyes and twitching lips are signs that children learn to read before the alphabet. Pauline smiled shyly and nodded slowly.

"Sit down," said Carrie, business-like. She took a tea towel to fetch his dinner from the saucepan and wipe the steam from the bottom of the plate.

"Do I get a kiss then, or don't I?"

Both girls, standing one on either side of Gramp's chair, leaned forward and planted a kiss each near his moustache, jumping and giggling as it tickled. Carrie, reaching over, plonked his dinner down with a thump – the plate was too hot to handle.

"And what do you think of this new house of yours then, eh?" said Albert, slowly lifting the pan lid from the plate. The steam rising with it carried a taste of the dinner to the hovering girls. Their mouths watered and they edged a little nearer.

"I like it," said Pauline in answer to his question, still quiet and a bit self-conscious in Grampa's company.

"And me," said her echo.

Albert ate a few mouthfuls in silence, noticing how their eyes followed his fork from the plate to his mouth. He smacked his lips tantalisingly and said, "Nice bit of dinner, Carrie!"

His wife didn't answer. She took that sort of compliment for granted.

The girls leaned an elbow each on the table and Albert took a few more mouthfuls, enjoying their torment and saying, "Mm!" He dipped a crusty piece of bread into the rich gravy and chewed it with exaggeration. Manners, he knew, prevented them asking. They swallowed surplus spittle and he could tease them no longer. He nudged Pauline and told her, "Go on, go and fetch two saucers and two spoons from the pantry."

"Now, Albert!" said Carrie. "They've had theirs not three hours since. You'll need that inside you, there's plenty of work to do over there."

"Hush woman," he grunted. Children and chicken were

always a-pickin'. "There's too much for me, getting up from bed."

Carrie tutted. He spoiled those girls.

CHAPTER 7

The Green Glass Jug

AT NINE O'CLOCK, Carrie took the children home washed, fed and ready for bed. Carrie had wanted them to stay. But she knew she mustn't push her luck with Ivy. Not yet. They were her children and even angels would fear to tread there without permission.

The girls had also wanted to stay, saying, "Please, Gran, can we? Aw, please!" Gran's beds were nicer than theirs. They were so soft and high, it was like sleeping on a cloud. The frames stood a good twenty inches from the floor, then there were springs on top, flock mattresses on top of those and finally milk puffs, shaken up and pummelled like dough every morning till their fillings pushed out at their cotton cases and they resembled gigantic white loaves, risen and ready for the oven. Gran had put a hot brick from the oven in for them every night at the cottage, wrapping it securely first in 'flannelette'. Sleep came quickly in Gran's beds. But for tonight, 'no' it was.

They got to No. 26, tapped the door and walked in. Ivy was in the middle room alone, unpacking dishes.

"Where are the men then?" asked Carrie.

"Guess!" said Ivy, in a short voice.

"Oh aye."

Carrie didn't need to be told. Colliers always had the ready excuse that they had to have a pint to dampen the dust. And fair play, who could argue?

"Nearly finished? It's looking nice." Carrie looked around. All the furniture had been put in place, the lino and assorted rag and coconut mats were down, the fires lit in the kitchen and middle room, the curtains and blackouts up. The house was now a home again. "The girls have had supper and a wash," she said.

"Good," said Ivy, still feeling far from happy. "Thanks Mam."

"Have you had any food?"

"No, I'm not hungry."

"I'll make some."

Carrie stalked purposefully to the pantry to make some toast on the gas stove. Ivy couldn't afford to go without food; there was more meat on a kipper. The girls, having looked around in the kitchen, were running into the parlour then out again and clattering up the stairs to see which room was theirs.

"Quiet, you two!" shouted Ivy, irritably. In a minute or two they came clattering back down, still full of noise and chatter.

"Now," Carrie scolded, coming in with a plate of hot toast for Ivy and trying to appeal to their better nature. "Mammy's been busy all day, look. She's tired out. Show her those little brooches you've been making, then straight up the apples and pears with you, eh?"

The brooches were made from tiny, red glass beads, threaded onto fine wire and twisted into butterfly shapes, so that the wire ends formed the antennae. Ivy had made them when she was small and smiled wistfully at the sight of them. Mam had plenty of patience with the girls, she'd say that for her.

"They are beautiful," she said. "Take them upstairs with you and put them somewhere safe." She hadn't thought to keep her own and regretted it now.

"G'niekobless," said the girls to their mother and gran as they kissed them.

"G'niekobless," answered the women.

Liz didn't have a clue what this strange word meant but it was the nightly knot that securely tied up each day of her young life. It was never missed out. If she forgot to say it or was pouting, then she would shout it down from upstairs before sleep overcame her. Deep down was an unconscious fear that without it, things might change. Children like consistency. This time, they walked up the stairs quietly.

An hour later they were still wide-awake. Carrie had gone home, Ivy had washed all her precious green glass tea and water sets – one of the wedding presents from her former master and mistress – ready to place them carefully in their usual place in the two glass-fronted cupboards, one on either side of the oval mirror in the top half of the dresser. She handled each piece delicately. She had never seen a glass tea set anywhere else. Everyone fancied it. It was her pride and joy.

Noise filtered down from upstairs, getting louder. Ivy walked to the foot of the stairs and whispered, "Be quiet up there!"

"It's our Liz, Mam, she won't keep still," Pauline responded.

"Li-iz!" shouted Ivy through clenched teeth, thinking of her new neighbours.

There was silence – for all of two minutes. Then the squabbling began again.

"Bring her down here!" Ivy said.

Her tone was menacing but the girls knew her bark to be worse than her bite, so down they came.

"Now, sit there in that chair, both of you." She gave them the comics she had bought earlier. "Ten minutes! Any nonsense and you go straight back up!"

They sat and were quiet.

Ivy resumed her labour of love, sorting the beautiful dishes as if she was back in her years in service. How she had enjoyed those years working for the Goldbergs. Oh, and that house! To think she had actually lived in a house like that. The work had been hard, very hard. But her mistress had appreciated her. Every now and again, she would come down stairs to the kitchen with some items of clothing that she no longer needed over her arm, saying, "Ah, Ivy, do you think you could make use of any of these?" Could she! There was absolutely nothing wrong with them. Ivy soon had several sets of the most beautiful silk or satin underwear in every possible pastel shade you could think of. She still had them but rarely wore them – they were far too good to wear about the house.

Another time, she got two paisley patterned dresses, one on a green background, the other on blue. Once, her mistress had even given her a coat of navy-blue, thick, crumpled material, fastened with glass bow-shaped buttons and with a luxurious big fur collar. Whenever she opened her wardrobe door, she couldn't resist running her hands through it. She kept them all for a special occasion, should one ever arise.

Liz soon lost interest in looking at pictures and reading the smallest words, and since Pauline was engrossed in reading every word of her comic to herself, she slid off the chair and stood by the table. Over the mantelpiece there now hung a big oak-framed mirror and she suddenly noticed that she could see the dresser mirror through it, together with several reflections of herself. She bobbed this way and that trying to see how many Liz's she could count.

Smash! The green glass milk jug lay in smithereens on the stone floor. Smack! went Ivy's hand, with force, on Liz's fat thigh. Before Liz had time to let out the terrified yell of pain, she was yanked up and plonked down next to Pauline again. Rushing to the kitchen to fetch a pan and brush, Ivy threatened, "You stay there till I get this glass up. Then it's bed. For both of you. Sleep or no sleep. And if I get just one peep out of you..." The rest of the sentence was left to their imagination.

Liz was bawling her eyes out with the sting and the shock. Pauline put her arms around her and rocked her gently. When the sobbing subsided a little through sheer exhaustion, Liz lifted her nightie to see the damage and rub the hurt. Ivy, on her knees collecting the last of the glass fragments, saw the risen outline of her hand on the child's leg and was filled with shame and remorse. In that same second Pauline saw it too – and her mother's guilt.

"You," Pauline said quietly, "you're worse than a stepmother, you are!" She could have found no worse adjective with which to accuse her.

Grasping the two of them tightly to her and trembling from head to foot at the horror of what she had done, she blurted out, "I'm sorry, Lizzie love, Mammy's sorry. I didn't mean to do it!"

In bed later, Pauline told Liz that she had seen their mother's eyes brimming with tears. Liz hadn't seen them for the tears in her own. Served her right, anyway, she thought. There are no shades in the colour of childhood judgement.

CHAPTER 8

Beginning to Settle

DURING THE NEXT few weeks, the graph of the Edwards' family life more or less settled back into a straight line. Jim started work at the colliery, Pauline started school and Ivy, still wracked by her conscience over the jug incident, made a supreme effort to banish all thoughts and regrets of her former home from her mind by vigorously establishing those Victorian standards of housework learned and adopted during her years in service. The front step and a half moon of pavement below it were blue-stoned regularly, the wooden lavatory seat in the *ty bach* at the top of the garden was scoured almost white with Vim, the ironwork of the grates was zebo-ed and buffed with scraps of velvet and all the brass work burnished to put the sun to shame.

Liz was left to her own devices for most of the time. Other times, she went shopping with her mother, took Pauline to school with her mother or went over to Gran's with her mother, but she wasn't allowed out on her own.

"You're too young, you don't know the place yet. You could get lost," said Ivy to her persistent pleadings.

So Liz played with her dolls or coloured in Moonface and Sylvie and all the gang from the *Magic Faraway Tree* in the centre pages of her *Sunny Stories*, or she painted pictures in her painting book, rubbing the brush hard in the squares of paint till it resembled a tiny flue brush, and invariably tipping paste pots of muddy water all over the table in her efforts. When it was fine, she wandered in the garden, spending some time on the strong swing Jim had fixed up for her, or gathering beetles and spiders to keep in matchboxes as pets, which Ivy immediately threw out again.

But the weekends showed more promise. There were dozens of children of all ages in Stephen's Street alone and Pauline now knew a lot of them through school. From nine o'clock on a Saturday morning, weather permitting (which meant anything other than a downpour), there would be a rat-tat-tat on the letterbox from some child or other, followed by: "Is Pauline coming out to play?" Being new to the place she was a novelty and therefore in demand.

Automatically, Liz ran to get her coat when Pauline got hers. She'd hold it up impatiently for Ivy to help her put it on and tie the strings of her pixie hood. Pauline didn't complain of her tagging on. All her new friends had brothers and sisters in tow, too. Sometimes they played with the little ones, sometimes the little ones played by themselves, but not far from the top of the street. Winter weather called for games of action and they ran their feet off after balls or each other.

The Edwards' house and its neighbour, the last house, were semi-detached and slightly bigger than the rest of the terraced street. Their two front doors opened directly onto the pavement, whereas the others all had tiny front gardens with iron railings and a gate. From the top of the street, the ground levelled out into a large open field. At its far end sat a popular pub, the Navigation. A corrugated iron fence bordered the right-hand side of the field, protecting the neat allotments behind it from the freely roaming sheep. It ended a few yards from the pub where a stile gave access to a path that led to a wooden bridge over the railway and another, much steeper path down to the river.

On the left-hand side of the field, a wide path led down behind the street – a shorter route to Crymceynon Infant and Junior School – and up, past the pub and Carrie's old cottage, to the next village. Below this wide path was a stretch of marshy ground and a yard wide stream – all that remained of the canal of bygone days. The stream was still called the canal and the path, the canal bank. The shrinking had been so gradual over the years that it had passed unnoticed. The children learned to weave babies' rattles, tiny umbrellas, whips and baskets from the rushes that thrived there.

Across the stream were the little woods where bluebells, harebells, milkmaids, primroses, violets and many other kinds of wild flowers grew. Then came the farmer's field, tempting to all to trespass in for the simple reason that it was forbidden. Behind and to the left of that was the mountain, a place to let imagination run wild. The girls knew the whole area well by the middle of December.

CHAPTER 9

First Christmas

CHRISTMAS WAS DRAWING near. Liz and Pauline believed in Santa Claus, as did everyone under twelve, and tried hard to be exemplary in their behaviour. Every mother in the street was inundated with enquiries from their broods as to what they could do to help, over and above their normal duties.

The children learned young that their help was expected in family life. Each one had their allocation of chores from a very early age – it was part of life's process, part of growing up, and never looked on as an imposition. Demands such as, "Look after the baby for me," or "Run down the shop," or "Help me put this ton of coal in," were obeyed – even in the middle of a good game – though grizzled at under their breaths. They learned through participation, responsibility for themselves and others, and a degree of self-discipline.

The mothers, busier than usual with all the extra preparations, were not above exploiting their children's beliefs, Ivy and Jim included. One step out of line brought the dire warning: "He can hear you, mind!" God was irreverently deposed during those weeks before the festivities.

Liz and Pauline had woken at dawn on Christmas Day, their eyes wide to gather the weak light. The night before, their father had nailed two of his long, woollen working socks to the small wooden mantelpiece over the bedroom grate. They were the last things the girls had seen before their eyelids became too heavy to hold back. Now, even in the almost dark room, four eyes focussed on the target. Yes! They had been filled.

Quick and quiet as mice, they scampered out of bed and reached for them, fearless of the shadows till their toes bumped into unexpected obstacles on the small hearth. They looked down then stepped back, their hearts in their mouths. There was somebody sitting there! Two somebodies, in fact. Liz threw her arms around Pauline's waist and buried her head in her chest, trying to make herself invisible. Goblins!

"It's alright, Liz," said her brave sister, "they're only dolls!"

But such big ones! Two celluloid, life-size baby dolls sat fully dressed on two small stacks of books. They carried them to the window for closer examination, Pauline climbing on to a chair to throw back the curtains. Both dolls were dressed in hand-knitted proper baby clothes: leggings, dresses, coats, bonnets and mittens; one in pink, the other in blue. The pleasure Liz felt was almost a pain. She picked up the pink one, more than half her size but feather light, and clasped it to her with a sigh that rose from her toes.

"She's the most beautifullest baby I ever saw!" she said.

Pauline had the blue doll.

With their new annuals to look through, dolls to play with and Pauline home every day for company, the Christmas holidays flew by for Liz. In no time they were over and school had started again. She missed her sister more than ever now. The weather worsened so that even trips over to Gran's were fewer. There was nothing to do, all day to do it in and no-one to do it with. The winter dragged. Liz wished she could go to school too; she wished she could read and do real writing with a pen and ink. She wished it would stop raining or blowing or snowing. Such is life, she discovered: up in the air one moment, down the next. She was soon to learn things could get worse, much worse.

"Aw, never mind love," said Carrie consolingly, "we'll soon have the light nights here. Once Christmas is over, every day gets longer by a chicken's calm."

Well, Liz had seen those chickens walking and they did it in very slow motion indeed, from what she could see. One foot up, stretch a bit, stop, stretch a bit, then down, the other foot up, stretch a bit, stop… At that rate winter was never going to go.

CHAPTER 10

Vera's History

GRADUALLY, AND ALMOST against her will, Ivy found herself being drawn into the pattern of everyday life in the village. Inclined to keep herself to herself, having more Albert's nature in her than Carrie's, and still bearing resentment towards the place like a dull ache deep inside her, she made no conscious effort to become involved. But it was unavoidable. On those long sojourns to the shops and school and even longer ones home again, uphill and loaded down, she met so many people that it would have been downright churlish not to pass the time of day by hurrying on ahead, and one word would always lead to another. She had made one friend, a Mrs Roberts from four doors down.

"Mm," said Carrie, fully in favour of her choice. "Vera Roberts. A nice girl, Vera."

Everyone under forty was still a girl to Carrie. Ivy had only to mention meeting someone and it was enough to send Carrie off, filling in their details with a quick précis of their background and circumstances. Not that she was a gossip – she only ever repeated what she knew to be true. She had no time for rumour. Interested, that's all she was. One village being much like another in the valleys and having always lived somewhere in the area, Carrie knew several of the inhabitants or their relatives from years before. She found the kaleidoscopic patterns that were shaken up by births, marriages and deaths in such close-knit communities, intriguing and absorbing.

Others, like Ivy, found it claustrophobic. She had been away from the mountains since her early teens and had experienced, to some degree, a more cosmopolitan way of life in the metropolis. In the village, she felt a bit out of touch, out of tune and out of step. A fish out of water.

"You don't remember ol' man Merryman?" asked Carrie, still on the subject of Vera.

Ivy was blank. Carrie proceeded with a quick summary of enlightenment.

"Yes you do! Used to live not far from Auntie Martha's. His wife was a small, dainty woman from a good family. They had two daughters. One was a teacher, the other married a doctor. Remember?"

There were vague stirrings in Ivy's memory.

"Well, that's Vera's father too, that old man living with her." Carrie's voice dropped to a whisper. "Not that he'd ever own up to it." Her voice shutting off completely, she mouthed the word 'illegitimate'.

Despite herself, Ivy's face showed a spark of interest. It was enough to encourage her mother.

"He would have been just about fifty then. The shock killed his poor wife in the end. She was never the same after she found out. Our Martha said she never got over the shame of it."

"But I don't understand," said Ivy. "If he doesn't own up to Vera's existence, how come she's living with him now?"

"Oh, it's a long story," said Carrie.

"I'll make us a cup of tea," said Ivy.

They settled themselves, one on each side of Ivy's kitchen fire with their cups and saucers in their hands and Carrie continued.

"After his wife's death he wasn't very popular there, as you can imagine. And he had no intention of moving in with Vera's mother – that had all been over, long since, so he upped sticks and moved here, away from that area. Both his girls had left years ago to get away from the scandal." She paused to take a few sips of tea. "Anyway, about eight years ago, Vera's husband was killed in the pit. She had the one boy, Gareth, by then and was big in the way with the other one, David. She was destitute of course. No-one to turn to. Her mother had died when she was about sixteen and her mother's husband had left the day he found out about the affair, so she had no husband, no family, no money, nothing. Not knowing her father's address and in sheer desperation, she had written to Audrey the teacher, having got the address from a teacher friend of hers, to ask of her father's whereabouts, telling her of her plight and more or less pleading for help of some kind. Well, as luck would have it, about the time that she posted the letter the old man suffered a stroke. Bad it was, mind. Give the Devil his due. Now, the two ugly sisters as I call them – they're not very nice people – got together to discuss the situation."

"How do you know all of this, Mam?" interrupted Ivy.

"Oh, I took some sheets over as I don't have a sewing machine. You know Vera does sewing, do you, to earn a few extra bob?"

Ivy nodded.

"I wanted them turned sides to middle. There's years more wear in them now. If there's ever anything you want done like that, she's the one to ask, mind. Now, where was I? Oh, then she asked me if I would teach her to crochet and we got to know each other and she confided in me. This is all in the strictest confidence, mind. I don't want it broadcasting!"

"Mam, as if I would."

"I know. I know I can trust you, otherwise I wouldn't be telling you. Anyway, to get back to where we were. They couldn't have their father coming to live with either of them and bringing his past with him, not with the kind of circles they move in, but they couldn't afford to ignore him either. There's quite a bit of money to be had after his days and they are the sort who never get enough. So it suited them to offer Vera a roof over her head and a small pittance to look after him. Mr Merryman, of course, had no say in the matter and Vera holds no threat to their inheritance. All she means to him is a daily reminder of his guilt. God knows what will happen to her and the boys after his days. She'll be out on her ear, you mark my words."

"Sounds to me like Vera's got the worst end of all this."

"Well, she couldn't afford to refuse, could she? And despite everything she has still got feeling for him. Must do, or she wouldn't tend him like she does. He's made a complete recovery from that stroke, thanks to her. The ungrateful ol'..." Carrie failed to find words to voice her contempt. "Have you noticed? He still calls her Mrs Roberts. He will not admit to her being his."

"Poor Vera."

"Aye, she deserves a medal, that one. And one as big as a bloody bakestone, to make me say such a thing! She's his alright, you only have to look at her to see the resemblance." Carrie put her feeling into poking the fire. "Vera has been a better daughter to him than those other two put together and those two lovely boys of hers are the only grandchildren he will ever have. I dread to think what the future might hold for them all."

CHAPTER 11

Ankle-Strapped Shoes

MARCH CAME, WITH spring and Liz's birthday just around the corner. Ivy, caught off guard in a magnanimous moment, said she could invite two friends to tea on that day. Liz knew immediately who she would ask: Wendy Williams and Brian Pierce.

Wendy was an only child and lived opposite with her mother and two lodgers – 'Uncles' she called them. Her father had died from TB when she was a baby. Wendy looked pale and delicate with a mass of brown fizzy hair swamping her small face. It was the hair that Liz had noticed first about her. Her own was short and wispy and white-ish fair. Ivy cut it regularly in a crop across her forehead and bobbed to just below her ears, hoping it would thicken. Every morning she tied in a ribbon to add a bit of interest, pulling it tight and anchoring it with grips, but it was useless. The ribbon slipped at the slightest movement and Liz soon tired of pushing the heavy bow up the skinny tail. Once out of sight, she yanked it off and shoved it up the leg of her knickers.

Pauline's hair was thick, dark and long. When it rained, little tendrils broke loose and coiled like springs about her face. She wore it in two fat plaits that ended in 'S' curls below the ribbons. If the plaits swung forward, she lifted them by the 'S' and with a flick of her wrist and a toss of her head, sent them flying back over her shoulders. How Liz envied her that flick and toss! Having a friend richly endowed with a crowning glory helped to quell it a little.

Wendy's looks were deceiving. She was brimful of nervous energy – a real live wire – and her passion was tap-dancing. That too, Liz admired and envied. Well, her desire for curls was futile but tap-dancing she could learn. She practised incessantly, getting on everyone's nerves. She dropped hints as big as bricks about her birthday present, desperately wanting a pair of black, shiny, patent-leather ankle-strapped shoes with tiny buttons, just like Wendy wore. They made your feet look just right for tap-dancing. Her own were clumpy lace-ups and the laces kept coming undone and getting in the way.

"You'll be starting school soon, Liz. School shoes are what you need. You can't have both. Money doesn't grow on trees," said Ivy.

"Wendy Williams got a pair."

"Has got," said Ivy, never missing a chance to correct her grammar. She had always been good at English and Composition when she was in school and wanted her girls to do even better. "Wendy Williams' mother only has one child to keep," she said firmly and on the defensive, adding to herself, "and more money than sense with two generous lodgers to help her to do it." Carrie had filled her in on that score, too.

Liz tried her father, the night she had toothache. She knew he was at his most vulnerable when one of them was 'bard'. But to no avail. She sat on his lap, with one of his woolly socks filled with hot salt from the frying pan held against her cheek – an old remedy, and probably a gipsy one, thought Ivy wryly, though it always seemed to work – and pleaded her case.

"Oh now, Liz, that's your mother's department."

"But Dad, I can't dance in these clodhoppers!"

"Ankle straps wouldn't last, Miss. You would be through them in a week. Then what would you do? No, school shoes it is."

So that was that, then.

Brian Pierce also lived on the other side of the street but halfway down, where there was an elbow bend directly opposite Lowe's corner shop. His older sister, Margaret, was now Pauline's best friend. The Pierces were ten children altogether, only the twins being younger than Brian. He was as dark as Liz was fair but their natures were much the same.

"Aye, I'll come," said Brian when she asked him. "We never have parties in our house. My father says every day's a bloody party with ten kids sat round the table!"

Neither Wendy nor Brian had started school yet and during the last few weeks Liz had enjoyed their company for the best part of every day. They played outside when the weather permitted, providing they went no further than Price's pine-end – the smooth end wall of No. 27 – and in Liz's or Brian's house when it rained. They never played at Wendy's. Apart from one of the 'Uncles' always working nights, Mrs Williams' house was full of little knick-knacks and ornaments, which didn't mix well with boisterous young children. Besides, she had "no shape with little 'uns," as Carrie said.

Ivy never minded having them on 'days' or 'afternoons' shift. They played in an empty bedroom with their shoes off. She found it easier to get on if Liz was occupied, and Brian's mother hardly noticed if a few extra joined her throng. Liz liked playing at Brian's house best. Mrs Pierce, or Elsie-May as she was better known, was the most easy-going of mothers. "Come-day, go-day, God send Sunday!" said her neighbours, summing up her attitude to life. Fair play though, it was no wonder she was *didoreth* (half-soaked) they said, with a husband like hers and a houseful of kids. It was enough to *dant* any woman. Some felt sorry for her, some admired her and some even envied her and her attitude towards life, but nearly everyone liked her. She was that sort of woman. There was always someone or other popping in for a chat.

CHAPTER 12

Elsie-May Pierce

CARRIE HAD KNOWN Elsie-May (Jones, as she was then) and her family from way back, before she had married Tom and moved to Crymceynon.

"Oh, she was such a pretty young girl," she told Ivy, when she learned they had got to know each other, "and with a nature to make a saint jealous, even then. All the young lads fancied her, but none more so than Tom. You could see he idolised her – always carrying her shopping for her or pushing her bike up the hill – anything!"

Ivy loved these mental picture drawings of her mother's. It gave the individuals she described a three-dimensional character and gave a more immediate understanding of what they were really like, though she could be infuriating at times, wandering off the story just as it became more interesting. Ivy swore she did it deliberately, just to aggravate her.

"Before anyone could make a move in that direction, though, she upped and away to service – like you did," Carrie continued, adding with a grin, "though she didn't quite make it to cook!"

That was understandable, thought Ivy, having been over there several times. Still, that didn't detract from her personality. You just couldn't help liking her.

"Four years later, she was back. Pregnant!"

"Aw no!" Ivy hadn't expected to hear that. "What happened, poor thing? Was it adopted or brought up by her parents, or is that her eldest child now?" she asked, since babies born out of wedlock in those days often became a 'sister' or 'brother' to the new mother.

"No," said Carrie, with sadness in her voice. "It was still-born."

"Oh, that's so sad, to lose her first baby."

"Mm." By the look on her face, Carrie was imagining just how one could deal with such a horrendous experience. She drew in a deep breath. "I remember it well, like yesterday. It just broke her heart. No-one ever discovered the circumstances or who the father was. And it wasn't for want of trying – you know what some people are like!"

Ivy nodded knowingly. Elsie-May must have gone through it enough, without having all that to put up with. When she was in London she had known of girls in the same predicament who had been taken advantage of, seduced or even raped. In some cases the employer, or a member of his family, was responsible. What could these girls do in such situations? Who would believe them? Your word against theirs – and they were the ones with the money for clever lawyers. Looking back now, Ivy realised nothing prepared you for the risks. A promise of marriage and a better life, taken at face value, was very tempting to a young, totally naïve girl. She realised that she had been very lucky in the Goldberg household. She could so easily have ended up like Elsie-May, through no fault of her own.

"Poor Elsie-May, what a start to her young life," Ivy said, thinking out loud.

They both sat silent for a while, Carrie thinking along exactly the same lines as her daughter. There but for the grace of God, eh? Before she had gone into service, Carrie's last words to Ivy as she had kissed her goodbye at Cardiff Station had been: "Look after yourself now, love, and keep yourself to yourself." It was the nearest she could get to a warning. What else could she have said? She just couldn't go into detail about things like that, then. Not with her fourteen-year-old daughter. She had never been sure if Ivy had understood what she was getting at. Ivy hadn't. She knew next to nothing about the facts of life and was unable to make any sort of connection between her mother's words and the dangers facing her. Ivy thought she had meant 'mind your own business' or words to that effect.

Carrie couldn't bear thinking about what could have happened; she wouldn't think about it. All had turned out all right, thank goodness. She took another deep breath and changed to a lighter mood in her story. Now that Ivy was married and had children of her own, their conversations could cover any risqué topics.

"One bright spark who had previously had his eye on her, scathingly remarked in the pub one night: 'Elsie May? Elsie has, by all accounts, boys!' Tom Pierce happened to be there and gave him a broken nose for his wit. He married her not long after."

"Good for Tom!" Ivy's opinion of him moved up a notch.

"And look at them now," Carrie opened her palms as if displaying them, "with all those lovely kids, each one as fit and strong as a young pony." She paused a while, thinking. "She's a wonderful mother, mind, Ive," she concluded, then added as an after thought, "in her own way."

Yes, thought Ivy, nodding in agreement. Mam's right to say 'in her own way'. "They seem very happy together, anyway," she said aloud, "I get the impression that they are well suited to each other."

"Oh yes. She's grown to love him, you can see that. She won't hear one word against him and he worships the ground she walks on. His only drawback, as far as I can see, is when he gets drunk."

Ivy's notch took a nose-dive. Jim and he were now good mates and were often out together for a drink when they were on the same shift.

"Not that he gets worse for wear often, mind," Carrie said. "They couldn't afford that, anyway. Oh, but when he does have a skinful it's a pantomime over there!"

"How do you mean 'a pantomime'? He's not violent is he, when he's drunk?" Ivy was thinking of the hours that Liz spent over there playing with Brian, and the evenings that Pauline and Margaret spent together doing homework or just chatting.

"Naw! Nothing like that," Carrie giggled. "No worries on that score. He's never once laid a finger on Elsie-May or any of the kids."

"Well, what does happen then?" Ivy needed to know.

"It's a regular thing, by the look of it. It's happened more than once, to my knowledge."

"What? What?" Mentally, Ivy's finger was on the notch again.

"I was over there this day, when he lurched in, bumping into furniture, knocking things over and shouting to his wife, 'Elsie-May, my little flower, your beloved is home. Where are you, my Betty Grable of the valleys?' We had been in the garden collecting eggs and she was still out there. That's what I'd gone over for. You know how your father loves a fresh egg for his breakfast. Fair play, she always lets me have one or two when the hens are laying." Carrie was enjoying this now, stretching it out to keep Ivy's attention. She had it.

"Mam! Get on with it!"

"Right. In she came and went straight up to him with her finger on her lips. 'Tom! Tom! The neighbours will hear,' she scolded. Whereupon Tom opened the back door, the front door, lifted the sash on the parlour window, stuck out his head and bellowed to all and sundry, 'Let the buggers hear!'"

Ivy shrieked. Partly from relief at the outcome. Some men, she knew, could be really aggressive with drink. Up went the notch again.

Carrie hadn't quite finished. "Then he flopped into his armchair, bent down to unlace his boots and leaned back. All around him now, he could see the criticising, accusing faces of his brood. It was plain to see what they were all thinking – our Dad being daft in front of people. Then he slammed his fist on the table, making the dishes bounce, and shouted, 'There are too many bloody kids in this house!'"

Both women were laughing out loud now. When they got their breath back, Carrie added, "As if he was the last to blame for that!"

CHAPTER 13

High Hopes

LIZ'S BIRTHDAY FELL on a Monday – washing day – and it was raining.

By the time the girls got up, there was already a bucket of whites boiling on the fire and a boshful of towels soaking. The kitchen was cluttered with a zinc bath and rubbing board balanced on two chairs, a small Acme wringer on its stand with a small bath beneath to catch the drips, a bucket of blue in the corner for final rinsing, and on the table an enamel bowl filled with starch, mixed and ready for the cottons. Sorted piles of dirty washing littered the floor. Ivy was flushed, her damp hair shoved up into a net, her hands red and cushiony. The girls' breakfast was laid at the far end of the table away from danger. Ivy was poking at the whites on the fire with a thick bleached stick when they came in.

"Happy birthday, Liz," she said, kissing the top of her head. She poured the tea and took a plate of hot toast from the oven. "Get a move on now, the pair of you. I've got a lot to do today."

By dinnertime the kitchen fire would be totally obliterated from view, with damp washing hanging from the airing rods near the ceiling and draped on the fireguard around the grate. Already the air was heavy with the pleasing clean smell of soap and hot metal.

There was a narrow oblong package by the side of Liz's plate. Ivy, lifting the heavy bucket from the fire and tipping it carefully into the bath, kept an eye on her as she opened it and saw the mixture of disappointment and delight on her face. It was a wooden two-tiered pencil box, varnished and decorated with painted flowers. Sliding the lid forward Liz found two pens and four bright silver nibs in one compartment, an indelible and an HB pencil in the other. In a tiny compartment at the top was a pencil sharpener. Swivelling the top layer to one side revealed six coloured pencils and a rubber. It was a lovely thing which Jim had made well. Ivy stood behind her, wiping her hands on her pinny.

"Like it?" she asked.

Liz nodded.

"For when you start school. Look after it now."

Liz nodded again, taking out a pen and fitting on a nib. Ivy smiled. Liz did like the box, but the edge of her pleasure was blunted. She had so wanted those shoes.

"Can I write with ink?" Her pleasure was sharpening. She got up to fetch the bottle from the windowsill.

"Not now, Liz. Later."

"Only to try."

"When I've finished."

"Only my name."

"No! Not now, later."

Liz sucked the new nib as she had seen Pauline doing with new ones. The ink would stick better. Again, she coaxed, "Only once!"

"Li-iz!"

When Ivy stretched out her name, Liz knew she was stretching her mother's patience. She got back to her chair and contented herself with wetting the indelible pencil and writing her name on her hand. Ivy and Pauline were stifling a giggle over something.

"Give her yours then, Pauline, and hurry up or you'll be late for school."

Pauline handed her sister a small package wrapped in red crepe paper.

"She made that all by herself," said her mother.

'That' was an envelope-sized purse knitted in red wool, fastened with a red button and with a long strap to fit over her shoulder.

"It's to keep your hankie in and your ribbon. It's not very lady-like to shove it up the leg of your knickers!" said Pauline in a superior voice, but laughing.

"On her head it's supposed to be!" said Ivy, joining in with the laughter.

Liz thought what a good mood her mother was in this morning, washday and all. Again they were exchanging glances and giggling. Something was going on and she was excluded. She didn't like it. She opened her purse, put in a clean hankie, slung it round her shoulder and crunched her toast.

After adding two large jugs of cold water to the bath, Ivy began rubbing the washing up and down the brass ridges of the rubbing board, while Pauline began clearing the table.

"Oh, I forgot," said Ivy, after a while, "your father said something before he went to work about a box in the parlour. You'd better go and look."

Hope rose in a lump in Liz's throat. She ran. Beneath the parlour window stood a hexagonal rosewood table. It had a little shelf set low down between its legs. On the shelf was a white box. School shoes. They must be. She took off the lid and lifted the tissue paper. A pair of ankle-strapped shoes shone up at her – smooth, black and beautiful.

"They're only on approval mind," said Ivy by the parlour door. "Try them on but don't step off the mat."

They fitted! Well almost. They were a little bit long in the toes but cotton wool would cure that. As her mother said, that was a good fault.

"You've got your father to thank for those. He's tapped your old ones for school."

It wouldn't do for Ivy to admit she had been won over. The time would come when she would have to say 'no' and mean it. It was always the mother who had to be firm. Fathers got off lightly with daughters.

Liz resisted the very strong temptation to try out a few taps then and there, putting the shoes carefully back in the box. Her cup runneth over.

CHAPTER 14

In Trouble Again

IVY HAD LIT the middle room fire and was laying the table for the party in between sprinkling and rolling the dry washing, and draping and turning the wet in the kitchen. Liz was upstairs on her own and out of harm's way, or so Ivy thought.

It was three o'clock and the others were coming at four. Liz finished dressing and stole into her mother's bedroom to see herself in her best dress and her ankle straps in the dressing table mirror, tilting it forward to see the whole ensemble. The shoes did look lovely. The wireless was on downstairs – her mother wouldn't hear. She tried a few steps on the rug. No good. She removed it and tried again on the oilcloth.

"Oh, I'm a little Dutch girl, a Dutch girl, a Dutch girl. Oh, I'm a little Dutch girl, a Dutch girl am I!" she sang, Shirley Temple minus the ringlets, "On the goo-od ship Lollipop."

On she danced, dwelling in the realms of fantasy and oblivious to everything around her, only to be brought abruptly back to reality by a smack on the bottom that brought the blood to her cheeks and a sting to her eyes.

"Didn't you hear me calling?" shouted her mother, breathless from running up the stairs. "The whiting is all flaking off the ceiling downstairs. All the party food is covered in it!"

As if she didn't have enough to do, she now had to pick whiting flakes off a bloody jelly!

CHAPTER 15

St Mark's

PAULINE AND LIZ started Sunday School at St Mark's just before Easter. They had plenty of company. The whole of the Pierce clan attended, as did Wendy Williams and several of the other children that they now knew from the nearby streets. Children didn't play out much on Sundays. There were too many adults about, hats on heads, books under armpits, on their way to various places of worship. Any misbehaving could be spotted and reported back to their parents. Freedom was restricted.

It was a long walk to the church, breaking some new ground for the Edwards girls. They crossed the stile, hovered for a bit on the railway bridge hoping for one of the frequent trains to come along and engulf them in sulphurous steam, and then followed the long steep path downwards to the black satin river below. They crossed this by a wooden bridge that was fenced and rested securely between two large iron pipes. Boys preferred to cross by balancing on the pipes themselves.

At the other end was a smallholding known as 'Gilbert's Ducks'. They gave this a wide berth as most of the 'ducks' were geese. They left the riverside path after about a hundred yards to scramble up the bank to the road above, careful of their Sunday best in the process. A little higher up from the road sat St Mark's. There were no other buildings nearby. The graveyard to the left of the church was cut into terraces. Funerals there were very difficult to negotiate, especially for the elderly. 'Penance steps' Carrie called them, on the principle that only the good die young.

The church was small, with grey stone and blue slate outside, pink walls and polished wood inside. It smelled of beeswax, brasso, musty books and flowers. Mr Pomfrey, the vicar, was in his early forties, single, dark and devilishly handsome. He delivered his sermons with dramatic enthusiasm and seemed genuine in his devotion. Miss Lewis, their Sunday School teacher, cream and ginger in both colouring and temperament, was in her mid thirties. She tackled their religious instruction with perseverance, fortitude and discipline but also with a kindness and concern. The children loved her and enjoyed attending, needing no coaxing. It was far better than staying home all day Sunday at their mothers' beck and call.

Even Vincent Griffiths attended regularly; though much good may it do him, Ivy thought. Six-year-old Vincent, from what she had heard, was fluent not only in bad language but foul language and you never heard those words used, not even from drunken colliers. Not in her experience, anyway. Butter didn't melt in his mouth, said her neighbours, it turned rancid! Well, any sign of her children picking up words like that and she would be across that road like greased lightning to complain to his parents.

carrying her basket. "He's yuh for good by the looks of things. They won't let him in up there," pointing skywards, "and they're afraid he'll take over down there!" pointing to the ground.

Ivy laughed. She couldn't help herself. That boy had a wisdom beyond his years, she thought. He would see Vera would be all right in the years to come.

Crymceynon Infant and Junior Schools sat facing each other, one at each end of an asphalt yard. Neat stone walls topped with rounded red bricks enclosed the playground on three sides, with railings and a huge gate on the fourth facing the road, allowing the children to look out during playtime and anyone passing to look in. This was a good arrangement in that pre-school children had a favourable first impression of the place, seeing all the pupils happily playing.

"Now be a good girl," Ivy told Liz, "and listen to what teacher tells you, mind!" She would live to regret those words. From now on, whatever teacher said would be Gospel, even when misconstrued.

She gave both girls a kiss and a quick hug, then she and Vera, waving Gareth off on his way to Senior School quarter of a mile further on, turned and climbed back up the hill to the main street and the shops for a morning of queuing and hoping.

CHAPTER 17

Infant School

DESPITE THE DELAY in getting to school, Liz and Wendy still had time to get their bearings before the bell went for lines. They discovered where the 'Girls' toilets were and, attracted by their small size, christened one each, more from novelty than need. Washing their hands at the little basins, they worked up a good lather from the rough cut yellow soap and left a damp, grey patch on the clean roller towel when they finished. They slotted their feet in the bars of the big school gates and scootered them open and shut till someone else demanded a turn, then explored the cloakroom, bending to see the wire cages beneath the benches where they were expected to keep their daps or wellies, if they had them.

Inside, during assembly, they sang the morning hymn with gusto, knowing all the words and tune from Sunday School, all the while absorbing the atmosphere of chalk, dust, milk and security around them. They adored Miss Stephens, the uncertified teacher of the 'babies' class, practically on sight. She was a born teacher who took to children like a duck to water.

The children of the two schools were encouraged to learn under the basic principle of reward and punishment. For good work, good behaviour, good deeds or good manners, everyone would obtain a reward sooner or later. It was always the same simple thing, yet revered and sought after: the rubber stamp of Headmaster GT Hughes' signature, thumped onto a pad of violet coloured ink and imprinted carefully either at the bottom of a sheet of work or drawing, or on the back page of an exercise book. They were displayed with pride and eagerly pursued.

Punishment was severe: a visit to Mr Hughes' office to stand alone before his big desk and face those piercing brown eyes that seemed to penetrate your very soul. There was never any need for the cane.

Chapter 18

Doctor Treadwell

LIZ WASN'T WELL. She was sickening for something. It's only to be expected, thought Ivy. Now that she's been in school a few weeks, she'll pick up everything that's doing the rounds. It was the same with Pauline when she started: one childhood ailment after another. But both girls had good grounding with plenty to fall back on and it was generally accepted that the younger they were, the better they got over these things. Pauline had come through unscathed. Ivy, as yet, wasn't unduly worried.

Liz had woken crying before Jim had gone to work. Ivy had brought her downstairs, opened up the bed-chair by the kitchen fire and settled her into it with two soft pillows and the 'cwtchy' blanket, crocheted from odd balls of wool. Both girls enjoyed this ritual when they were 'bard'.

Ivy would send for Dr Treadwell as soon as it was reasonable. It was too early yet – only just gone six. He was a good doctor, from what she'd been told, though apparently a bit on the odd side, which maybe came from living a bit too close to Annabelle Jackson, people said. They lived next door to each other in the two three-storey houses at the bottom of the street. It was well known that Annabelle's often strange behaviour stemmed from her drinking habits – she continually chewed cloves in an effort to disguise the fact.

Dr Treadwell, on the other hand, was simply a health fanatic, inclined to carry things to extreme. Well, fresh air was all right in small doses, but a person could freeze to death in that surgery in that bottom storey. If you had a cold going in, you'd have bloody pneumonia coming out! The waiting room consisted of a long bench in a passageway and people slid up a space each time a bell tinged. It could all do with a damn good cleaning, his more house-proud patients thought, noticing the cobwebs and dust in the surgery itself and associating health with cleanliness. But the doctor's housekeeper was forbidden to enter the surgery. Everything there must be left in exactly the same place it had occupied for years. That way, the doctor said, mistakes were eliminated. Well, there was logic in that, thought Ivy, mentally cataloguing all the bits of information she had gathered about the doctor before meeting him. Apparently, big brown bottles, all identical but each containing different remedies, sat on a high shelf ready to be dispensed, and people took their own assorted bottles to be filled from them. Whatever the neck size, he could pour from the big to the small without spilling one drop.

Then there was what Jim had heard about the doctor from Tom Pierce. They had been up the allotments getting their potatoes in and Tom was relating how his mate Ivor had got on when paying the doctor a visit back in March. Jim stopped digging and leaned on his fork to listen. He'd had no cause to meet the man himself yet, thank goodness, but it would do no harm to be armed with a little knowledge of him. Jim liked to know what to expect, being a collier, in case he had another accident in the future. He'd had quite a few accidents and visits to doctors in the past. Some of the treatment he had received had been good; some not so good.

"You won't pull the wool over his eyes, wuss, to stretch a bit of time off after a bump, or swing it a bit when you've had a few too many," Tom had warned him, while tapping his nose. "He's got ways! Ivor had fallen off the journey as it went up a steep slope. He was all right, mind, but had some nasty bruising on his back and thought he'd have a week or two off out of it. Fat chance!"

Tom explained how Doctor Treadwell had told Ivor to "drop your trousers then; let's have a look," and had proceeded to walk around him, touching a muscle here, pressing a bone there, before walking back to his desk to make a few notes. He then leaned back in his chair and studied the face before him. All this time poor Ivor still had his trousers around his ankles and was turning blue with the cold – the window always being wide open and the March winds blowing a gale outside. "Er, you can pull your pants up now," the doctor had said offhandedly, and the speed with which they were pulled up over those frozen limbs determined better than anything the degree of injury. Ivor was given a bottle of witch hazel to bring out the bruise and sent packing.

Jim chuckled but thought it was fair enough. He had learned from Tom's story that this doctor had no time for malingerers. Well, Jim had had enough genuine reasons to be laid off work during his life in the pits. He wouldn't and couldn't tempt Providence, so that didn't bother him. Nor did the fact that the doctor had a mind of his own and wasn't afraid to take decisions, whether they offended or pleased. Jim could respect that as well as the man's wry sense of humour, which was always a virtue.

Chapter 19

Ivy Sends for Bessy-Ann

In less than half an hour, Liz was worse – much worse – and Ivy didn't know what to do. She felt the child's forehead again, gently brushing the wet crop to one side. Her whole body was on fire, her nightie damp with sweat.

"Try a little drop of tea? Come on, just to please Mammy."

Liz took a sip. It squirted straight back into Ivy's face with a force that was frightening. Liz flopped back onto the pillows, gasping for breath and moaning pitifully. Terrified, Ivy ran up the stairs and shook Pauline awake.

"Get dressed quickly! Run and fetch Bessy-Ann. It's number thirteen I think, next door down to Lowe's shop. Tell her I want her. Hurry!"

The urgency in her mother's voice brought Pauline wide-awake in an instant. In less than five minutes she was dressed and off down the street.

Ivy didn't know quite what to expect from Bessy-Ann. Her mother always spoke well of her and so did several other people she had got to know over the last few months. She was a much valued member of the community they said, and a very intelligent woman, though you might think otherwise when you were in conversation with her. However, all she lacked was a formal education. That, and the fact that she didn't have a head for words, let alone a tongue. It turned around and tangled up even the simplest of them. Most people had learned to ignore it, Carrie had said, because her advice was always worth having. Not that Bessy-Ann noticed anything, anyway. She was totally and blissfully unaware of her bloomers and her meaning always got across, however deformed her words were. If a particular one eluded her any time, then 'watewclit' – her version of 'what do you call it' – always sufficed. Her trouble was that Welsh was her mother tongue. She had never spoken a word of English until she was seven and had tried hard to master it but had never quite got the hang of it.

Ivy knew that Dr Treadwell found her indispensable at a birth, death or even a post mortem, and being the cheaper option, people sent for her before consulting him in a crisis. You didn't have to pay Bessy-Ann – not in money, anyhow. Not that she was short of a bob or two. The doctor had secured a nice, lucrative little post for her, keeping an eye on Annabelle Jackson, the aristocrat down on her luck who had lived next door to him for the past seventeen years or so.

Ivy looked at the clock. It seemed ages since Pauline had gone to fetch her. Surely more than five minutes. The clock must have stopped. Ah, at last, here she was!

CHAPTER 20

The Crisis

IVY, ON PINS with worry, rushed to invite Bessy-Ann in. With surprising gentleness, Bessy-Ann put her two big, rough hands on Liz's throat, feeling for swelling. "Open wide, sweetheart. Let Bessy-Ann see your watewclits."

Wide-eyed and wide-mouthed, Liz instinctively obeyed, tolerating with great difficulty the spoon handle pressing her tongue down and making her retch. The big woman nodded her head knowingly and stepped back.

"I think it's diphtheria, Mrs Edwards," she said apologetically.

Diphtheria? Ivy's legs gave way. She sat on a chair with a thump, stunned. No! It couldn't be. The woman was wrong. It was tonsillitis or swollen glands, something like that – something familiar, something ordinary, something she could handle. Who was this woman anyway, to come out with such an opinion about her child? It was ridiculous. Just look at her for goodness sake! What could she possibly know? Ivy refused to accept her diagnosis though she didn't voice her thoughts. People round here were still in the Dark Ages, believing in witchcraft and old wives' tales. Why had she bothered to send for her? But fear gnawed at her just the same.

Bessy-Ann carried on regardless of the scepticism on Ivy's face. She was used to this reaction from newcomers. "What I would give her, if I was you," she said, authoritatively, "is half an eggcup of parafeen..."

Paraffin? Listen to the woman! That would kill her!

"...then half an eggcup of goose grease, which will bring it straight back up again and burn off the damage. Then the juice of half a Jaffa."

Ivy was not very far from hysteria by now. Half an orange! You couldn't get an orange anywhere these days for love nor money.

"But that's old fashioned now," said Bessy-Ann matter-of-factly, still unperturbed by Ivy's look of incredulity, "and I'm not infallijubble, I could be wrong." However, her tone said she knew she wasn't. "Best to get the doctor," she said, patting Ivy's hand reassuringly, "to make sure. Pauline can go. Her little legs will be quicker than ours and there's no-one about yet to spread the inflection." She turned to Pauline. "Go up the steps to the front door, sweetheart, and keep ringing the bell till he answers. Tell him Bessy-Ann sent you. He'll come." Her eyebrows lifted as she spoke with an air of assured expectation.

While waiting for the doctor to arrive, Ivy had to keep busy and occupy her mind and hands to control her anger towards 'that woman'.

"Can I make you a cup of tea?" she asked Bessy-Ann, crisply.

"Oh, yes please, I'd love one."

"A biscuit?"

"Mm, I'll have an unjiedestive if you've got one. They're my favourites."

"Unjeidestives!" said Ivy scornfully to herself, through narrowed lips. Nothing the woman could do or say now, despite Ivy knowing her history, was agreeable to her. She transferred the rage, fear and resentment swirling inside her head to the biscuit tin and its tight fitting lid then, when it finally opened, to searching among its contents for some bloody 'unjeidestives'. Bessy-Ann shouldn't come out with statements like that, Ivy thought. She was frightening people and upsetting them needlessly.

But the fear still gnawed away.

CHAPTER 21

Diagnosis Confirmed

DR TREADWELL THREW the wooden spatula onto the fire in disgust. Inflammation of the now grey mucous membrane was plain to be seen.

"It's diphtheria all right!"

He took a bottle of Izal from his bag, tipped a liberal amount of it into a bowl of water, dowsed his hands thoroughly and flicked them dry, sending the splashes to the four corners of the room.

"She will have to go to hospital, I'm afraid. Immediately!"

Hospital? Ivy's world was falling apart.

"Can't I nurse her at home?" she asked. "I'll do everything you tell me to."

"I'm sure you would, Mrs Edwards, but that is just not possible, I'm afraid."

"But she's only just five years old! To go all that way and by her…"

Dr Treadwell sighed. He hoped he wasn't going to have trouble with her, there wasn't time. He would have to put it more bluntly, that was all. Cruel, perhaps, but kinder in the long run. "Every hour now," he said patiently, "is of the utmost importance. This bacillus attacks the nose, throat and windpipe. It multiplies and spreads rapidly. Poison from it gets absorbed into the blood stream and carried to all parts of the body. It's going to be a long business and she is going to need constant supervision."

"But I can..." Ivy began.

"No. You cannot," he said firmly. "Her convalescence may be interrupted by certain forms of paralysis." He omitted to tell her the details of such paralysis: of the heart, the palate, the eyes, lips and diaphragm, the first critical around the ninth day and the last at the thirty-sixth. The very word had alarmed her enough to achieve his aim. He knew now that he had her full co-operation. He held up his hand quickly – he didn't want to frighten her too much. "It's usually temporary, sometimes only momentary, but do you want to take that risk?"

Ivy started to tremble, losing control, tears leaking from her staring eyes.

"No, of course you don't. And stop that!" he said sharply. "There is too much for you to do."

Now she would pull herself together. She could cry later. Hastily, he wrote some instructions on a pad, tore off the sheet and handed it to Bessy-Ann to deliver to his housekeeper. Verbal messages, he knew from experience, could be mutilated in transit. When she had been dispatched and while they waited for the ambulance, he turned again to Ivy.

"Everything," he said, "and I mean everything, will have to be washed and disinfected. Furniture, floors, curtains. Get rid of all unnecessary clutter. Bessy-Ann will show you and give you a hand when she comes back. She knows the routine. Pauline is to be kept in one room, all her utensils and linen kept separate from the rest. The window is to remain open day and night and no-one is to set foot over that doorstep until I tell you." He put his arm comfortingly around her shoulder. Time now to ease up a little. "Liz will be in the best possible place, Mrs Edwards, and she stands a good chance. She has a strong constitution." He delved into his bag and called Pauline to him. "Now, I'm going to give you an injection. Take off your jumper, there's a good girl."

She obeyed, docile under his command. As the needle went in, she flinched and wriggled, sending the long, thin steel veering off course. It scratched across her shoulder blade and she let out a piercing shriek of pain that summoned the goose pimples in her watching mother and sister.

Carrie had called in just after the ambulance and the doctor had left. Bessy-Ann had taken the trouble to inform her of the situation, thinking Ivy could do with her company, what with Jim being in work.

"Oh, Ivy *bach*, come here!" she said, holding out her arms.

Ivy, her head on her mother's shoulder, broke down. "Why, Mam? Why Liz? Why my child?"

"There, there. These things happen, love."

That didn't help quell the anger Ivy was feeling. "I try my best to keep them clean and well fed, to bring them up tidy. If it was one of the Pierce clan, I could understand it..."

"Now Ivy, that's just not fair, you know it's not. It's downright cruel. It's not like you. You're blaming yourself and clutching at straws. Think what you're saying."

Ivy was shaking her head. "No, I didn't mean it like that, Mam, honestly. You know what I mean, don't you?"

She was crying again now and swamped with guilt. Carrie gently rubbed her hand up and down Ivy's back.

"Yes, I know love, I can see your reasoning." She loosened her hold on her daughter, to look her in the face. "The only way I can describe things is, there's wild flowers and there's garden flowers, eh? And they're both beautiful and they both thrive in their own environments. But both kinds are affected by circumstances, aren't they? Both can suffer drawbacks, and this is one of them. But our little Liz is strong, Ive – she'll pull through this, you'll see. Don't you worry, now."

By the time Jim came home from work, Ivy had been ready to scream at him, "It's all your fault! This would never have happened if you hadn't brought us to this God-forsaken hole!" She still needed to vent her spleen on someone. But she couldn't do it. One look at him told her that he was already lashing himself with those same thoughts. She couldn't give him a further whipping with her tongue. The sight of him sitting there by the table in his pit dirt with his dinner pushed back untouched and sobbing like a baby with his head on his arms robbed her of all her venom. Instead, she put her hand on his shoulder and said, "Come on, Jim, eat your dinner."

Her father was the same. Not a bit of good. Oh, they could chastise the women easily enough in day-to-day upsets with the children. Always with Jim it was: "Where were you when this happened?" if one of the girls hurt themselves. But if he had been looking after them, the tune changed: "Accidents do happen, gel." Lords and Masters, aye! Children themselves, if the truth was known. But this was no day-to-day thing, this was different. This was life-threatening diphtheria and laying blame at each other's door accomplished nothing. It only served to isolate them from each other when they needed each other the most.

Ivy's own thoughts had been tormenting her ever since Liz had been sent off alone in the ambulance to strangers and a strange environment. It isn't your heart that aches at such times, she thought abstractedly, it's the base of your throat. She was the one to blame if anyone was. She should have had them immunised, she knew that now. But she had been afraid of it, it was too new and she had kept putting it off. She should have insisted on going to that hospital with Liz, no matter what they said. Now she would never rid her mind of that picture of Liz holding out her arms and crying, "Mammy! Mammy!" as the doors of the ambulance closed and she was whisked away.

Maybe, if she had tried Bessy-Ann's advice it wouldn't have had to happen at all, thought Ivy, clutching at thin air. Carrie had said since that she could vouch for the effectiveness of her cure in years gone by. And Ivy had to admit, the woman had been right in identifying the disease. She had seriously misjudged her.

CHAPTER 22

The Fever Hospital

LIZ HAD BEEN given a quick disinfectant bath on arrival at the hospital before being carried to an iron-framed bed with smooth clean sheets in a big, pale-green room full of other, mostly empty, beds.

"G'neikobless," she whispered mournfully to the young nurse who tucked her in, desperately wanting something familiar to hold on to in this alien world of strangers.

"Good night and God bless you too, hinny," the Scottish girl replied, banishing forever the mystery of the word and instantly tuning in to the child's need, though it was only just gone midday. "Try and sleep now and don't you worry. Your mammy and daddy will be able to come and visit you soon."

And they did come, every Wednesday and Saturday evening, to stand and wave and mouth messages to her from behind a huge window, both of them dressed from head to foot in green gowns for all-too-short half-hour spells.

"You be a good wee gerrl," said Nurse McClean cheerfully, "and we'll soon have you up and about again, you'll see."

Liz couldn't be anything but good, she could only lay there coughing and gasping for breath and using up any energy she had in the effort. At first, the foot of her bed had been elevated on two colliers blocks. She'd had blanket baths, liquid meals and daily injections in her bottom until it was sore. She never cried out, terror stopping her. She had to be good or who knows what might happen? So she rolled over onto her tummy when she was bid, gripped the iron bars of her bed and shut her eyes tight to try to block out the memory of Pauline's scream.

In the second week her bed had come down a block, though Liz hardly noticed the change. In the third week her bed was flat; the fourth she was given one pillow and in the fifth, a second one. The days, nights and weeks became one long, lonely void of misery. She saw her parents now and then through a mist of tears, then slept and looked to the window for them again, but they were gone.

When the thirty-sixth day had safely come and gone, she woke one day to find someone dressed in a long green gown with a mask over his nose and mouth, sitting beside her bed. Only his eyes were visible. They were shining wet and winked at her, while he lifted a bandaged hand and placed a finger where his lips should be. It was Daddy!

Jim had bribed the nurses with a persuasive tongue, some silk stockings and a few lipsticks. He still kept in touch with some of his old mates down at the docks. If you had money, most things were still available there – and Jim had the money. He had worked doublers at every opportunity since Liz had gone to hospital. Ivy had begged him not to. She didn't want another invalid in the family. Long hours underground combined with worry and exhaustion were bound to lead to carelessness and higher risks. The extra money wasn't worth it. They could manage all right, just as long as they had money for the bus fares. It was all they needed – they'd had so much given to them by their friends and neighbours: sweets, chocolates, flowers, slices of chicken breast, cakes – all sorts of things, some from people they hardly knew. Their kindness and concern had amazed Ivy. She looked on the village with different eyes these days.

Brian Pierce had been the first to call to the house. He had come that first afternoon, holding a brown paper bag containing two fresh brown eggs wrapped in newspaper.

"Mammy says to give 'em to Liz," he said.

Ivy took them and thanked him but he had waited, wanting to say something more.

"Mrs Edwards?"

"Yes, Bri'?"

"She's not going to die, is she Mrs Edwards." It was a statement, not a question. "Vincent Griffis says you die wiv dipferia. He's a liar, he is."

CHAPTER 23

The Gipsies' Remedy

JIM HAD HAD an accident. Ivy had known all along it was bound to happen but there was no reasoning with him. Shaping a pit prop, his razor-sharp hatchet had slipped and sliced through the cushion of his thumb. Dr Treadwell had refused to stitch it until every vestige of coal dust had been removed. Jim wasn't having any of that. By that time all the feeling would be restored to the wound and it would be too tender to touch. Stubborn, he had gone home, extracted some hot resin from the sticks in the oven, poured it straight onto the raw flesh, stuck back the flap and bound it up. "It's what the gipsies do, gel," he explained.

Well, of course, Ivy might have known!

"I saw them do it once, when I was a boy. They used to camp by the river not far from our house every summer."

The wound healed a treat and Jim never lost a shift through it, though the blue crescent scar would remain with him for the rest of his life.

Liz was gaining ground rapidly now and Jim continued his short, unexpected visits to sit by her bed and tell her stories – mainly about the gipsies' yearly visits – and slide chocolate bars under her mattress. Carrie sent her a black china doll (always a favourite with young girls) to keep her company and crocheted scarlet knickers, a dress and bonnet for it. Pauline bought her eight little celluloid figures of Snow White and the Seven Dwarfs from the market over-the-other-side.

"It is a fever hospital, remember," warned one of the nurses, "she'll have to leave everything behind her when she goes home."

So the little orange-framed picture of poppies, bought with a penny each from the children of Liz's class at Miss Stephens' instigation, remained at home to wait for her, as did the little navy-blue prayer book from Miss Lewis and the Sunday School. She would want to keep those.

Halfway through July, Liz had her last disinfectant bath, clutching Bashful in one fist and Doc in the other. The Scottish nurse, when she had found them, had checked them for cracks and given her a conspiratorial wink. So, secreted in her fists they had stayed, with Liz hiding her hands behind her back whenever anyone else appeared on the scene. Then, for the first time in nine weeks, she donned day clothes and shoes and socks. She was going home!

CHAPTER 24

Full Acceptance

DURING THE PAST few months the news bulletins on the wireless had grown increasingly grim. Back in April, Norway and Denmark had been invaded. In May it was France, then June began with the evacuation of British troops from Dunkirk. On June 27 the newspapers said a Welsh town had had its first air-raid warning. And then there had been a machine gunning and bombing raid by a lone plane down at the docks. Twelve people had been killed and twenty-six injured. There was no satisfaction for Jim in the knowledge that he had been proved right.

Ivy stood by the back bedroom window looking out at the now emerald green, fern-covered mountain which, at first glance last October, she had found so oppressive. But now that both her girls were playing happily and healthily with all their new friends in the summer sunshine, she felt her last shred of resentment melt away. This was the best place to be.

CHAPTER 25

Vincent Griffiths

ELSIE-MAY WAS PREGNANT again. Ivy called in on her way to the shops to see if there was anything she wanted. There probably wouldn't be with all those children of hers to run errands but it was an excuse to call in for a sit and a chat. She called in often these days. Mrs Griffiths was already there with her son Vincent. He was standing on the axle of Brian's tricycle as Brian pedalled it round and round the middle-room table.

"Be careful, Vincent!" said his mother from her vantage point in the kitchen. Dressed in shades of brown, she reminded Ivy of an edgy sparrow as she twittered and fluttered anxiously over her son. "Mind that chair!" She half rose from her seat at every exclamation. "Be a good boy," she coaxed. "Come and sit down. Please."

"They're alright," assured Elsie-May calmly, "leave 'em be in by there!"

She may as well, thought Ivy, since Vincent wasn't taking a blind bit of notice of his mother's pleadings. But Mrs Griffiths couldn't relax if she tried. She was constantly worried about what might happen next and Ivy knew why. Billy Griffiths had confided the full story to Jim one day on the long trek home from Crymceynon Colliery.

"We've got a big problem with our Vince, Jim," Billy had said. "We just don't know how to deal with it."

"Oh aye, what's that then, Bill?"

"He swears, mun! And when I say 'swears' I mean swears. As Mary says, we never know when the air around him is going to turn Reckitt's blue."

Jim had tried to look sympathetic.

"We keep getting complaints, mun. We're ashamed. Aye, ashamed of our own son. Now that's not right, is it Jim?" He hadn't waited for Jim's reply. "We don't know where he gets it from. Not from us, wuss!" He hesitated. "Well, not from Mary, anyway. And the worse I ever lay my tongue to is bloody, bugger and damn. And even those under my breath if he's about."

Jim rubbed his nose to cover his amusement. The thought of Mary Griffiths getting into a rip and sounding off tickled him pink. She, who looked like she couldn't say 'boo' to a mouse!

"None of the other kids use language like that, do they? The only person we know of that does, is that posh Annabelle Jackson that lives at the bottom of the street. Bessy-Ann says she can swear worse than a trooper. But she's never out and about. So where's it coming from, eh?"

Jim shrugged his shoulders. Most of the colliers, of course, were familiar with all the swear words under the sun, but to give the Devil his due, they were rarely repeated above ground, there being gentlemen in the lowliest of societies.

"He's been a worry to us one way and another since the day he was born, wuss! And that day was an outing, believe me." Billy's shoulders heaved and sank at the memory of it.

"How do you mean, Bill?"

"Well, he was an eleven-pounder, mun. He put poor Mary through hell even then. I stood on that landing for hours listening to her screaming and shouting. 'Turn that ruddy picture to the wall,' she yelled at poor Bessy-Ann when it was finally over."

Billy's hand flew to his mouth. He hadn't meant to mention the picture but the damn thing was always at the back of his mind. Jim had noticed his reaction and was intrigued.

"Picture? What picture?"

"Oh, just one her maiden aunt gave us for a wedding present," Billy mumbled. "It's embroidered with all butterflies and flowers and birds and bees and things." His voice barely audible, he added, "'Love one another' it says in cross stitch." Looking wistfully into the future, he murmured, "Chance would be a fine thing!"

Jim got the picture. "Have you tried giving Vincent a good clip round the ear, Bill?" he asked, changing the subject back to the swearing to save Bill the embarrassment of going any further down that road.

"No, not yet. But I've threatened him. He's only six, mun, Jim."

"Have you sat him down and given him a good talking too, like man-to-man sort of thing?"

"Aye, time and time again. And Mary has. She's told him straight: 'When you grow up to be a big man, I'll remind you how you used to shame your poor mother'. Nothing seems to get through to him."

Jim shrugged his shoulders again. "Well, I can't think of anything else, Bill," he said. "Ivy's the one you should talk to. She would sort him out for you, I bet."

They had reached the top of Stephen's Street. As he left Bill, Jim said, "You never know mun, he may grow out of it."

"Aye, maybe," said Billy, not sounding too hopeful.

CHAPTER 26

Recruitment

WHEN THE AUTHORITIES began recruiting members for the Home Guard, Jim, Tom and Billy were among the first to volunteer, quickly followed by several others from the streets around. Jim knew he was no use to the army. If flat feet exempted you, what chance did he stand with a right foot that had been crushed and a left shin that had been broken in two separate accidents he had sustained during his working life? But he needed and wanted to feel he was doing his bit towards the war effort. What man didn't?

The wounds from both his injuries had taken a long time to heal, longer than the bones had taken to knit, until Jim had taken the matter into his own hands, copying once again what he had observed from the gipsies in his youth. It was worth a try. Ivy could scoff but he had learned a lot from them during those years. Every day, on both occasions, he had walked on his crutches to the nearest pistle and held the bare wound under the ice-cold spring water until the area around it had gone numb and blue. He had then vigorously rubbed the skin, surrounding it with a coarse piece of towelling till the colour came back, bound it up with a crepe bandage and put two of his long, thick woollen socks over that to keep the heat in and the blood circulating. The doctors involved at the time were surprised and self-congratulatory at the sudden and rapid improvement. Jim didn't enlighten them.

The recruit numbers continued to mount and they all met

up on a regular basis for practise – one evening a week for those on the right shift. Sometimes this took place on the canal bank where they marched smartly up and down, drilled, set the 'canal' alight with paraffin and jumped over it, unrolled barbed wire, crawled through it and lay flat on their stomachs to fire rounds into the bank. A gang of young boys watched all their actions and orders closely, but from a distance.

When manoeuvres were finished and the group had dispersed, Bill, Tom and Jim climbed halfway up the mountain for a sit, a chat and a smoke before going home. Now it was their turn to watch as the boys regurgitated all they had assimilated and turned it into their own fantasies. The mountain soon became a bloody battlefield, littered with fern-bayoneted bodies or 'men' shot down by verbal machine guns – 'a-a-a-a' – from a camouflaged hide-out, or blown up suddenly (with a high jump in the air) by bombs or mines exploding with a loud 'pwwch!' Aeroplanes on two legs with 'wings' outstretched zoomed in from all directions.

For the duration of their game, it was obvious to the three men watching and subconsciously reliving their own youth that inside each boy's head was a 'soldier' fighting for his life and his country. Just let the Germans come! They and their fathers would give 'em what for.

CHAPTER 27

Olicka Bolicka

LIZ DIDN'T DO much tap dancing these days. It wasn't worth the state it got her mother into. The last time she had been caught at it was in the back yard, accompanying herself with the chorus: "An' curse away, my boys, an' curse away!" Her mother had thrown open the back door and shouted: "Will you keep still! You'll shake away the only bit of flesh you've got left!" Liz's appetite was all right but she had gone to nothing in Ivy's eyes. "And it's anCHORS away!" she added. No, it wasn't, Liz had said, adamant. Teacher said. They had sung it in school. So there!

"That child is getting spoilt," said Carrie, who had been there. "You want to put your foot down with a firm hand, Ivy, or you'll be making a rod for your own back."

"Oh yes?" retorted Ivy. "And who was it who walked the whole of town till she found another black china doll?"

Liz soon found another craze to fill the void: two balls. She had stood for hours watching the bigger girls play against the smooth wall of Price's pine-end. "Olicka bolicka zooka zolicka, Olicka bolicka knob!" they chanted, throwing the balls alternatively and sending the last one high up to land on an enamel plate advertising Holdfast Boots with a knotted rope. Clang! Fortunately, Mrs Price was stone deaf and her husband was up the allotments. They repeated the verse to 'oversies', 'bouncies', 'legsies', and other variations, till a ball was dropped and they changed turns.

Liz was soon practising with two balls against any smooth bit of wood or wall in any spare moment she had, chanting as she threw. It wasn't long before Ivy pricked up her ears at the words. She didn't like the sound of them; they could be misconstrued. It was too similar to another word she had heard Jim say when he had hit his thumb nail instead of the metal one with the hammer while making the garden swing. The nails had been big ones that needed a good whack.

"Sing something else," she said to Liz, lightly.

"Why?" she asked.

Why did children always have to ask 'why' when you tried to tell them something for their own good?

"Because I don't like the sound of it."

"Why?"

Ivy was stuck for once for an explanation. How could she go into detail? Lamely, she said, "I don't think it sounds very nice."

Liz thought it sounded lovely, just right. The rhythm matched the throws. "I don't know nothing else," she pouted.

"You don't know anything else," said Ivy, automatically. "Think of something."

What was the matter with her mother? Liz wondered. Why was she having a row? She hadn't done anything wrong as far as she could see. Her bottom lip stuck out further.

"What about, um, salt, pepper, vinegar, mustard?" Ivy suggested.

Liz's eyes were down, feet scuffling. "That's for skipping," she said. Stupid, the tone implied. Besides, that didn't fit the rhythm. "Why can't I say it?" she persisted. "I like it!"

"And I don't, I tell you." Ivy was cornered. "It sounds too much like swearing."

Oh, so that's what it's all about.

"It isn't, Mam, honest," Liz said, reassuringly.

Ivy wanted an end to this. What would people think?

"You are not to say those words and that's final," she said. There was enough said about Vincent Griffiths and his tongue. She wouldn't have put it past him to have composed that verse himself.

Relating the episode to Jim later that day, he surprised her by not being in the least put out about it. In fact, he had burst out laughing and told her, "That's been going around for years, gel."

Well, she had never heard it.

"It came over with the Belgian refugees after the last war. They're Belgian words. They mean sweets or chocolates or something. I used to work with some of them in the colliery when I was young."

Not that it made a jot of difference to Liz. She carried on regardless, either out of earshot of her mother or under her breath in her presence. But several times in the days that followed, Liz was caught blithely singing the forbidden words as her mother passed to peg out some washing, pay a visit to the *ty-bach* or pick something from the garden. Liz would halt in mid-bolick, drop the ball and wait for the row. It never came.

Olicka bolicka knob!

CHAPTER 28

A Letter from Liverpool

IT WAS NOVEMBER and Carrie was sweeping up the fallen leaves outside her front door.

"Letter for you," said Jenkins the post, "from Liverpool. I think that's your Doris' handwriting, isn't it?"

Nosey bugger, thought Carrie, it would pay him to keep his opinions to himself. Now Mrs Davies from next door, who had been talking to her while she swept the front, would want to know all the ins and outs of a cat's arse! Well, she could wait.

Carrie went in and poured herself a nice cup of tea, in fine bone china of course, before settling down to open the letter. This was too rare an occasion and she intended to savour it. She sipped the tea delicately as she read the first few lines, and then let the cup drop back in its saucer with a bang. Doris was getting married to some bloke in the merchant navy next May! And about time too, was Carrie's first thought. She had been engaged three times. If Doris was looking for perfection in a man, she wouldn't find it!

"I'm making my dress, Mam," she wrote.

My godfathers, she must be serious, Carrie thought. She had never known Doris to thread a needle before.

"It's powder-blue crepe-de-chine. Mr Sykes let me have it as a special favour. He owes me that much. I've carried that shop of his for years. I've enclosed a postal order towards your train fare, Mam, and I'll be sending more as the time gets nearer because I'd like very much for you and Dad to be there, if you could possibly make it. I've written to our Ivy too, to invite them and my two little nieces, if they can possibly make it. I'd love to have those two little ones as bridesmaids. But I said I'll fully understand if they can't come, what with the move and hospital and everything."

Well, as far as Carrie was concerned, wild horses wouldn't keep them away.

"You'll like David, I know you will. He's a bit taller than me, fair, and something like our Glyn to look at – and I've always said our Glyn reminds me of Errol Flynn, so you can see he's HANDSOME! His father died years ago and his mother a few months back, so I've moved in with him."

Oo, the headstrong little…

"Don't worry, his sister Joyce lives here too, so tongues won't wag!"

Well why couldn't she have said that in the first place? Getting me all worked up…

"Joyce is courting strong so we hope to have the house to ourselves within a year. There's plenty of room here, it's a big house so could you all stay for a week, perhaps? We'd love it if you could. Make a little holiday out of it. After all, it's a long way to come. What do you think?"

Oo, a holiday! Now wouldn't that be a treat. In Liverpool! Almost like going abroad! The furthest Carrie had ever travelled up to now was Cardiff and that was only to the station to make sure Ivy got on the right train to London to go to service.

"I thought I'd let you all know now in plenty of time, so you can get used to the idea."

Carrie was used to it already. She couldn't wait. Would

they be allowed to go though? London and the provincial cities were now being bombed regularly. 'Is your journey really necessary?' asked the posters. Well, if it wasn't necessary to attend your eldest daughter's wedding, she didn't know what was.

Carrie's mind was made up. She was going. She was quite excited about the prospect. She loved 'jaunting'. Albert didn't, and hadn't for a long time now, not since he'd come back from the war. She knew that's what was at the bottom of it – the war. But she could never get him to explain or talk to her about it. Best to leave sleeping dogs lie, she concluded, rather than bring back bad memories. It must be that: bad memories. She used to think in the first few years afterwards that he would tell her eventually, but he never had. Whenever she had broached the subject he had fobbed her off one way or another, so she had just got used to it and accepted it.

Carrie had found it very strange in the beginning because Albert never used to be such a recluse. She couldn't even get him to come to the pictures with her and he used to love that just as much as she did. Still, he never stopped her going. "If Albert was to say I couldn't go somewhere, I'd go twice," she'd say jokingly, to hide her worry. "I was in enough with the kids while he was in the army." Though she never was. She had carted them with her wherever she had wanted to go. Ivy could vouch for that.

Carrie had often dwelt on Albert's reluctance to go any further than where they had actually lived. It was such a contrast to what he had been like before. When they were first married and the children were small, he liked nothing better than an occasional trip out on the bus or the train to a nearby town or a visit to relatives. They would save up and look forward to a little outing. She just couldn't understand

– and Albert couldn't say – that all he wanted and all he could cope with since his return from the battlefield was peace, quiet and routine. Chitchat and small talk was too much of an effort for him with all he had inside his head. Day to day, that was his life now. Each day was a mountain to climb, but over the long years he had managed to make some kind of path for himself that made the ascent a little easier.

Albert was resigned to Carrie's 'jaunting' now. Why should she suffer, after all? But, to be truthful, he did miss her when she wasn't there. The house was too quiet. Carrie was so full of life, full of fun. There was always laughter around where she was. He dealt with her absences by making a joke of it, like she would, and had a stock answer for anyone who called while she was out: "She's not in. She's gone north to play for Wigan!"

When Albert came home from work that day, Carrie was upstairs. She had been to her sister Martha's and back. (Her sister had married well; Joe was a surgeon, or had been, and had served in the First World War. He was retired now.) On the bed were three large crumpled brown paper bags. Inside were three expensive, rather flamboyant hats. Carrie couldn't decide which one she would wear for the big day. She was determined now, come hell or high water, that she and Albert would be at that wedding.

CHAPTER 29

The Glass Of Port

JIM EDWARDS AND Tom Pierce had become big butties at work. They had also become big boozing pals and most evenings found them either up the Navigation or down the Station or the Miners', shift permitting. Jim had asked Billy to join them several times as he was good company, but he had always refused.

"Has he signed the pledge or what?" Jim asked Tom.

"Naw, it's worse than that!"

"Worse?"

"It's a very long story, wuss."

They were strolling all the way down to the Station Hotel.

"Well, go on then, I'm all ears. We've got plenty of time."

Tom began. "He used to like his pop once, when he was younger. It all stems from then, from the time he played cards for money. Illegal in those days, see, wasn't it? Outside the cemetery and in the middle of winter."

Jim was immediately interested and Tom continued.

"Then one of the group said, 'Damn! That lot in there behind that bloody cemetery wall are warmer than us. We'd be better off in there with them.' Well, a week later, wuss, that bloke was dead and buried in that exact spot behind the wall!"

Was Tom pulling his leg? He seemed serious enough.

"Things got worse a month later when Bill went to the local barber's funeral. A spiritualist he was. 'Rejoice!' said one of his fellow worshippers as the barber was planted. 'Do not be downcast. We have not lost a brother. He is here with us now!' And right on cue, said Bill, a robin on a branch nearby started whistling and twittering, and that's unusual on a cold windy day, isn't it? It put the wind up Billy alright! 'Here I am,' it seemed to be saying, 'here I am.'" Tom could hardly tell the story now, for laughing.

"You're having me on, wuss!" said Jim.

"No I'm not, honest to God, Jim! This is exactly what Billy told me. He'd had a few before going, to ward off the cold and the dread, but ever since he's given up drink and gambling. He won't touch a drop. He spends all his time and energy now in the garden and doing up the house. Mary wishes he wouldn't, mind. His enthusiasm outdoes his ability. The sheep keep climbing over dumped rubbish to get in the garden, and have you been in his house yet?"

Jim shook his head.

"Well, that looks like a patchwork quilt!" Tom had a way with words. "Stitched in the dark!" he added.

Ivy didn't mind these nights out too much to begin with. It was nice to see Jim making new mates and settling down, just so long as he didn't come home drunk or sleep late for work. She enjoyed a bit of solitude with the wireless and her knitting after the girls had gone to bed. She was making a matinee coat for Elsie-May's new baby and the pattern was intricate feather and fan. You needed a bit of quiet for that. Ivy was a good knitter and took great pride in it, keeping the wool in a pillowslip on her lap the whole time so that the finished garment was always immaculate. She put the finishing touches to it and wrapped it in tissue paper.

Ivy knew the little coat wouldn't look new for long. Just one wash and it would probably be thickened from being dowsed in water that was too hot for it. Still, who knew what her standards would be like if she had a houseful? Ivy considered that prospect for a moment or two but reached a rapid conclusion. No, she could never be as bad as Elsie-May. She would still be particular, especially about food and her washing, even if the scrubbing and polishing had to go by the board. Jim would see to that. Big as he was, he had an Achilles' heel – a very weak stomach.

She remembered the time they had lived in a basement flat and Jim had discovered black pats (beetles) in droves in the *cwtch* under the stairs. He had heaved helplessly at the very sight of them. Someone had told him that a hedgehog would soon get rid of them, so he had caught one and installed it, thinking no further than that its mere smell or presence would be enough to rid them of the menace. But when he found the animal crunching up the crisp, black delicacy with relish, Jim had had his dinner up, quickly followed by his breakfast.

No, Elsie-May, it had to be said, was far from hygienic when it came to food. Only last week Ivy had seen her 'drawing' chickens for her Christmas orders on the kitchen table ready for storage in Parson the butcher's cold room, then give the wood a scanty wipe down with newspaper, followed by a none-too-clean dishcloth, before blithely proceeding to cut bread and jam culfs for the children. Jim wouldn't tolerate that in a month of Sundays!

Ivy put the spotless parcel on the dresser and went to fetch her coat. The baby wasn't due until next week – Christmas week – but she may as well deliver it now, then that job would be done and out of the way. The girls were fast asleep and she would only be half an hour at the most.

"Oh, Mrs Edwards! It's lovely, beautiful!" Elsie-May was genuinely pleased and touched by the gift. She held it up by the tips of her fingers. "All that work," she said enviously, seeing the pretty design. "Oh, I could never do that. Oh, you are clever. And so kind. Thank you." She leaned forward and gave Ivy a peck on the cheek.

Well! Ivy hadn't expected that. But it was nice to be appreciated, it gave you a nice feeling, but it was only what Elsie-May deserved when all was said and done. Ivy would never forget her kindness and concern over Liz last summer. All those kids of her own and she could still find it in her to worry over someone else's. No wonder people liked her.

"Come on," said Elsie-May, "you must have a little drink with me. A port. I've got some somewhere and it's Christmas in two days after all."

Ah, friendship had its limits. But how could Ivy refuse without hurting her feelings? "Er, well just a small one then," she said. "I must get back, I've left the girls in bed on their own." Oh well, she told herself, alcohol was an antiseptic wasn't it?

After a rummage in the depths of the sideboard cupboard, two dusty glasses and a bottle were unearthed and placed on the table. Ivy didn't like the look of them one little bit. She swallowed, practising. Elsie-May reached up to the airing rods and pulled down a damp cloth, huge and salmon pink and proceeded to give the glasses a cursory wipe out. Ivy looked and looked again, disbelieving her eyes. The 'cloth' was a pair of winceyette knickers! She shut her eyes, not daring or wanting to look. What the eyes don't see, the stomach won't worry about.

"Please God," she murmured under her breath, "don't let the gusset come anywhere near..."

CHAPTER 30

Ivy's Solution

IVY LOOKED AT the clock on the mantelpiece. Nearly half past five and still no sign of Jim. Oh, this was too much. She'd had enough of this now. Out Christmas Eve, out after dinner yesterday and out again since first thing this morning. Carrie and Albert had called over before ten o'clock, supposedly to stay for the day, but they hadn't been in the house five minutes before Jim and her father put their coats on again and were off out through the door. And he'd had no breakfast. He'd be ill, drinking on an empty stomach, as sure as God made little apples. Well, it would serve him right. She wouldn't tend him. He could stew in his own juice as far as she was concerned. She would have no sympathy for him.

A quarter to six! The evening session would be starting soon. Where the hell was he? No pubs were open now as far as she knew. If they were in Tom Pierce's company, they would probably be in one of his mates' houses helping to dispose of a secret horde. His nose was like a divining rod where alcohol was concerned.

Ivy lifted the saucepan lid off the dinner she was keeping warm for him on the hob, sitting on a saucepan of hot water so that it wouldn't dry out. A nice dinner going to waste. The last of the chicken and stuffing, crisp roast potatoes (rapidly losing their crispness), mashed potatoes, sprouts (going yellowier by the second), peas, carrots and a lovely drop of gravy, if she said so herself. She moved the saucepan a little further back from the fire. The girls and Carrie had gone over to Duke Street, carrying a dinner for Albert after they'd had theirs – Carrie's intuition telling her Ivy would be best left on her own in the circumstances. Sparks would be flying there soon, by the look on her face. The girls would be better off out of it.

Ivy wondered if Tom Pierce had come home yet. She doubted it. And their baby due any minute. Men! The selfish... Marching to the *cwtch*, she grabbed her coat and crossed the street to Elsie-May's.

"No, not yet," Elsie-May said, totally unperturbed and with an indulgent smile in answer to Ivy's inquiries. "No sign of the ol' drunkards since two o'clock!"

Didn't this woman ever get cross?

"Did you say two o'clock?" Ivy asked. She hadn't seen them since ten.

"Yes. They called in then, the three of them, on their way to somewhere over-the-other-side. They wanted a bite to eat first, though. They were starving!"

"A bite to eat?" repeated Ivy, disbelievingly.

"Yes. Talk about famished! They polished off all my pork and stuffing and my last jar of pickles. You should have seen the pile of sandwiches I made and they were all gone in no time."

Mm, were they now? It was Ivy's turn to smile. Jim had already been drunk by two o'clock, then. He must have been, he would never have eaten at Elsie-May's in his right senses. She had him now – she'd cure him!

Back at home, Ivy settled herself by the fire, switched on the wireless and took out her embroidery to stitch some more lilacs on the small tablecloth she was making from a bleached flour bag. She hummed to the music as she stitched. At half-past six she heard the front door open. Jim staggered in warily, with a grin like the Cheshire Cat's on his face.

"Alright gel?"

Ivy grinned back at him. "Yes, fine!"

Jim, fully expecting fireworks, was slightly nonplussed by the affability in her voice.

"Do you want dinner?" she asked, getting up and switching off the wireless. "I've kept one warm for you."

"Aye, aye, yes please, gel." He concentrated hard on making his legs and tongue work as near to normal as he could as he walked unsteadily to the bosh by the back door to wash his hands, venturing further conversation on the way. Perhaps he wasn't looking quite as drunk as he felt. "Wherrer the girls then?"

"Over at Mam's. They won't be back now until bedtime, I expect."

"Oh." Pity, that, he thought. It meant there was plenty of time yet for Ivy to explode. It was bound to come. If the girls had been here, she would have retreated as she usually did into wounded, stubborn silence. He didn't know what to expect now. She had something up her sleeve though, he was sure of that.

"Sit down. I'll get your dinner for you," she said.

Cautiously, Jim sat with his back to her, half expecting the hot dinner to be tipped over his head or dropped with a crash on the floor behind him. Instead, it was placed quietly before him and Ivy sat down again to resume her needlework. He relaxed a fraction and smiled across at her.

"Ah, this looks good, gel!"

"Eat up then, while it's hot."

Threading her needle with more mauve silk, she stitched away patiently, one eye on him, the other on her work, until he had cleared his plate.

"By damn, I enjoyed that!" he said, pushing his plate to one side. He got up and moved to the armchair opposite hers, loosening his belt and relaxing his guard as he went. What more could a man want, he asked himself as he laid back contentedly by the fire and shut his eyes. A good home, good mates, good food, a few drinks – and an understanding wife! It was Christmas and the war and all it meant seemed very far away for the time being. His breathing slowed. Yes, life could be sweet on times.

"There's some Christmas pudding left if you want it," said Ivy suddenly, penetrating the soporific haze that swam inside his head. He couldn't be allowed to go to sleep. Not yet.

"Er, no thanks, gel. Later. I'm as full as an egg right now."

"I didn't think you'd have room for it," said Ivy quietly, "not after all you've eaten today."

On the edge of unconsciousness, Jim tried to work out what she was on about.

"Mmm?"

"Well, all those sandwiches you scoffed."

Sandwiches? He hadn't scoffed any sandwiches. Had he?

"Pork sandwiches, with pickles. And stuffing."

Sandwiches. No. He couldn't remember. God, his eyelids weighed a ton!

"Yes, you must remember." I'll make you, thought Ivy! "At Tom's house. His wife made them, dinnertime."

He sat up, suddenly wide-awake now. "I ate pork and pickles? In Elsie-May's?"

"And stuffing," added Ivy, rubbing in salt.

It took Jim all of five seconds to reach the drain in the backyard. She spared a sympathetic flinch at his painful retching, then picked up her bundle of Clark's Anchor silks and searched for a suitable shade of green. She doubted very much if Jim would be going out again this evening. And she had a feeling it would be a very long time before he'd get too drunk to keep his wits about him in future. She wet the end of the length of silk she had selected and slid it accurately through the eye of the needle.

Chapter 31

Another Spring

THE CLOCKS WERE turned forward again, making the daylight stretch into the evenings and the children harder to get in for bed. From teatime to dusk on weekdays and morning till night at weekends they were out in droves, weather permitting, covering the mountainside and outnumbering the sheep. Relishing the fresh air and freedom again after the long winter months, Liz and Pauline were eager to rejoin all their friends to play through the ritual procession of games, most of which the girls had never heard of until they moved to the village, until the days shortened once more. Boredom was a word that never entered their vocabulary these days. If there was any likelihood of it rearing its head and they started to bicker with each other, Jim would say sternly: "If you two can't find something useful to do, then help your mother!"

With the temperature still nippy, the first things to appear were skipping ropes, footballs, rounder bats and balls, hooks and wheels, whips and tops and anything else that involved running about. As the air warmed, these would be followed by two balls, jackstones, marbles, stepping games or hide and seek.

Towards the end of July, all their time would be taken up picking the mountain's lush harvest of whinberries, then toting them round the houses to sell. There was always a ready market for this produce. The end of August meant the same procedure for the plentiful supply of blackberries growing in the hedges of the farmer's field and three sides of the allotments. "Bar cwtch, bar cwtch, nobody come to my cwtch!" the children chanted if they found a well-laden bush of either fruit, and it was obeyed without question.

The last week or two of the school holidays usually found them scavenging pieces of cardboard or 'borrowing' a tin tray without their mothers' knowledge to use as sleds to slide down the dry grass mown short by the sheep, from the top of the mountain to the bottom, choosing clear pathways for their descent. Hour upon hour they burned up energy, only going home when they were hungry.

Liz and Pauline, copying the other children, had learned to stave off their hunger pangs while they played. Depending on the time of year, they nibbled on what nature provided all around them. The 'bread and cheese' – as they called the leaves on the hawthorn trees – were delicious when young; their bright red berries likewise in the autumn. 'Sweet leaves' – the little dark green rosettes of leaves growing in the big field – were bitter to begin with but turned sweeter the longer they were chewed on. Then there were the allotments to visit to coax for young carrots, peas or beans, which were nicer raw than cooked. 'Scrumping' fruit of all kinds from back gardens was another, though more dangerous, source of food. You might be spotted and clecked on. Stumps of cabbages and cauliflowers, peeled to their soft centres, tasted like the sweet young kernels in the hazelnuts that grew in abundance not far from the river – as did groundnuts, identified by their clusters of small white flowers.

As dusk turned to dark, parents gathered at the top of the streets to shout or whistle in their children. In most cases, wherever they were and whatever they were doing, they came running. It was folly not to obey the 'call'. If they were too far away to hear it, it was relayed to them by others:

"Matthew, have you seen John? His mother's on the warpath, tell him!"

"If you see Rhys, tell him his dad's been shouting for him for ages. He'll cop it!"

Jim had a piercing two-note whistle, low then high, blown with his fingers on his tongue. It carried far on the air and the two girls easily recognised it among all the others. A slow response led to Jim's right eyebrow descending over his eye, his left remaining unmoved. This was to be avoided at all costs. It was enough to subdue them and get them in quickly – washed, teeth brushed, undressed and ready for bed in record time. It always amused Jim because if it hadn't had that effect, he would have been lost. He could never lift a finger to them, unlike Ivy, who could give a stinger if she was riled – but only ever on the thighs or bottom, the well-padded areas, and never around the head. Jim smiled to himself. If he had ever given them a smack he knew he would have had a right hook from Ivy. Men's hands were too big for smacking. On the fairly rare occasions when they had been late responding to his whistle and had been sent off to bed without supper, he had sneaked up a little later with a plate of thick toast and dripping. Still with that eyebrow down, though.

CHAPTER 32

Tragic News

TELEGRAMS TERRIFIED CARRIE; they never brought anything but bad news to the likes of her. She put the one that had just been delivered onto the mantelpiece against the clock and stared at it, debating the lesser of the two evils: to open the thing herself or to wake Albert, who was on nights and had only been in bed for an hour or two. No, she couldn't do it. Albert would have to. Just holding the thing gave her the shakes. She went upstairs into the bedroom and shook him gently, whispering his name. "Albert? Albert!"

"Mm? What?" His eyes, still black rimmed after his bath, opened slightly then closed again.

"We've had a telegram."

Albert grunted and rolled over, pulling the bedclothes with a jerk over his ears.

"Albert!" Louder now and rougher shakes. "It's a telegram! I think it's from our Doris."

"Then open it woman!"

"I can't. You do it."

"Dear God! Can't a man have a bit of sleep in this house?" He sat up and snatched it from her, tearing it open. "It's probably to say she's changed her bloody mind again!"

It was a Saturday at the beginning of May. There were less than three weeks to go before the wedding, but she had done it before. There had only been a fortnight to go that time. Albert's outburst had an instantly calming effect on Carrie.

Of course! That was the reason for it. She had been worrying for nothing. Hadn't Doris assured her time and again in her letters that she lived far enough away from the city and all the dangers of those terrible bombing raids? She sat on the side of the bed and watched Albert's face as he unfolded the paper and read the stilted sentences. His features slackened suddenly into a look of utter despair, and fear again gripped Carrie's stomach as her mind raced.

"What is it? What's wrong? It is from our Doris, isn't it?"

Albert looked up at her but could say nothing, do nothing. His silence petrified her. Her mind searched frantically for some explanation and she pounced on one, willing it to be true.

"She's pregnant, that's what it is, isn't it? And that waster's gone off and left her in the lurch. I knew it. I knew it would happen, moving in with him and everything, the headstrong little..." It was no good, she wasn't deceiving herself. She could see the truth in Albert's face but she couldn't admit to it or accept it. She prattled on, panicking. Once she stopped, Albert would say something and she couldn't bear to hear the words. While they remained unsaid... "She'll have to come home to us, that's all. We'll manage somehow. A nine days wonder that's all it will be..." Her voice was shaking and getting higher with each word. She had a last attempt: "You let anyone say anything to me about her, that's..." She trailed off, giving in, as Albert reached out to put his arms around her.

In 26 Stephen's Street, Ivy was folding the pretty dresses Vera had made for her two girls to wear to the wedding before putting them away. They were so sweet, pale eau-de-nil seersucker with smocked yokes. Vera had finished them the night before and had brought them up for them to try on, and Ivy had finished off the two little white boleros she had knitted to be worn over them. It could be chilly up there in

Liverpool, Doris wrote.

Just over a fortnight to go now! They were all so excited, especially her mother and the kids. Pity Jim couldn't come. He couldn't get time off work. They couldn't have afforded his extra fare anyway, but it would have been nice to go as a whole family. Vera had said she'd cook a dinner for him for the couple of days they'd be away. She was such a good friend. She had also made a little dress for Elsie-May's youngest out of the leftover bits as a favour to Ivy. Elsie-May had spared her some coupons so she could get a pair of shoes for Pauline. She couldn't wear those school shoes. Liz would wear her ankle straps, that would be right up her street! She could see her now, showing off her tap dancing to Doris and Dave. And Ivy had her 'special occasion' at last. She would be wearing a pale-blue satin underset, her blue paisley dress and her navy coat with the fur collar. Auntie Martha had supplied Mam with a smart outfit, also in navy blue, and Vera had made her a very pretty corsage to pin on the lapel out of scraps of pink velvet. She would take that over to Mam's now to show her. Doris was going to be so proud of them all.

She got to Duke Street just half an hour after the telegram had arrived.

The following day brought a letter from Joyce. Her brother had been expected home on leave that night and Doris had spent the day out shopping and getting her hair set. It was getting dark by the time she returned and the sirens must have started just as she got off the train. Doris hadn't gone to the shelter, probably wanting to get home as it was only a short walk to their house. Joyce had found her in the street later, when the all clear had sounded. A stray bomb had fallen in the next street and she was lying in a pool of blood, a piece of shrapnel embedded in her jugular vein. She must have died almost immediately.

CHAPTER 33

Dealing with Death

CARRIE FOUND IT impossible to accept Doris' death. Her beautiful eldest daughter had been cut down in her prime when she had everything to live for. All her relations would soon be gathered for her funeral when it should have been her wedding. The cruelty of it was unbearable.

While Ivy tried her best to comfort her mother over the rest of that dreadful day, it was her father who worried her the most. He wandered around the house like a lost sheep. She had tried to comfort him as well during those first hours and had put her arms around him to hug him close. But he hadn't responded or shed a tear. All he did was pat her hand and say, "I'm alright, love, you see to Mam. She can't cope with all of this. She needs you." And you don't? Ivy thought.

Daughters are always more in tune with their fathers. Always a quiet man, Albert's silence was now extreme. She knew instinctively that this lack of evidence of his grief didn't mean that he wasn't deeply affected by the loss of his child. She also knew it would make him ill if he didn't let go soon.

CHAPTER 34

Still No Tears

THE NEXT DAY, after sending the girls down to stay with Vera, Ivy and Jim went back over to Duke Street. Carrie was busying herself when they arrived, half-heartedly and randomly tidying up – clearing the table, gathering and folding old newspapers, washing dishes. Carrie's way of handling things, Ivy knew, was to stay inside her own four walls and stick to some sort of routine until she could come to terms with whatever had happened. There was comfort and security in that. Ivy's mind went back to the time her grandmother died. Carrie had behaved in the same way then.

Her father, on the other hand, was still pacing about like a caged animal. He needed to get out in the fresh air and open spaces away from this horror and confinement, to try to lose himself and his thoughts in nature – walking on grass, among trees, under the sky; to be distracted by his surroundings if only for split seconds. He didn't need people, he didn't want company; in fact he was afraid of it – afraid he'd lose control completely. The closer one got to anyone else, the more pain it brought. He could stay in control if he distanced himself from involvement with the others.

"Dad," said Ivy, sensing his needs, "why don't you go up the allotments or somewhere for an hour or two, eh? The fresh air will do you good. God knows you don't get your fair share of it stuck in that mine day after day. Don't worry, I'll stay with Mam till you come back."

"Aye, aye, I think I will. Is that alright? Are you sure?"

"Of course. There's nothing you can do, Dad, is there, not at the moment."

He needed no second bidding.

As soon as he left, Ivy had a quick word with Jim, who then followed Albert discreetly a little while later. Watching from a distance, Jim saw him collect his garden fork from the allotment shed and start digging, slowly at first then frenziedly, with a ferocity that achieved nothing but damage. Suddenly he stopped, his head tilted back, his knees gave way under him and he sank to the ground. Thankfully, there was no-one else around this early in the morning.

When Jim reached him, he had his eyes tightly shut and his fists pressing hard against his mouth as if trying to stop himself from vomiting. There were no signs of tears. Jim lifted him to his feet and walked with him to the allotment shed.

"You alright, Dad?"

"Aye, Jim, aye. I'm fine. Just felt a bit faint, that's all."

Jim passed him the flask of precious whisky he'd purposefully brought with him. Later, he told Ivy in detail what had happened. She was then more worried than ever.

CHAPTER 35

Getting Things Ready

DURING ALBERT'S ABSENCE and with Carrie's grateful assent, Ivy saw to the funeral arrangements. The Co-operative Wholesale Society would handle it all. Bessy-Ann, who had called to give her condolences and to offer to help in any way she could, stayed with her for company.

Ivy sent telegrams to her two brothers, Glyn and Daniel in America. There was no possibility of them coming home, she knew, but they had to be told. She also sent one to Auntie Martha and her husband Joe to ask if they could come to stay with her parents for a few days. She would have to have help from someone. She couldn't be in two houses at the same time, and Jim would be off to Liverpool later in the week to accompany Doris' body home on the train. David and Joyce would be coming as well and they'd have to stay at her house, which would take some organising. But it was the least she could do. They couldn't travel all that way and go straight back on the night train.

Joe and Martha arrived late that night and would stay in Duke Street until a few days after the funeral. They had brought all sorts of things with them, including suitable black clothes for Carrie, both sisters being of much the same 'stamp'. Albert was alright in that department, his one and only best suit being kept mainly for funerals. Trust Auntie Martha to turn up trumps, thought Ivy, thankfully. You could always rely on her to think things through and to be practical as well as helpful.

In the days leading up to the funeral, Ivy had no time to grieve. It had to be pushed to the back of her mind so that she could concentrate on what had to be done. The house in Duke Street had to be cleaned right through and made to look its best for a start. To be poor and show poor was the Devil all over, Carrie always said, and Ivy wasn't going to let her down. While Martha kept Carrie company, cushion covers and runners were washed, starched and ironed; curtains from the three downstairs rooms were laundered and re-hung; windows were cleaned and two nice rugs that Joe and Martha had brought were put in place of some rag mats. The best china was collected up from Vera's, Bessy-Ann's, Ivy's and Carrie's and was carefully washed, polished dry with tea-towels and packed away in readiness for the traditional post-funeral sit-down meal.

Ivy couldn't have done it all without Vera and Bessy-Ann's help. People were right about Bessy-Ann, she now realised, as they all polished the furniture together. She still felt guilty about her previous thoughts of her. But if Bessy had sensed anything of Ivy's attitude when Liz was so ill, she had never shown any sign of it. They had since become good friends.

CHAPTER 36

Uncle Joe

SINCE JIM HAD found her father acting so strangely in the allotments, Ivy's concern for him had deepened. Since coming back from the war he had seemed different, and the more she dwelled on it, the more she realised that he had been keeping things back from them and suffering in silence all these years. Doris' death, a direct result of this war, had brought all that death and destruction from the last one flooding in on him and he couldn't cope with it. Ivy was terrified at the thought of what might happen but was helpless to prevent it. She had tried all sorts of ways to get him to 'open up' but was frightened to delve too deeply. His reluctance to have any sort of conversation about those years or about war itself left her bereft. She wondered if Uncle Joe could somehow get through to him. He had served in the Great War, too. That at least was a common denominator between them. Ivy had never taken much notice of him before. He was a very shy, reticent man who always kept in the background – the total opposite of his wife. She decided she would have a chat with him at the first opportunity.

It came quicker than Ivy had expected. Joe was standing alone in the backyard smoking his pipe when she had gone out to shake some mats.

"Uncle Joe!" she said, impulsively. "Could I have a quick word with you? It's about my Dad."

"Of course you can, my dear. What is it? What is the matter? How can I help?"

The eagerness in his voice told her that he had sensed something was wrong too, and that he was half expecting her to ask. Reticent he may be, but he obviously pondered over things a lot and saw much that others might miss.

"I'm so worried about him." Ivy rolled her lips together in an effort to stop herself crying, but her chin quivered. "I'm afraid he'll make himself ill." The effort hadn't worked and the tears came spilling out.

He put his hand on her arm. "Let's take a little walk over to your house, eh? Then you can tell me what's worrying you without fear of interruption."

They left by the garden door and walked up the gulley to Stephen's Street. Two hours later, he left Ivy's with the words, "Leave it to me, my dear, and try not to worry. I'll do my best."

"Thanks, Uncle Joe."

Ivy was exhausted with it all. She closed her front door and went back inside to have a few moments to herself. She couldn't relax at all. Had she done the right thing? Was now the right time?

Back at Albert's house, Joe had a quick chat with Martha in the pantry, then they walked back into the kitchen.

"Look," said Martha, casually, "why don't you two men take yourselves off for a walk or something, up the mountain or somewhere? You're no help here at the moment with all us women about the place. You're just getting in our way and under our feet."

"Come on then, 'Bert," said Joe lightly. "We shan't stay where we're not wanted, shall we!"

CHAPTER 37

The Catharsis

JOE, KEEPING AN eye on Albert, waited until they were halfway up the mountain before uttering a word. Albert was also silent. Then quietly, Joe said, "Bloody wars!" Would Albert respond? They walked on about a hundred yards, Joe waiting patiently. He wouldn't rush this.

At last, Albert replied. "Bloody wars, aye." The anger in his voice was palpable. "And it's only a handful of the buggers at the top who decide it all. We don't get a say."

They climbed on again in silence but at least Albert had responded. Joe hoped it was a trickle that just might lead to a stream. Five minutes passed before Albert spoke again.

"You don't see many of them or their bloody relatives involved in the sheer bloody misery of it though, do you?"

Joe nodded, but Albert wasn't looking for a reply, it was as if he was talking to himself, voicing his thoughts at last.

"And what happens when it's all over? When we've done all their dirty work for them? We've outlived our bloody usefulness, that's what!" Albert's face twisted into rage. "You can all clear off now back to your sad little lives. There's no jobs for you, no grub, no rejoicing for you lot. We get all of that. You're no use to us anymore." He stopped in his tracks. "We're no use to any bugger, no use at all!" What use was he to Carrie, Ivy or anyone else? He couldn't talk to them or console them about Doris, much as he longed to. He was useless, a waste of space.

Joe didn't know what to say. Best to say nothing then, he decided. He didn't want to stop this flow, not now it had begun. Albert needed to talk about his feelings, preferably to someone like himself – someone who could relate to what it was all about. Someone who had been there. Not that Joe had suffered like Albert. His own part in the war had been on the medical side, trying to save lives not destroy them. That in itself put a different aspect on things in retrospect: there had been so much to do, he hadn't had time to dwell on things. Oh, he'd had his share of nightmares in the first few post-war years but they were balanced out by the fact that he had been in a position to help and do some good. God knows how much worse Albert's experience must have been out there in the slaughter of the battlefield, seeing and being forced to take part in the killing, maiming and suffering of one's fellow man, knowing there was nothing you could do about it but try to save your own skin to fight another day, and another.

Joe was beginning to feel nervous. What if the flood of Albert's thoughts overwhelmed him, dragged him further down, drowned him? He would have to tread very carefully from here on.

Albert had quickened his pace, turning from the sheep path they had been following and heading straight up now on all fours as if he wanted to get away from everything as quickly as he could. He muttered to himself continually as he struggled upwards: "…and here we are again, back to where we started. Nothing gained. All for nothing. All that filth and obscenity and ruined lives, all for nothing. Wasted!" Up and up he climbed, his mouth moving as fast as his feet.

Joe was really worried now and being of stocky build he could not keep up. He stopped, resting his hands on his knees to get his breath back. When he looked up again, there was no sign of Albert. Now Joe tackled the ascent on all fours. When he reached the summit he could see Albert a few yards below him, sitting on a clump of young green ferns, his knees up to his chest, his arms clasped tightly around them, his body rocking back and forth like a boy when he's fallen and hurt himself but there's no-one around to comfort him. When Joe reached him, he was shocked at the state he was in. His eyes and nose were streaming wet, his mouth full of bubbling saliva. He turned his head as Joe sat beside him and put his arm around his shoulders.

"Doris, my lovely little Dory! Why her, Joe? What had she ever done? Why couldn't it have been me instead? Look at me: this hopeless wreck of a man! I'd be no loss to anyone. It's all still there inside me screaming to get out and I can't shift it. It's taken my life from me, Joe. I'm no bloody good or use to God nor man!"

"Hush, 'Bert, hush. That's nonsense. Ivy and Carrie need you, and your two lovely little granddaughters. You're a lucky man to be surrounded by such love." Joe and Martha had never had children. "And they all need you now more than ever."

There was no pacifying Albert, his whole body was still wracked with his sobbing. Joe tightened his grip on his shoulders and said, "Let it out, 'Bert! That bloody scream inside you. Let it out, man. Get rid of the bloody, poisonous thing. There's no-one up here to see you or hear you. Let it go, once and for all!"

To Joe's surprise, Albert's sobbing slowed and gradually stopped. He sat for a while just staring ahead, then suddenly stood up. A low rumbling sound, from deep in his guts, gathered and rose. Like an erupting volcano the noise belched out – long, high and piercing. It was a scream the likes of which Joe had never heard, even when having to amputate limbs with little or no anaesthetic in the makeshift field hospital. He stood up too, grabbing Albert by the shoulders. "There, man, there. That's good, that's better. Well done!"

For several minutes neither man moved. Then Joe took out his tobacco pouch to fill his pipe, offering it first to Albert. "Let's sit down, Alb', eh? Have a quiet smoke."

They sat and they smoked, back to silence but a different, more comfortable one. All the tension seemed to have left Albert's body. Joe prayed it would last. They finished their pipes and tapped them out on a stone. Joe got to his feet.

"Well, shall we go back for a bit of dinner now?" He looked at his watch. "We'd better not be late or we'll be in for a right rollicking!"

Albert actually smiled.

"Come on, then," said Joe, "but don't think we're having a race. I'm not built for racing!"

CHAPTER 38

The Two Sisters

MEANWHILE MARTHA, NOW knowing all about Ivy's concern and the reasons for it, sat with Carrie in her kitchen while Ivy and Vera sat in the parlour making lists of what was left to do. Martha was five years older than Carrie and knew her sister well – knew just how far she could go without overstepping the mark. It was always best to come straight to the point with her, no beating about the bush if something needed to be said. So she leaned forward in her chair and said gently, "You need to help Albert over this, Carrie. It's taking its toll on him."

Carrie looked up, startled by this announcement. Martha shuffled to the edge of her seat, reached out, took Carrie's hands and said, "I know, I know that you must be suffering too, what you must be going through. Don't think for a minute that I don't. But you are strong, Carrie. You may not realise it now, but you are and you're stronger than Albert. This terrible accident that has happened has brought back to him everything about war and all its consequences. All the cruelty that he witnessed and was part of in the last war, and now to lose his lovely, beloved daughter through this one..."

She deliberately left the sentence unfinished so Carrie would focus on what she was saying and think about it. Understandably, Carrie was so wrapped up in her own grief that she was oblivious to that of those around her – those closest to her. If Martha could remove a little of that wrapping, she knew it would benefit her sister. Only good would come out of it.

"All the grieving in the world won't bring Doris back, love," she continued. "It's the living that need you now: Albert, Ivy and those two lovely granddaughters of yours. Who do they look to? Who have they always looked to in times of any sort of trouble? And this is of the worst sort, isn't it? They all need you to be there for them, just as they are all there for you, if you give them a chance. But Albert needs you most of all."

Carrie said nothing for minutes but she stared at Martha's eyes, searching her face, analysing what she had said, knowing that her sister always meant well for all concerned. With a huge sigh, she finally nodded in agreement. "You're right, our Martha, I know you are right." She broke down in tears again and Martha squeezed her hands. "It's the thought that I'll never see her face again, hear her voice, touch her again. It's breaking my heart."

Martha slid off her chair onto her knees before her sister. "Oh, Carrie *bach*, our dear Carrie." She squeezed her hands tighter as the tears spilled from her own eyes, wishing she could somehow ease this terrible pain for her. "Listen, love, you've got memories, Carrie – loving, happy memories. Try and focus on those and you will see her, hear her, touch her whenever you want to, love."

Pictures of Doris at different ages immediately started flitting through Carrie's mind at this suggestion. She stared into the distance, seeing them clearly and reliving the moments. Martha was right again. She was always sound, sensible and sincere. She was so lucky to have a sister like her, she realised. It was such a shame, such a waste that Martha had never been able to have children. She was so wise and caring of others.

Carrie nodded to Martha, loosened her hands from her grasp, then held her beloved sister's hands tightly to her bosom.

CHAPTER 39

The Children's View

IVY HAD TOLD the girls of Doris' death the day she had learned of it. It was always best to be honest with children, she felt. Death to the Edwards girls had, until now, meant the accidental discovery of a dead bird or animal slowly decaying in the undergrowth and crawling with maggots. On such occasions they chanted as they had seen the other children do: "Fever, fever, don't come to my door!" Then they spat and threw stones on it to cover it up. They never associated such sights with the death of people. The whole concept of mortality among their own kind was beyond them as it hadn't come into their lives before. Grampa Edwards had died before they were born, Wendy Williams' father had died before they knew her, and as they had only met Auntie Doris once, when they were both too young to even remember what she looked like, her sudden demise did little to further their understanding of the great mystery. It remained as remote as ever for the time being.

What did upset the girls was their mother's and grandmother's grief. To see grown-ups crying inconsolably really unsettled them. They felt shut out, fearful and helpless while it went on. They wanted them back as before. The whole business reflected itself at bedtimes for weeks afterwards. They talked about it to each other, trying to reason out and come to terms with the reality of death. They said their prayers more frequently than before, listening to the words they were saying instead of rattling them off in parrot fashion.

"As I lay me down to sleep,

I pray the Lord my soul to keep,

And should I die before I wake,

I pray the Lord my soul to take."

They felt their security threatened. Prayers were their insurance. If the worst should happen then Jesus would look after them.

"There are four corners to my bed,

Four angels round my head,

One to watch, two to pray,

And one to carry my soul away."

Away to Jesus, of course, in Heaven. The burning fires of Hell held no threat for them. You only had to worry about that when you grew up, because Mr Pomfrey had told them that Jesus said, "Suffer little children to come unto me."

Their last prayer was of their own composition.

"Please God, take care of Mammy and Daddy and Gran and Grampa and Grannie Edwards and Uncle Glyn and Uncle Danny..." and anyone else who was important in their lives, finishing with: "...and please look after them for ever and ever. Amen."

CHAPTER 40

The Funeral

CARRIE WAS SITTING on the settee in her parlour between Albert and David, staring at the coffin, waiting for it all to begin and be over, while the men from the village gathered quietly outside the house. Vera and two of Carrie's neighbours were busy in the kitchen slicing tongue and ham (supplied courtesy of Martin the grocer, who waived the necessary ration coupons for 'friends in need'), cutting loaf cakes donated by friends and sorting out the borrowed cups and saucers, ready for the traditional post-funeral sit-down meal when all the men returned from the cemetery. Women never attended a burial. They were present at the beginning of life, men at the end.

The vicar of St Mark's arrived. Carrie gripped Albert's arm tighter and let out her breath in an audible, involuntary sigh. Everyone rose to their feet. Liz, ensconced with Pauline in the kitchen with the helpers, was all eyes and ears in this new, awesome experience. She could hear the disembodied voice of the vicar and the muffled sobbing of her mother and gran. Then the voice stopped and everyone said, "Amen." Suddenly, there was a tremendous low rumble from outside the house, gathering and rising in volume, and the most beautiful sound she had ever heard enveloped her. The hairs on her arms stood straight on goose-pimpled skin and she caught her breath. The men had started singing – tenors, baritones and bass blending in beautiful harmony:

"The da-ay Thou ga-avest Lo-ord is ended,

The darkness fa-alls at Thy behest,

To The-ee our mo-orning hymns ascended…"

Never before in all of her six years had Liz experienced such powerful emotion. Tears fell like little peas from her eyes, yet she wasn't sad. She would never hear that hymn again without it having the same profound effect on her.

The service over, the coffin was carried to the hearse and the four bearers – Jim, Tom Pierce, Billy Griffiths and David – took up their positions around it. Dr Treadwell had kindly offered his car and had supplied a driver to carry the main mourners. There were only two: Joe and Albert. Albert's brothers, all four of them, had been killed in the war. He had no sisters. Jack Jones was invited to join them in the car. He was as close as any brother could be. Besides, it was such a long walk to the cemetery and though Jack would have done his damnedest to get there, he wouldn't have been able to keep up with that club foot of his. All the rest of the men gathered in neat, orderly ranks behind the car and the procession moved slowly off.

The route would take them down the long street to the big vicarage on the corner, then turn left to a wide bridge over the river before eventually reaching the road to St Mark's – nearly two miles in total. All the walkers would return home by the same route that the children used coming home from Sunday School.

As soon as the hearse was out of sight, Carrie headed for the kitchen and ensconced herself in her usual chair by the kitchen fire. There she remained until everyone but her family had gone. Albert had been back and forth several times to squeeze her shoulder, kiss the top of her head and inquire if she was, "Alright, love?" She had nodded with a weak smile and replied, "And you?" He had nodded too, before rejoining Jack and Joe in the yard with his pipe. Martha, Ivy and Vera had shielded her to the end, accompanying those who wished to pay their personal respects and goodbyes, steering them in and out of the room as quickly and efficiently as possible.

It was over. It was done. Their child was in the earth. Rest in peace, our beautiful Doris.

CHAPTER 41

Evacuees

A MONTH AFTER Doris' death, things were slowly beginning to return to normal – very slowly in Carrie's case. She would get up early, moithered and unable to sleep, and start rising the ashes and cleaning the grate ready to light the fire. Halfway through, she would sit back on her haunches and stare ahead. Half an hour or more would pass before she could resume. She'd start preparing dinners then forget them, catching the smell of the saucepans boiling dry just in time. Never having been much of a smoker and not even starting until her grown-up children had encouraged her by extolling all its 'benefits', she now smoked, or rather wasted, more than she had ever done – lighting one and putting it down on an ashtray or the edge of a piece of furniture then forgetting about it, leaving it to burn its length.

Albert, now more in control of himself since the mountain climb with Joe, grieved over his daughter just as achingly as his wife, but both were able to find comfort in talking to each other about Doris at mealtimes or in bed at night, going over all the happy and sad events of her growing up. They chuckled at some and cried at others. When emotions are high, laughter and tears are never far apart.

Ivy, with her young family to see to as well as regular visits to her parents' house, discovered she could push it to the back of her mind for longer periods every day. But the empty feeling of loss still remained, engulfing her sometimes just as she was about to fall asleep, especially on night shift when Jim wasn't there to *cwtch* her to him.

Now she had even more on her plate to concentrate on. It was Crymceynon's turn for an allocation of evacuees and they came from all over Britain, from the north to the south. Ivy said she would take two in. She had to, she had no choice. She wasn't 'working', both her girls were now in school and she had a spare bedroom. Not that she minded, really.

The ones allocated to her were from a middle-class family in Cardiff. Two little girls, much the same age as her own: Dorothy and Mary Barksted. Their parents had delivered them in their own car! Nice people, Mr and Mrs Barksted. They reminded Ivy of her master and mistress in London. You could always tell breeding. They had stayed to tea and Ivy, using one of her precious tins from her rapidly depleting store cupboard, had made them salmon and cucumber sandwiches – with the crusts cut off, of course – and then went mad and opened a tin of peaches to follow. (Hopefully, Jim would be able to replenish her stock when he next had chance to visit the docks.) Such sweet little girls they looked; well mannered and very well spoken. They would be a good influence on Pauline and Liz. Ivy was sure they would all get on like a house on fire.

CHAPTER 42

Cock-a-Reeling

"CAN YOU DO 'cock-a-reeling'?" asked Liz of Mary, the younger of the two newcomers, as the four girls walked up to the big field.

"What's that? I've never heard of it."

"I'll show you." Liz tucked her dress up into the legs of her knickers ready to show off and stood facing the corrugated fence of the allotments. She jumped onto her hands and sent her feet flying over her head, landing with an echoing 'clang' on the metal. "And I can do Chinese bend," she said from her upside down position, letting her feet walk down the fence until they reached the ground and her stomach faced the sky. With a kick she was upright again, then Mary tried.

"Push harder, don't be afraid," encouraged Liz, "it's only grass, it can't hurt you."

Wendy Williams and Margaret Pierce joined them and before long six pairs of heels were ringing in quick succession on the fence. For an hour or more they played. Clang-clang, clang-clang! The summer sunshine shone warmly on them and they were enjoying themselves when two gnarled, dirty hands suddenly appeared, gripping the top of the iron from the other side, followed by an apoplectic face.

"Clear off, you noisy lot of buggers!" said Mr Jones, who had come to the allotments to pick his kidney beans and have a bit of peace away from his nagging wife, not to put up with this continual clatter. It was giving him a bigger headache than she had. “You hear me?” he bawled. “Now clear off!”

Gesticulating with one arm, he lost his hold and balance and fell off the pop case he had been standing on. The girls went into fits of giggles with the crash. The head re-appeared and they scattered.

“And pull your clothes down!” he shouted after them. “Girls you are, mind!”

Upstairs that night, Mary and Dorothy decided they needed more practise in ‘cock-a-reeling’ if they were to become as proficient as the others. The bed was the ideal place for it, as it stood sideways on against the wall. Standing on the opposite side of the room left plenty of space for a running jump and the springs gave them extra bounce for their take-off. Pauline and Liz crept in to instruct them, keeping their voices down and stifling their giggles as time and again the two learners collapsed in an untidy heap. Suddenly, there was a cracking, splintering sound and the bed tilted with a jolt to one corner. The Edwards girls flew back to their own room and pulled the bedclothes up to their chins as Ivy came storming up the stairs.

“What is going on up here, for goodness sake?” she asked. “The leg of the bed has come right down through the parlour ceiling!”

Liz and Pauline waited with baited breath as Ivy’s footsteps passed their door and stamped on to the disaster area in the smallest front bedroom. They would all cop it now!

“I don’t know what happened, Mrs Edwards,” they heard Dorothy say in a cool, calm and collected voice. “We were just lying here when all of a sudden…” she shrugged her shoulders. “One of the floorboards must be rotten or something.”

Innocence personified. Pauline couldn't help but admire Dorothy's bare-faced lying. It took the wind right out of Ivy's sails.

"You weren't jumping about or anything?" she asked, searching the wide-eyed face for signs of guilt. She could always detect it in her own two. She found none but wasn't convinced yet.

"No, Mrs Edwards." How could you suggest such a thing, her tone implied.

Ivy remembered the woodworm she had seen the day they moved in. The child could be right, she supposed. She would have to give her the benefit of the doubt. Now her anger was replaced by worry. If it was the woodworm, none of them would be safe in their beds. She would have to see the rent man about it when he called next week. And Jim, out as usual on dayshift, would have to take the oilcloth up after work tomorrow before his nightly refreshments (though he went out later and came home earlier these days!) to check all the boards. They would all have to be treated with creosote or something, she supposed. There would be a mess and a smell to put up with for days. She looked around. They may as well distemper the room out while they were about it. They had intended doing it before the evacuees arrived but they hadn't felt up to it or hadn't had the time. There was a distinct grubby patch on the wall by the bed, though how it had got so dirty so high up, and how she hadn't noticed it before, she didn't know. She pulled the blankets back off the two girls.

"Get out," she said, defeated and deflated, "you'll both have to help me to lift it and shift it."

CHAPTER 43

Cracking the Shell

IT WAS THE first of December. They would all be glad to see the end of this year. Knowing that Carrie was dreading Christmas and all it entailed, her grief still enveloping her like a hard shell, Ivy decided to invite her parents over to their house for the day. That way, with the four girls filling the house with their chatter and laughter (and squabbles) and with neighbours popping in and out, they wouldn't have much time to dwell on things.

Grateful not to have to think about the festivities and all the preparations, Carrie did her best to help by offering to keep the four girls happy and occupied over at her house for a few hours now and again to give Ivy a chance to get things done. She was a bit behind with everything these days what with the extra washing, ironing and cooking for the evacuees and having to spend such a lot of time queuing for any little extra Christmas treats. Most of her housework was left until the evening now, when four boisterous youngsters about the place made things twice as hard and took twice as long. She still had four three-ply cardigans to finish, one for each of the four girls as an extra Christmas present, and all the buttons to sew on. Fast knitter though she was, she would have a heck of a job to finish them all on time. Ivy solved this problem by taking her knitting with her to the queues. That way, she felt, the standing about for hours wasn't a complete waste of precious time. Especially when, just as she was about to be served, whatever 'luxury' they had been waiting for ran out.

The four girls sat around Carrie's big kitchen table which was covered in remnants of wallpaper rolls, some old catalogue books, red tissue paper, scissors, crayons, dolly-pegs and two pots of flour and water paste. They were going to make Christmas trimmings.

Liz fidgeted in her seat, anxious to get started. Gran always had good ideas. She was going to enjoy this. First, Carrie showed them how to cut four oblong pieces of wallpaper, then an inch strip from the short side of each one; they turned them over to the plain white side to colour them in, making up their own designs but using lots of colours. This took a while and Carrie sat back in her chair to stare at the fire and retreat back into her shell.

"Gran, we've finished!"

She got up automatically and showed them next how to fold them length-ways and cut, at inch intervals, slits from the fold to within an inch of the ends, open them up, paste the short ends together, paste the ends of the strips and attach them as handles. They stood them on one side to dry. They were Chinese lanterns.

The girls sat back in their chairs, very pleased with themselves. The coloured pages of the catalogues were torn out now, cut into strips, pasted on the ends and joined together, interlocking to form paper chains. While they were drying, they began making butterflies from the pegs and tissue paper. Cut into oblongs again, the children made running stitches up the centre of the folded tissue with darning needle and red wool, pulling the wool to ruche the paper. This they inserted between the legs of the pegs and with the wool still attached, secured the wings to the 'necks'. Several strands of black cotton were knotted, cut into lengths, moistened with paste and left to dry, then were stuck to the heads as antennae. A little tweak on both sides of the tissue and behold! The butterflies were in full flight.

Carrie went to the pantry and returned with four small, empty meat paste pots, an inch of candle stuck firmly into the bottom of each one. With one of Albert's spills from a jar on the mantelpiece she lit the candles, placed a lantern over each and switched off the light. The effect to the girls was magical as the candle light shone through the slits in the coloured paper. They whooped and squealed and clapped their hands. Carrie's spirits lifted at their reaction and she felt herself smiling broadly. The shell had begun to crack a little.

CHAPTER 44

Pearl Harbour

DECEMBER THE SEVENTH brought the terrible news that the American Fleet at Pearl Harbour had been bombed by the Japanese, the result being that the United States was now at war with Germany and Japan. That was the one positive thing to come out of this atrocity: America, with all its might and numbers, was now Britain's ally.

Carrie and Albert listened to the announcement on the wireless, full of apprehension. Both their boys would be involved from now on. They had left home sixteen years ago, being disillusioned with Britain and disgusted with the way ex-servicemen and colliers had been treated, and having no other prospect other than a life underground (and even those jobs were scarce and fought over). In the occasional letters their parents had received since, they had learned that the two of them had joined the American Army as soon as they had been eligible. They had both done well for themselves, Carrie had to admit. She was so proud of them. Neither of them had married yet but Danny was courting strong, so you never knew. It would be nice to see them settled with their own families.

Since Doris' death their letters had been more frequent and she was so grateful for that. They were good boys. She had even received parcels from the two of them recently, with lovely little American luxuries of sweets and biscuits and things. And photographs! Oh, they looked so handsome in their uniforms and she wished she could see them and touch them in the flesh. She had kept the photos in her pinny pocket since, taking them out at regular intervals to stroke their faces with her fingertips. Albert said she'd rub them blank if she wasn't careful. He hadn't looked at them much. She had handed them to him when they arrived and he had stared at them for quite a while but handed them back without a word. He'd just put his hand on her shoulder, given it a squeeze, then gone out the backyard to clean his boots.

Glyn's photo was taken in a place called Atlantic City and Danny's in Boston, both on the East Coast but a few hundred miles apart. They said they didn't get to see each other often as they were in different units, but they kept in touch regularly by phone. Carrie had asked Bessy-Ann if she could possibly ask the doctor if he had an atlas she could look at, then she and Albert had spent hours pouring over it and absorbing all the information about the areas. It seemed to bring them that little bit closer.

Men didn't write gossipy letters like women, Carrie mused. There was never enough information nor enough letters to satisfy her. But all of them were full of enthusiasm and praise for the new country. She was glad of that, glad they were happy there.

"Gee! It's a great life here!" Danny wrote. "You can't imagine it! Army life is full of opportunity for promotion and travel. We've both been all over the USA from north to south. Can you imagine that?"

But there was hardly a word about Miriam, his girlfriend, or about their plans for the future. Why couldn't they write more chatty letters like our Doris does? Carrie's hand flew to her chest at the unexpected thought. Used to – her brain corrected her.

Glyn's letters ran along the same lines, usually finishing with, "Don't worry about us, we're having the time of our lives!"

She was happy that they were settled, that everything was fine for them – that's if they weren't just saying that to stop her worrying. It was selfish to want them back. Much as she hadn't wanted them to go, she had realised at the time that she couldn't stand in their way or stop them. What did Britain have to offer them back then? Strikes, unemployment, poverty and soup kitchens! They had made the right decision.

But that was before the attack. Now they would be at war, fighting in the thick of it. She gasped for breath at the thought.

Chapter 45

Albert's War

Carrie and Albert had married young and had their four children in their first five years together. Then, said Carrie, Albert had come to his senses – though the truth was that she was very fond of children and after the birth of her two sons had desperately wanted a daughter. Then she wanted another daughter to keep the first one company.

For the next few years they were poor but blissfully happy, until 1914 when war broke out and Albert had volunteered. Carrie had begged him not to go, but he said if he wasn't prepared to fight for his own family, who else would be? He had ended up at Sulva Bay, Gallipoli. On the second day his horse had been shot from under him. He had been lucky, by God he had been lucky. The only physical injury he had sustained then – and for the duration of the war – was three broken fingers which were caught in the reins when the horse fell beneath him.

However, the mental damage he suffered was crippling. Each and every sight and sound of human suffering he had seen and heard during those horrific years had taken root in his memory like tiny seeds and try as he might he could not weed them out. Just a word in a normal conversation could trigger a picture of devastating mutilation; a sudden shout or bang could start another period of a continuous tinnitus of agonising screams and moans inside his head. He had survived but God knows there were times when he wished he hadn't.

He no longer had control over his thoughts. When the images flashed he had to find a place to be on his own as quickly as possible, switching to automatic pilot until he got there. He was terrified of losing control of his voice and that the screams would make themselves audible to others. Once on his own, he could screw his eyes tight shut, press his knuckles into his closed mouth and force himself to breath deeply and slowly till the horror dimmed again. There was no cure for this kind of injury and he could tell no-one. Who, unless they suffered it too, could understand?

The only time he had ever come near to telling anyone was when he arrived at the stattion. The first person he met was his best butty, Jack Jones from Crymceynon, who had been visiting his parents where Albert and Carrie were then living. (Jack had volunteered too, but the authorities said he would be more hindrance than help with his club foot. It had broken his heart when all his mates from the pit had left for France.) Jack shook Albert's hand firmly and grasped him by the shoulders, slapping his back. "Albert Thomas! Welcome home, wuss!" he said. "How are you mate? God, it's good to see you!" The friendliness, the familiarity, the very normality of being back home again was too much for Albert. His eyes brimmed. "Jack," he said, "I've been to Hell and back."

Albert was certain of one thing: he would not be responsible for bringing any more children into this world. He had two sons and God forbid they would have to endure war in their lifetime. He had no doubt though, Germany would rise again as sure as night followed day.

Carrie's idea of war and army life was limited, based mainly on the sanitised newsreels and fictional films she saw at the cinema. She had nothing else to go on. Albert had come home in one piece and had never spoken about it. The letters she had received from him had only mentioned his concern for her and the children and told her not to worry – everything was fine and it shouldn't last much longer. He had sent them Christmas cards and birthday cards – so pretty and unusual that she had kept them all – and had brought home for her a beautiful red satin, heart-shaped pin cushion with a design picked out in colour-topped pins which she treasured, it being from abroad. She had missed him and longed for his return, but there was nothing she could do about it except what Albert had told her: concentrate on looking after the children and wait for time to pass. So she had.

CHAPTER 46

Albert and Carrie's Night Out

CHRISTMAS HAD COME and gone. Carrie hadn't been out once, not even over to Ivy's. The shock of Pearl Harbour, coming on top of losing their daughter, had driven her back into a deep depression. She couldn't stop worrying. She continually questioned Albert about war: what it was really like, what the boys would be getting into, what the risks would be and what chance they would have. He did his best to answer her as truthfully as he could while trying not to add to her worries.

Since his walk with Joe, the oppressive pressure in Albert's head had dropped a little and the obsession slackened, allowing him to interact more with life around him. It was still there, threatening to overwhelm him, and he knew he would never get rid of it, but he was beginning to feel that he could be in charge of it and not the other way around. Carrie, he realised, had a right to know. Ignorance is bliss only up to a point. But fear and worry could do strange things to the mind, with the same thoughts going round and round and leaving no room for others. He had to help her off this roundabout somehow, before it took hold completely.

"Things are different this time, love," he told her, "especially now that America and all its might and numbers have joined in. They've got masses of machinery, arms and new equipment. It shouldn't last long. Our boys will be in and out before we look round."

She was looking at him, searching his face.

"Let's cross our bridges as they come, eh?" he suggested. "It's pointless worrying now, isn't it? It doesn't solve anything, does it? You are the one who always told the kids, 'Don't trouble trouble till trouble troubles you,' eh? Well, take some of your own advice!"

Carrie nodded but was unconvinced; it was easier said than done for both of them these days. There were constant butterflies in her stomach. Albert had noticed that she wasn't sleeping too well and that she picked at her food.

"Look, love," he said, "Glyn and Danny are not kids anymore. They are grown men and intelligent. They won't do anything foolish or take risks, will they, eh?"

She nodded again.

What else could he say or do to reassure her? His mind raced around for an answer as he watched her slowly clear away the tea things. He realised that she needed to get out from these four walls and do something different – something she could derive some pleasure from, however small, to give her a lift.

"Tell you what," he said suddenly, "how about a night at the pictures? You haven't been for months and months. That would take your mind off things for a bit, wouldn't it?"

Carrie waved her hand and shook her head before removing the tablecloth and shaking it by the back door. She never shook it in the grate – there were birds out there looking for crumbs.

"No. I don't feel up to it. I'm too tired."

"I'll come with you, if you like," he said, smiling and hoping this was an offer she couldn't refuse.

Now it was Carrie's turn to placate Albert. It dawned on her that he was fretting about her. Though she really didn't feel up to it, she made a huge effort and smiled back. "Would you? Oh Alb'! That would be nice." She put her arms around his neck and kissed his cheek. She was beginning to warm to the idea. "Just you and me. And Tuesday is the quietest night. It will be dark going and dark coming home. Oh, I'd like that, Alb'!"

"Right then!" He smacked her bottom. "Go and get your glad rags on woman, before I change my mind."

Sitting through the short picture, comfy together and surreptitiously holding hands, Carrie relaxed. It was the Dead End Kids. She liked them and even managed a chuckle now and then, nudging Albert and whispering to him. Oh, it was nice to be out together like this. Just like old times. The *Pathé News* was next, ahead of the main picture with Bette Davies. Carrie settled back in her seat as the white cockerel crowed. She liked seeing the news, even though it was a few weeks out of date by the time it reached Crymceynon.

The first item came as a shock to both of them. It showed the actual attack on Pearl Harbour. The pictures had an even stronger impact on them than the wireless report had done, bringing back all the initial fear and pain and multiplying it. All those aeroplanes and bombs, all that destructive power! Nobody had stood a chance.

They couldn't stand it. Simultaneously, they got up and started pushing past people to get to the aisle, oblivious of objections, desperate to get out.

They walked home at a rapid pace still holding hands, not one word passing between them. They reached home, undressed, climbed into their nest of a bed and *cwtched* up together, wrapped tightly in each other's arms and in their own thoughts.

CHAPTER 47

The Gathering

THE FIRST AIR-RAID warnings in Crymceynon had sent the villagers scurrying like frightened rabbits to the shelters that had been built near the railway station, the schools, the cinemas and other strategic places, or into the tiny rooms beneath their own staircases. Time and again they had sat them out in these cramped conditions, only to find on emerging that nothing had happened. Familiarity with the wailing sound soon brought contempt for it. They were alright, nothing was going to happen here. As time went on they rarely ran for cover. Instead, groups of men and women would congregate at street corners after the children were in bed, to watch and listen to the sounds of attack away in the distance. They gauged the source and the amount of damage being done to 'some poor devils' by what they saw and heard, and talked over their fears and feelings, finding some relief in sharing them.

At the top of Stephen's Street, they gathered outside Nos. 26 and 27, resting their bottoms in turn on the two parlour windowsills. During these vigils, someone or other would invariably slip indoors to make a pot of tea and bring out a tray of steaming cups to hand round.

They stood watching in February 1942 when for three consecutive nights the town near the docks was bombarded incessantly. They saw the incendiaries fall like rain, saw the searchlights near the coast sweep across the sky and heard the thunderous booms of the bombs and guns. Some of the men climbed the mountain to stand in impotent silence and look down into the distance at the burning devastation, the horror drawing them like a magnet. There, but for the grace of God... The women looked up at the red sky to the south for evidence of what was happening and smelled the burning on the passing breeze.

One night as they gathered together, there was a sudden new sound in the air, much closer than the general uproar. Short, quick, blasts of wind, like breath from some gigantic running animal, came whistling nearer. The sound stopped and the watchers held their breath. A heavy crump, followed almost immediately by an enormous explosion that rattled the windows all around, mobilised them into action. The children!

Ivy ran up the stairs shouting urgently to Mary and Dorothy, then grabbed her own children, one under each arm. With superhuman strength, she ran down again and practically threw her daughters onto the spare blankets on the *cwtch* floor, pushing the evacuees in after them. Jim, having run all the way home from the mountain, found them there, the girls already settling to sleep again, head to toe like sardines. Ivy was sitting just inside the doorway, the handle of her broken cup still hanging from her thumb.

The following day, word reached them that a landmine had been dropped on the common in the next village, the explosion leaving a crater big enough to bury a double-decker bus. Miraculously, no-one had been killed. The newspapers never mentioned the place by name in their reports. Carrie told Albert that their next-door neighbour had said to her earlier: "I could have been there, Carrie! *Rebecca* is on there with Joan Fontaine and Laurence Olivier. Oh, I would die to see that!"

Chapter 48

Pink Bluebells

On a sunny Saturday in May, Pauline and Dorothy sat on the stile by the Navigation pub reading Enid Blyton books they had borrowed from the library, while their two younger sisters burned up their brimming energy doing 'gymnastics' – cartwheels, handstands, Chinese bends and 'cock-a-reeling'. Ivy hated that expression too and had tried her best to get Liz to call it something else, but to no avail. "Everybody calls it that," Liz had said. So Ivy had given in gracefully before all the 'why's' started.

While upside down against the allotment fence, Liz spotted Brian Pierce's sister coming down from the woods on the other side of the canal, her arms full of bluebells. Upright again, she ran to Pauline and said, "We're going over the woods to pick some bluebells!" Gran would love some of those. She ran off with Mary close behind.

The woods consisted of about twenty trees in all, mostly hawthorn (or may, as the children called them). The blossom was 'going over' now, dropping tiny white petals on their heads like confetti at the slightest breeze. Thick on the ground beneath, the bluebells bloomed. The two fragrances together were intoxicating. Just a whiff of them in later years would be enough to transport Liz back to these days.

Michael Richards, who was in Pauline's class in school and was the eldest son of the Navigation's landlord, had spotted her sitting on the stile. He came out and strolled over to her in an overtly casual manner. He liked Pauline. The two of them were top of their class and he enjoyed pitting his wits against hers, though she did have the edge over him.

"Hiya!" he said, climbing up between the girls.

"Hiya!" they both answered.

"What you reading, then?"

They showed him the covers.

"Are they any good?"

They nodded. "Yeah, not bad."

There was a moment's silence while he thought of something else to say. Eventually, he said, "Been anywhere?"

Pauline answered him. "Only down to Lowe's shop for my mother and down the library to change our books. What have you been doing?"

"Nothing much. Had to take my gran's dinner down for her, that's all." Silence again. He searched his mind quickly for another topic. "Where's Liz then? She's usually not far away from you!" Worst luck, he thought.

"Oh, she's gone off over the woods with Mary. They're picking bluebells."

Ah, here was a chance! "Do you know how to turn bluebells pink?"

"What?" said both the girls together, looking at each other and wrinkling their noses. "Don't be daft! How can you turn them pink? That's rubbish!"

"No it's not. It's easy," he boasted. "Come on, I'll show you, if you like." His father had shown him when he was little and he had been fascinated, though his father couldn't explain to him how or why it had happened. He hoped the 'magic' of it would impress the girls – Pauline in particular. "Right, come on then!"

The three jumped off the stile and ran to the woods. When they had picked a good handful of the sweet-smelling flowers, Michael wandered off, looking for something. "Ah, here's one," he shouted.

"One what?" said the girls together.

"A red ant hill." He found a stick and dug a hole in the top of it.

"What are you doing that for?" they asked curiously.

He put the bunch of flowers into the hole, head first. "You'll see!" he said, mysteriously. Pleased with himself, he brushed the dirt from his hands on the sides of his trousers. "We'll come back later and I bet they'll be pink."

"Yes, and pigs might fly," said Dorothy, sceptically.

"How much do you bet?" said Pauline.

He thought quickly. He couldn't bet with money since they never had any to speak of. Besides, the experiment might not work and he'd look a right fool if he couldn't pay up. Then he had a brainwave! The Saturday matinee at the Palace cinema was always well patronised, so he said, "Tell you what, if you get to the pictures before me next Saturday you've got to keep me a seat, and if I get there first I keep one for you!"

They shook hands on it. Either way, he would win and he might even get to put his arm, nonchalantly, along the back of Pauline's seat!

The girls couldn't believe their eyes when they retrieved the flowers. The bells actually were a beautiful shade of pink, with just a few tiny patches of blue here and there. Dorothy called the others to come and see. Wonders would never cease! Liz, awestruck by this remarkable transformation, commandeered them immediately. "I can have 'em, can't I

Mike? I want to show them to my gran."

He'd proved his point and got what he wanted, so he wasn't bothered. "Aye, go on," he said.

On the way down to Duke Street, Liz met Vincent Griffiths. "Look, Vince. I've got pink bluebells. Bet you haven't seen these before!"

He crossed over to her and inspected them. "Oh aye? Where'd you find those then, Liz?"

"I didn't find them. Michael Richards made them."

"Made them!" Vincent scoffed. (He didn't like Michael Richards. More than once he had told Vincent: "Go and wash your mouth out, you dirty pig!") "Huh! And how did old clever-clogs do that, then?"

"He put them in an ant hill."

"An ant hill? That's a load of bull...! He's played a trick on you, mun. I've heard geese fart before!"

Liz's eyes opened wide. Wherever did he get these expressions of his from? Good job her mother wasn't here to hear him.

"Yes he did," said Liz defiantly. "We saw him, so there!" She stuck her tongue out at him.

Vince frowned. He had to dislodge Michael's halo somehow. "Oh, I know what happened, mun!" Instinctively, and without having so much as a clue about chemical reactions, he jumped to the right conclusion. "The ants piss all over 'em, that's what's happened. I'd throw 'em away if I was you." He figured he could pick them up and boast that he had done it. That would be one in the eye for old Mike!

Had they? Liz wondered. Is that what happened? She looked down at the flowers, feeling slightly disillusioned and held them a little further away from her. Vincent saw her and added, "*Uch-a-fi!*" Liz dithered. They were pretty and she could still give them to Gran. She didn't have to tell her about Vincent Griffiths' theory.

Ivy, on her way out of her mother's house, spotted Liz talking to Vincent. She called to her to come to her side. Liz had been told not to play with that boy. To clear herself from any blame, Liz ran to her and blurted out, "Mammy, Vincent Griffis' been saying naughty words again!"

Right, thought Ivy. She marched home with Liz, deposited her with Jim and asked if Billy was at home. Jim raised his eyebrows at her thin-lipped expression and answered, "Aye, he should be." She marched out again and slammed the door behind her. He guessed what was up and thought, I wouldn't relish being in your shoes, Billy boy!

Ivy crossed the road, opened the gate and knocked loudly on the Griffiths' door. Billy answered it, taking an involuntary step backwards and the enquiring smile quickly fading from his face when he saw hers. Without hesitation, Ivy started in on him. "I'll come straight to the point Mr Griffiths." (She thought 'Billy' would have been too friendly for this occasion.) "Your son has been using swear words again when talking to my youngest daughter. I will not tolerate it!"

Billy was immediately apologetic. He opened the door a little wider and motioned for her to step inside. "Oh, not again, not another one! I'm so sorry, Mrs Edwards. Come in, please."

"I'm not the first to complain then?" She remained where she was. "No, I won't come in thank you. I can say what I want out here."

"I'll have words with him again, I promise."

He couldn't placate her that easily.

"I think it needs more than 'words with him', Mr Griffiths."

Billy's face had a look of utter despair. He said miserably, "He doesn't hear it in the house, Ivy, I can assure you of that." He urgently needed help from someone. Ah, Jim had said Ivy would sort him out! Well, now was his chance. He looked at her appealingly. "I honestly don't know what else I can do to stop it, short of gagging him."

Ivy's voice softened. He really was at the end of his tether, she could see. She had an idea that just might work. "Have you thought of having a word with his headmaster, preferably with Vincent present? That might shame him."

Billy's face lit up. Jim was right! "Ivy, that's brilliant! I'll go with him tomorrow morning. Oo, I could kiss you!"

"Mm, better not," said Ivy, "Jim might not like it!"

CHAPTER 49

The Target

THE FOLLOWING MORNING saw Billy and Vincent in the school corridor outside Mr Hughes' office. Billy, holding his son's hand firmly, tapped on the door and entered on invitation.

"Oh, good morning, Mr Griffiths and you, Vincent. What can I do for you?"

"I think Vincent had better tell you that, Mr Hughes."

"I see. Well, come and sit down, both of you."

They sat, nervously. There was no going back now.

"Right then, Vincent. What is the problem?"

Vincent looked at the floor. "I been swearing, Sir."

"Speak up, please."

Just a fraction louder, Vincent repeated his crime.

"I see." Mr Hughes leaned back in his chair, rested his elbows on its arms and brought his fingertips together, tapping them. "And do you think it's clever to do that?"

"No, Sir."

"No, it isn't, is it? In fact it is quite the opposite. It shows a distinct lack of vocabulary and imagination. Do you understand what I'm saying?"

Vincent didn't.

Mr Hughes put it another way. "It means you could think of other, better words to put in their place. There are thousands of them, you know, in the English language."

He let that sink in, while Vincent squirmed, waiting.

"Do you know any other children in the school who resort to bad language?"

"No, Sir." Vincent had his principles. He wasn't going to cleck on anyone.

"Well, there you are, you see. Try listening to them when they are talking to see how they avoid using swear words." He sat silent for a minute or two, his eyes on the boy. "I'm going to set you a target, Vincent, and we'll see if you can be clever enough and determined enough to reach it. Agreed?"

Did he have any choice?

"Every Friday you will bring a sealed envelope to me from your father. Depending on its contents, you will or will not receive a stamp on your exercise book and we will see how far you get by the end of the term. It could mean ten stamps."

Ten! Vincent had never managed more than three in that time.

"Starting from now," said Mr Hughes, getting up and shaking hands with his father and giving him a quick wink.

Billy called straight to Ivy's on the way home to relate all that had been said and to prove he was trying to solve the problem.

CHAPTER 50

The School Holidays

HOORAY! NEARLY SEVEN weeks off school. Liz and Pauline were looking forward to this summer up the mountain even more than the previous two. They could introduce Dorothy and Mary to the 'delights' of picking whinberries and blackberries and selling them round the doors with the rest of their friends. They would be rich with the four of them picking. They could go to the pictures more often. Perhaps their mother would even let them catch a bus to town by themselves. They couldn't wait to get home and started.

Neither could Vincent. He kept looking at the back of his exercise book and showing it around the class, boasting. He'd only gone and done it, hadn't he? He'd only bloomin' well done it! He had ten stamps! Only two kids had beaten him, and only by one stamp. It had been easy: all he'd had to do was substitute his usual swear words for bloomin', blinkin' and ruddy. That's what Mr Hughes must have meant when he'd said to copy the other kids. It had worked like a dream. Mr Hughes had said he was proud of him and asked if he was now proud of himself. He sure was. Just wait till he showed his father. He ran all the way home up the canal bank and burst into the kitchen, opening his exercise book and yelling as he went: "Dad! Dad! Look, Dad! I've done it! I've got ten f..." His hand flew to his mouth to shove the word back in. In the same split-second, Billy's hand flew to his son's ear.

Nevertheless, whether it was Ivy's idea, Mr Hughes' words of praise, or the clip across the ear that did it, Vincent never swore again.

A few years later, it was Vincent himself who told his band of new-found friends (including Pauline and Liz now, with Ivy's approval) how he had acquired his debauched vocabulary. The summer before he started school, he had wandered down the canal bank behind Stephen's Street to the two big houses at the bottom. Annabelle Jackson's garden door had stood open and peeping in, he noticed lots of gooseberry bushes, all laden with fruit. Vincent loved 'goosegogs'. In he went, intending to fill his pockets and run. They were soft, ripe and golden. They would squash in his pockets, so he filled his mouth instead. He'd only managed two mouthfuls when he heard someone talking. He peeped through the bushes and saw a skinny old woman (Annabelle was in her early sixties) coming very unsteadily down the path, waving her arms about as if swotting flies and talking what seemed like gibberish to herself. If he made for the door, she would see him, so he backed into a corner and crouched down. The 'new' words pouring from her lips seemed to be about someone called Dudley. He watched and listened, fascinated.

Every day, for as long as the goosegogs lasted, he returned to stuff himself and spy on this strange woman, absorbing the words and repeating them. Gradually, he began repeating them to other kids, showing off and getting a reaction every time. Gradually, other kids' parents got to hear them. By now, he was addicted. It was exciting, getting people all worked up! It became second nature and he couldn't stop – until Mr Hughes had come on the scene.

Chapter 51

Ivy Steps In

David Roberts was in a state. He had run up to Ivy's and went straight in through the passage to the back kitchen where she was ironing, calling her name as he ran: "Mrs Edwards! Mrs Edwards! Please come quick!"

Ivy put the flat-iron back on the hob as he tried to grab her arm. "What is it Dave, what's wrong?"

"It's Mammy, Mrs Edwards. She's holding her stomach and it's hurting her and she's nearly crying!"

So was David, Ivy saw, so she ran back with him to see what she could do. She knew Vera suffered regularly from an 'acid stomach'. She was forever mixing a little bi-carb in some warm water to settle it. Gareth was in the middle of mixing some for her as they entered the house. One look at Vera and Ivy could see she was in agony. She had never been as bad as this with it before. Something was seriously wrong.

"Go and fetch the doctor, Gareth, I'll stay with Mam."

Mr Merryman, she noticed, was sitting comfortably in his usual chair, scowling at it all.

"How long has she been like this?" Ivy asked him.

He shrugged. Ivy's lips thinned. That man was a waste of breath. Seeing her annoyance, he grudgingly answered: "About five minutes. What's all the fuss about? She's had it before."

Ivy gritted her teeth.

"I hope this performance isn't going to go on much longer," he continued. "I haven't had my dinner yet and look at the time!"

David moved forward, about to say or do something, but Ivy quickly snatched his arm, restraining him.

"Oh, I am sorry," she said sarcastically. "Just hang on a little longer, till we get Vera sorted, then I promise I'll get you sorted! Alright?"

The old man wasn't quite sure how to take that.

"Priorities first though, eh?" she added with a smile, and much to her satisfaction, heard him mumbling under his breath.

Dr Treadwell arrived in his car with Gareth. After a thorough examination of Vera as she lay on the couch, almost screaming out in pain as he gently pressed her stomach, he turned to Gareth and asked him to get his mother's coat.

"She's going to hospital," he said. Seeing the startled look on the two boys' faces, he quickly added, "Now, don't you worry. This can and will be fixed and she will be home again in no time, but the sooner it is seen to the better."

"But I can't," said Vera, still doubled up with pain, her arms folded tightly across her stomach. "What about my boys and Mr Merryman?"

"They will have to see to themselves. It won't harm them. Let's put it like this: they will be in a much worse predicament if you don't get it seen to." There was no beating about the bush with him, especially when there wasn't time to dither. "No 'buts' woman. Into the car with you, now!"

Ivy, holding Vera's coat out for her, reassured her. "Look Vee, I can see to everything here. You look after yourself. And don't worry. Like he says, it won't be for long."

When the car had gone she turned to Gareth and David. "Now then, boys, you must be starving! Let's see what we've got." She looked around the pantry but there wasn't much choice. The shelves were like her own – mostly bare. There was some macaroni, a heel of cheese, quite a lot of milk and four small rashers of streaky bacon. Right, macaroni cheese peppered with fried, diced bacon it would be then. That should fill a hole or two. The old man watched as she prepared it and the boys laid the table.

"What's that?" he grunted, as the dish went in the oven.

"Macaroni cheese," she said, smiling.

"Hmph!" said Mr Merryman, unimpressed, then in a barely audible voice: "Thought she was supposed to be a good cook!"

Ivy heard; now she'd have him. She whispered to David to slip up to her house and fetch some parsley from a pot on her windowsill in the kitchen. Dishing up a little later, she winked at the boys and placed a sprig of parsley neatly on the top of each helping.

"What's this supposed to be?" said the old man, holding it aloft derisively between thumb and finger. She had known he would.

"It's garnish," she said. "It's what good cooks do!"

Both boys fell about laughing. Mr Merryman was not amused.

During the time Vera was in hospital, Ivy cooked them a main meal every day, did their washing and ironing and some of the cleaning. Relationships between the boys and the old man deteriorated gradually during her absences. Things came to a head on the first Friday morning when, regular as clockwork, Vera's postal order from Audrey and Marjory arrived. When Gareth went to the front door to pick up the post, it wasn't there. He confronted Mr Merryman.

"Where is it?" he demanded.

There was no answer, just a contemptuous look.

He said again, louder, "Where is it? Where's my mother's money?"

"Your mother's not here," was the reply, "and me being the only adult present in this house, my house, the post is my responsibility."

Gareth couldn't believe it. His mother's wages weren't the old man's responsibility.

"What did my poor mother ever do to deserve you, eh?" He surprised himself with his composure. "You treat her like dirt, yet she's been even better than a daughter to you. Better than those other two put together. Think about it – they wouldn't put up with you. My mam is their easy way out!"

The old man ignored him and picked up his newspaper. But Gareth had his dander up now.

"She isn't here because she's in hospital. And why? Because of the bloody strain of looking after you and trying to make ends meet all the time. And you steal from her, you tight bastard!"

Gareth shocked himself but it needed saying. Mr Merryman rose menacingly from his chair, lifted his hand and took a swipe but Gareth saw it coming and ducked.

"You watch your language, boy!"

"Why should I?" Gareth asked defiantly, "You deserve it. And my mam's not here to hear me or stop me."

"Oh I shall tell her, make no mistake about that!"

"Aye, and I won't care if she beats the living daylights out of me! It just hasn't occurred to you, has it, that Mrs

Edwards has taken Mam's place and has been tending you hand and foot? She doesn't have to do it. She doesn't owe you anything. And what thanks has she had, eh?"

"Hmph! I never asked her to!"

"Don't you think out of common courtesy that you could at least offer to pay her? She just might think better of you for it!"

The old man shifted in his chair till his back was towards Gareth and resumed his reading. But Gareth hadn't finished.

"I don't know of anyone else who is such an ungrateful, selfish..." he searched for adequate adjectives, "...horrible parasite. You're self first, self second and any over, self again!" The words came flooding out now. "You've no thought for anyone in this world, except yourself. Grizzle and pick faults, that's all you ever do. None of my friends like you. Nobody likes you. They all laugh at you. 'Mr Sadman' they call you. 'Imagine having him for a grampa' they say."

Mr Merryman had had enough. He took another swipe. And missed again. "You brazen little scamp. Your mother should have taught you to have respect for your elders!"

"She did and I have, for those who deserve it."

"You know nothing, boy!"

The guilt of the affair with Vera's mother, which his two daughters said caused his wife's early demise, was still nagging at him after all the years. He didn't need this boy to show him his faults. His eyes shone with anger at him.

"Oh, I know a lot more than you think," said Gareth, quieter now. He had put two and two together from the bits of conversations he had overheard.

CHAPTER 52

Mr Merryman's Decision

THE FOLLOWING MORNING, Carrie was coming out of Martin's the post, when she almost collided with Mr Merryman. She still did her shopping first thing in the morning, trying to minimize the number of people she would meet who may sympathise over Doris' death. The mere mention of her name was enough to upset her still. But Mr Merryman had taken her by complete surprise. The farthest he had been for years now, was up to the Navigation and back.

"Good gracious!" she said. "You're out early and far from home. What brings you down this far?" She knew Ivy did all his shopping.

"Business!" he snarled, pushing past.

Charming, thought Carrie.

Ivy had a surprise too, when she called down to Vera's later that day with a big saucepan of broth made with a marrow bone. She hoped it would last them for two days – broth always tasted better on the second day, anyway. Mr Merryman was waiting for her and the boys were out playing. Scowling, he held out the postal order.

Puzzled, she asked, "What's this?"

"It's what Vera gets every week from my daughters for looking after me."

So, he still had only two daughters then. What was this man like? She saw the amount. It was a pittance for the work involved. She wouldn't do it even for a king's ransom, day in and day out, like Vera.

Still holding it towards her, he continued: "You had better have it this week. I don't want anyone to say I don't pay my dues."

The bare-faced cheek of the man! The postal order, though unsigned, was still Vera's. Pay his dues? He didn't know the meaning of the words. If he had put his hand in his own pocket she might have been tempted, but this outraged her.

"No, indeed! I won't take that. Don't insult me, please!"

"But you must be out of pocket. I don't want you spending anything on me."

Don't worry, if it wasn't for Vera, I wouldn't be, thought Ivy. "Nonsense," she said, fixing her smile again, "I've had all your ration books and Jim's allotment's made up the rest."

"Mm, well, you've washed and ironed and..."

"What I've done, I've done gladly for Vera's sake and I know that she would do the same for me. That's what friends are for, isn't it?" But you wouldn't know that having none of your own, you miserable old bugger, she thought. "Put it aside till she comes home."

As she was about to leave, he collared her again. "Uh, Mrs Edwards," he cleared his throat, "could you and your husband call down later tonight? After the boys have gone to bed?"

The look on his face said he was very angry about something or other. What could it be? Me and Jim? She was puzzled but curious.

"Well, yes." She hesitated, then nodded her head. "I suppose we could." She could tell that whatever it was, it was killing him to have to ask her.

At half-past nine he was waiting for them on his doorstep,

just in case the boys heard the knocking and came down. With no hint of pleasantries or small talk, he ushered them straight into the parlour where a white, official-looking document, half covered by a newspaper, lay on a small table. Mr Merryman took a fountain pen from his waistcoat pocket, unscrewed the cap and signed the form before them. Then he handed the pen to Jim and motioned for him to do the same.

"Uh, if you and your wife wouldn't mind signing just there," indicating where he had just put his name, Walter Jeremiah Merryman, "on the dotted lines."

Jim now knew exactly what this was all about but wasn't going to oblige him that easily. "Hey, now hold on a minute!"

The old man frowned deeper and put a finger to his lips then raised his hand to the ceiling, his finger still pointing. He didn't want the boys woken up and Gareth spouting to Ivy about the row they'd had. Not until tomorrow, anyway.

"I don't sign my name to anything until I know what it's all about," Jim carried on in a stage whisper.

"It's my will! And confidential!" said the old man, trying to control the anger and impatience in his voice.

"Oh. Right. That's alright, then."

Jim and Ivy exchanged meaningful glances as he handed her the pen. She looked Vera's father straight in the eyes before adding her signature and said, "I hope you've had a really good think about this and that it's not something you've done on the spur of the moment."

He waited until she had signed before replying. Blotting the ink carefully, he turned to her with a wry grin, saying assuredly, "Oh yes! I've done nothing but think about it lately!" He omitted to say 'over the last twenty-four hours or so'.

Walking slowly back to their house, Ivy said, "He was in a funny mood tonight, wasn't he? Whatever brought all this on? I would have thought that he'd have sorted all this out years ago."

"Perhaps he's changed his mind about something, you never know and it's never too late to try and put things right. With Vera, anyway. Perhaps he's realising just how much he depends on her."

"Oh, I doubt that very much," said Ivy. "He looked to me like he was in a right rip about something." She paused, puzzling over what it might be. "Perhaps he's disillusioned with the fact that his daughters didn't step in to look after him when Vera was taken ill. I know he resents me being back and fo. Perhaps he's left everything to a cats' home or something!"

"Aye," agreed Jim, "he's a spiteful ol' bugger. I wouldn't put that past him!"

"It would serve them right though, the ugly sisters, eh, Jim?" She stopped and said, "Oh, I hope we've done the right thing tonight."

"Look, Ive, if we hadn't, he'd only have asked someone else."

"There is no-one else though, is there, with him? It's all down to us now, whatever happens."

"Now Ive, don't be daft. Don't start worrying over that. He could have asked someone in the solicitor's office, anyone in Martin's or Toni Morelli's."

Ivy resumed walking. "Mm, I suppose so," she said.

CHAPTER 53

Twins in the Family

CARRIE HAD FINISHED her housework for the day. She hadn't done much. She didn't have the *hwyl*. Her mind was on other things – mostly her boys. Where were they now? What were they doing? The letters still came fairly often, though each one left her wanting more information about anything and everything, especially about Danny, her youngest son. He had got married straight after Pearl Harbour. She hoped it wasn't a spur of the moment thing. Marriages were meant to last. A decision like that needed time to think about.

Her name was Miriam, that was about all Carrie knew about her. She'd had a photo of the two of them taken together. She took it from her pinny pocket to look at it again. She looked nice enough, but what can you really tell from a photo? She had short, thick, very black hair and a nice smile, but Carrie couldn't tell what colour her eyes were. She looked small, dainty – fragile even, dwarfed by the side of her tall, blond, smart son. She had been pregnant for nearly nine months now. That snippet of information had come with the letter before last. Carrie hoped everything was going well. She hadn't had a letter from him for nigh on five weeks. They were busy training, Danny had said, and there was little time left for anything else.

Oh, God, she wished it would all be over soon – an end to this constant worry. She and Albert were living on their nerves. Where was the postman? Had he been? She hadn't missed him, had she? She went to the front door and looked out to see if she could spot him. No, no sign. He must have been by now, there was nothing again today, then.

She couldn't settle to anything. She sat herself down in the parlour, picking at her fingernails and watching through the window. Ah! There he was! Would he pass or open her gate? She heard the squeaks and was on her feet and by the door as the letter came through the letter-box. Her fingers trembling, she eased up the flap, thinking, as she always did, funny bloomin' letters, written on the envelopes themselves. You had to be so careful not to rip them.

Carrie squealed. Twins! Miriam had given birth to twins! Oh, bless her heart. She didn't look big or strong enough to have one and she'd had two – a boy and a girl, born on the fifth of August. She'd called them Daniel Junior (that wasn't his second name, surely!) and Doris. Ah, Doris. The tears leaked in gratitude and joy as she pressed the letter to her heart for a few seconds. She read on. Doris weighed three pounds four ounces and Daniel four pounds. They were totally different to each other, the little girl taking after her mother and the little boy after his father. All three were doing well. Carrie couldn't wait until Albert came home. She suddenly had a surge of energy and busied herself to pass the time, giving her *ty-bach* and front step a 'birthday' – they hadn't seen a drop of water for weeks, and she had only done it half-heartedly before. When she had finished and dinner was nearly ready for Albert's arrival, she took the letter out of her pocket to read again. Tomorrow, there might be one from Glyn.

CHAPTER 54

Jim Starts the Ball Rolling

JIM'S 'ROOTS' IN the village were deepening and grabbing a firm hold. He really felt part of it now, both in work and out. Ivy and the girls seemed happy too. They never complained anyway. He had known – well, had felt strongly – that the move here would work out. He hoped it would be the last. The pit was in very good nick and should last for years to come, and conditions underground weren't too bad. He'd worked in worse, much worse. They could finally settle, perhaps.

Both the girls were doing very well in school and it was a good one. He knew Ivy was well pleased with it. If you don't have the talent yourself, as she said, it didn't stop you recognising it in others, but that headmaster certainly had it in her opinion. She had made a lot of new friends herself, with quite a few 'close' ones amongst her neighbours in the street: Vera, Elsie-May, Bessie-Ann. She may have got off on the wrong foot with the latter, but Ivy had been the first to admit she had been wrong about the woman and had jumped to conclusions on that first meeting.

Jim's thoughts rolled gently through his mind as he indulged in his favourite hobby – carpentry – in the back garden shed. It was good to have a hobby, he thought; everyone should have one to unwind, take stock, think things through, make judgements and take time to appreciate the good things in life, because they were there, however small, if one took the trouble to look. And after those hard, physical, mind-numbing hours in that dark dungeon of a pit, he derived total pleasure from his own hobby. It involved serenity, creativity, satisfaction and, of course, an end product. Most of the colliers had a hobby of some kind or other: choirs and bands, keeping pigeons, gardening, furthering their education with the help of the local library, billiards – the list was endless, so there must be something in it, he reasoned.

Jim was good with his hands. It had started when he was very young, making pegs with the gipsy kids in their summer stays. He had kept his mam, gran and aunties fully supplied. He smiled to himself, remembering. Ivy and Carrie had a good stock of them too. Now he was making a fort for one of his mates, Davey Davies – or 'Dai Twice' as he was better known. Davies – like Jones, Evans or Williams – was a common surname, and it being necessary to differentiate one from another in times of pit accidents in total darkness underground, nicknames were rife in the valleys. Dai Twice had started the fort but had broken his wrist in a 'bump' at work, so Jim had offered to finish it for him. It was intended as a birthday present for Dai's one and only son. He'd had three daughters quite a while before his arrival and they all doted on the boy.

Jim often had company in the shed while he worked, his mates popping in and out through the permanently unlocked garden door. That's how it had all started.

"Hey, that's nice Jim!" Billy said to him one day. "How's you looking to make one for me for our Vincent for Christmas? There's bugger all to be had in the shops now, is there? And he's been such a good kid since your Ivy sorted him out for us. We haven't had one complaint, not one!"

"Aye, alright. You get us some plywood and I'll have a go. Better still, I'll show you how to make one and give you a hand."

"Oh, great! And plywood's no problem. I know where I can lay my hands on lots of tea chests."

The same thing happened when Tom called.

"Nice. Do you make aeroplanes as well, wuss?"

Here we go, thought Jim, give 'em an inch and they'll take a mile.

"Aye, go on then, get me some balsa wood and I'll have a go."

"Balsa wood? I can get you loads of that. I know a few blokes who work in one of the factories outside town."

It was the start of what turned out to be the best Christmas the children of the three streets (and further afield) had ever had, despite it being war time. The whole thing mushroomed. Soon, several of the fathers and grandfathers were making toys, coming up with new ideas, sharing knowledge and 'acquiring' the necessaries. The women soon caught the bug, making dolls, gollies, tiny cot and pram covers, dolls' clothes – the varieties were endless. Scraps, and sometimes yards, of material suddenly 'materialised' from some source or other. Nothing was wasted and nothing was paid for! Everything was profit because everything was pinched, even the nails, wire, paint and glue. But all in a good cause, fair play, and as Jim always said, "Fair play is bonny play and good sports are good company!"

What was made was either for their own children or for sale, so they were making or saving money either way – a very profitable initiative and invention resulting in a pretty good Christmas all round.

Chapter 55

Herculean Journeys

THE BIGGEST HARDSHIP for the villagers was the food shortage; it was getting worse by the week. Jim never missed an opportunity to visit his butties from the docks. He would be off on his Hercules bicycle whenever he had the chance and Ivy wouldn't see him from early morning until late at night. Last time he had brought home a huge slab of cherry-genoa cake. She had put it in an airtight tin, still in its cellophane wrapper. It would keep like that for weeks. Best to keep something in reserve and not eat everything at once, even though she was dying for a nice big slice of it. One never knew these days.

This latest visit in early December was in the hope of getting some Christmas treats. He got two: a half bottle of whisky that fitted snugly into his jacket pocket and a whole crate of gorgeous, rosy-red Canadian eating apples, each one individually wrapped in squares of violet-coloured tissue paper. God only knows how he had managed those on his bike, thought Ivy. She didn't dare think and he didn't enlighten her. To help him up the hills – of which there were plenty and many of them steep – Jim had waited for a passing double-decker bus and had hung on to its boarding bar, guiding the bike and its heavy load with one hand. This saved his energy but he risked life and limb in the process every time the bus stopped – as well as his freedom. If a policeman had spotted him, he would have been arrested on the spot. Ivy was better off not knowing. And Jim was better off not telling her.

The apples were shared out and sold to neighbours in price and quantity according to the number of children they had. Jim would recoup his money but profit didn't bother him. There were favours done for his family by others. Share and share alike. His only stipulation was that the apples were sold minus their tissue paper. This was kept, smoothed out, strung on string and hung behind the toilet door for his personal use. He felt he deserved that. After all that cycling, newspaper could be a bit harsh on the bum!

When Pauline, Liz and the evacuees had taken their Canadian apples to school, they were soon surrounded and bombarded with requests to 'give us a bite!' or 'keep us the stump!' Liz would always share hers with four or five of her friends, holding on tightly to the apple so that the biter didn't get too good a hold, the various salivas making a cocktail with the juice. Ivy would have been furious if she had known – mixing all those germs! Carrie, on the other hand, would have looked on it as a strengthening of her immunity. "You can be too clean with kids," was her philosophy, "and we'll all eat a peck of dirt one way or another before we die."

CHAPTER 56

The Central Welsh Board Exam

PAULINE HAD COME home from school with a sealed envelope from Mr Hughes asking if Ivy could call to see him the following morning. What was wrong? What could it be about? All it said was 'concerning Pauline's education'. Surely her daughter couldn't be in any sort of trouble, could she? Perish the thought!

She tapped apprehensively at the door of his office at nine-thirty the next morning. She hoped she wasn't too early – or late.

"Come in!"

She opened the door and popped her head around.

"Ah, Mrs Edwards. Good morning."

She took Mr Hughes' outstretched hand and he motioned her to sit down.

"Now then, I'll come straight to the point. I'm thinking of entering Pauline for this year's Central Welsh Board exam," he said.

Grammar school? Her daughter might be going to grammar school! But she was ten and a half, not eleven-plus.

"Her standard of work shows she is quite capable of it, no worries on that score and she would be, let me see," Mr Hughes looked at some papers on his desk, "almost eleven by the time she started in September. If by any chance she should fail, then she would be entitled to another chance next year, of course. The decision is up to you, your husband and Pauline herself. But I have to have your permission before I can put her name down." He paused, waiting a little for Ivy to take it all in. She was pleased and proud, he could see that. There was one snag though, that had to be mentioned. "You do realise, don't you, that if she passes, you will have to pay towards her education there?"

Ivy was determined – they would manage that somehow. She was a good manager of money. She'd had plenty of practise in making a little go a long way over the years. Wages at the colliery were better now than they had ever been, such was the demand for coal. Pauline wasn't going to miss out on this opportunity. Ivy herself would have loved a chance like this. She had loved school – English, Composition and Arithmetic being her favourite subjects. But things were different then. She was working by the time she was fourteen, keeping herself and making a small contribution to her parents as they had been in desperate need of every penny they could get just to keep a roof over their heads. But she didn't regret it. Her time in London had been an education in itself.

"There is one other point," continued Mr Hughes, "that I feel I should mention. The boundary line that determines which grammar school she attends runs through the top half of Stephen's Street. Pauline would attend the one in the next village up the valley while the rest of the street and, of course, the whole of Crymceynon remaining attends the one on the outskirts of town. So she may not have much company, if any, to begin with. But I'm sure she would quickly settle."

Ivy hadn't realised that; it put a different aspect on things. She had seen children in the emerald green and black uniforms of the local grammar school when she had been shopping. She hadn't seen any others. What if Pauline had to travel alone? It was a long lonely walk before you reached the railway station or a bus stop. Suddenly she wasn't too keen on the idea. Now, one step at a time, she told herself – see what Jim says.

Mr Hughes was speaking again. "So, if the three of you could discuss it tonight and let me know your decision as soon as possible?"

He rose and held out his hand and she nodded, taking it.

"Um, yes. Um, thank you, Mr Hughes."

She walked home, apprehensive but proud as Punch.

That evening, they broached the subject carefully with Pauline as she sat at the rosewood table in the parlour doing her homework. She may feel she wasn't up to it yet. She might not want to do it at all.

"So, how is school these days then?" asked Jim, entering the room.

"Fine."

She didn't look up.

"Any problems?"

"Nuh."

Ivy followed in behind him. "Soon be time for the eleven-plus now," she said lightly, "just over a year to go!"

Pauline reacted; they had her full attention now. She swivelled round in her chair to face them both.

"No!" she stated adamantly, and for a split second, Ivy and Jim thought she was against the whole idea of it. "I want to do it this year! Michael Richards is and he's only a fortnight older than me." Her face said 'don't you dare say no!' "Besides," she added, strengthening her case, "I've got more violet stamps in my record than he's got!"

Michael Richards, mm. They knew him of course; he was

from the Navigation, a nice boy, a tidy boy. She would have company then, good company. Problem solved. Her parents exchanged relieved looks. That's that, then.

CHAPTER 57

The Yanks are Coming

THE YANKS WERE coming! The people in the village had known for a while that their arrival was imminent; news travelled fast up its grapevine, from shop to post office, to church, to surgery, to pubs and back again, embroidered and embellished, sometimes getting a bit tangled and mangled in the process like Bessy-Ann's language, but the gist usually got through.

The exams were over, summer holidays just around the corner, the sun was shining and the children were in the schoolyard for their dinner break. They ran to the railings as the first jeep turned from the main road and came slowly down the little hill towards the school. Jeep after jeep passed, each holding four men in uniforms that were different from those the British wore – and much smarter.

"Those are jeeps, those are!" said Vincent, knowingly. He was up-to-date with all things military. Lorries were passing now, one after another, some loaded with supplies, others with lots more men. Now and again a fistful of chocolate bars or packets of chewing gum were tossed to the children, sending them scattering like squirrels to retrieve them, squealing and shouting with glee.

By now, Mr Hughes was standing in their midst. He simply held out his hand, raised his voice a little and called out, "Bring them all to me please!" and was instantly, though grudgingly, obeyed. Pausing in the act of pocketing, they meekly walked over to him and handed over their 'finds' without exception, knowing full well that if they didn't someone would be bound to cleck on them. God forbid they should incur his wrath. In fact, as far as they were concerned, he was God. Besides, they knew for sure that all the goodies would be shared out equally before they went home. So it was only fair, they supposed. Mr Hughes, just like God, may have been feared at times but he was also loved.

Billeting officers had been around the streets in the last few weeks, knocking on the doors of the finer, larger residences over-the-other-side, looking for suitable lodgings for the higher ranks of the United States Army. The park had been commandeered for the lower ranks to set up camp. Not that the community was to suffer any deprivation from this; on the contrary, over the coming weeks once things were up and running, villagers were invited to join the troops in games of football, baseball, rugby, cricket and even boxing, the rudiments of each country's games swapped and learned.

On weekends, the children were invited to explore the 'adventure playground' of their training area, the biggest attraction by far being the contraption for practising parachute landings. It consisted of a thick cable stretched tightly from one very high platform to a very low one about thirty yards away. From morning to dusk every weekend, the children turned up in droves, all ages and both sexes, to queue patiently in a long snake-like line for 'goes' on this exhilarating new experience. Liz, Brian and Wendy were among the first to arrive. Their turn completed, they ran back to the end of the queue to wait for another, and another, never tiring of the excitement.

The community reciprocated with 'open house' at the Workmen's Hall for snooker, billiards, dramas and dancing.

More and more soldiers kept arriving by train, marching smartly from the railway station to the camp, much to the delight of the factory girls hanging from the windows to cheer, whistle and wave.

Saturday nights and dancing soon became the highlight of the week. Several of the Americans could play some kind of musical instrument, so there was no shortage of bands. Glen Miller had never sounded as good on Sunday afternoon's *Family Favourites* or on records, if you were lucky enough to own some.

All the Yanks, without exception, looked attractive in those classy uniforms and all had plenty of money in their pockets, so even if they had a face like the back-end of a bus, they still drew the girls. The novelty, the newness and the excitement soon led to 'romance'. Some of the colliers, and any British soldier lucky enough to be on leave, soon had their noses put out of joint – sometimes literally – but the Military Police, always in the vicinity, dealt with any disturbances with short shrift. Harmony and good relations had to be maintained at all costs.

"Hmph! It's the beginning of the end of moral decency, if you ask me!" said Madge Lloyd, though nobody did ask her. Watching couples strolling up the canal bank of a Sunday, she would tut-tut to anyone near: "It will all end in misery, you mark my words!"

Time would tell. But who could blame anyone snatching a little happiness wherever and whenever it was on offer? That too, was in very short supply these days.

When Carrie heard of Madge's condemnation of the American soldiers, she thought it was a good example of a pot calling a kettle black, though she didn't repeat that to Ivy. Carrie had known Madge all her life and knew her history.

What she did tell Ivy was: "A bigger hypocrite than her, God never put breath in. You steer clear of her, if you're wise!"

Madge lived a few doors up from Carrie. On the surface they seemed friendly enough but were really arch enemies. There was no love lost between them and things were bound to come to a head one day.

CHAPTER 58

Prejudice

THERE WERE SEVERAL coloured soldiers amongst the Americans but there was nothing strange in that to the villagers. All nationalities had lived in the dock area for as long as they could remember: Chinese, Indian, African, European and Irish coming with the ships; many of them staying and marrying local girls and rearing families. Gradually, they had filtered up the valleys. Men were men, was the general opinion, no matter what colour, creed or class, just as long as you were a decent human being. It was how you were, not who you were, that counted. You were judged on your merit. So it came as a great shock to find prejudice towards the coloured soldiers from some of their own countrymen. The locals wouldn't tolerate it.

Ivy was shocked to witness one incident of bigotry from a white American when she was coming home from town one day on the bus. It was quite efficiently dealt with, though. A coloured soldier had been in the queue in front of her and he had stood aside for her to board first. She thanked him and did so. There were two seats left and she sat by the window while the soldier sat next to her. As the bus progressed, four or five grammar school boys boarded, filling the aisle, followed by a white soldier. Seeing there were no seats, he motioned abruptly with his head for the one at Ivy's side to get out of his, which he immediately did. Ivy almost grabbed his arm to pull him back down but didn't quite have the courage at that moment. But the conductor had seen this and quickly intervened. If he hadn't, then Ivy would have been bound to open her mouth in protest as the white man sat down. As Carrie always said, she was never backward at coming forward when there was any sign of injustice!

"Er, excuse me, mate," said the conductor, ringing the bell for the bus to stop, "this man has bought his ticket and stays in that seat till he reaches his destination. You haven't bought one yet and I'm sorry, mate, but we're only allowed six standing. I'm afraid you're going to have to get off!"

The soldier could count, so could the rest of the passengers. There were five in the aisle including him, but seeing the sea of angry faces, he decided against protesting. The conductor took out his pocket watch as the man dismounted.

"There should be another one along in about, um, half an hour or so, buddy," he shouted cheerfully as the bus pulled away. Ding, ding!

CHAPTER 59

The Special Occasions

THE YOUNGER (AND not-so-young) generation now lived for the dancing on Saturday nights. Jim took Ivy a few times. The first time, she wore her green satin underset beneath her green paisley dress, a pair of silk stockings from the docks and black court shoes. Her brown hair hung loose and wavy to her shoulders, upswept at the front with side-combs. With some Pond's vanishing cream on her face and a little lipstick, she was ready. Jim said admiringly that she would knock 'em all for six! She did feel good. The sensual touch of the satin on her skin as she moved gave her a strange sensation. She couldn't quite put it into words. It made her feel… naughty, yes, that was it.

When they got to the hall and walked in, the atmosphere and the music washed over them. Jim lost no time in sliding his arm tightly around her, pulling her close to him and guiding her expertly around the crowded floor through the throng of dancers, proudly aware of the envious glances she was attracting from the Americans. You can look boys but you can't touch, said the look on Jim's face. If they fancied a dance with her, they'd be lucky!

The four girls were sleeping happily over at Carrie's ("For your mam and dad to have a bit of a lie in for once," she'd said) and wouldn't return until late morning. Carrie told Jim and Ivy: "You're still young and you're only young once in your life. Live for today," she said, a catch in her voice as she did so, "because you never know what tomorrow might bring." Jim liked his mother-in-law, he couldn't pick a fault with her.

They strolled home slowly in the warm air, feeling like newly-weds again, Jim's arm still tight around her small waist. They had thoroughly enjoyed themselves – and the night wasn't over yet. They had the whole house to themselves! Once inside the front door, Jim took her gently in his arms and kissed her long and tenderly, Ivy fully responding. The embrace became stronger, more intense. His hand fumbled with her buttons.

"No, Jim, no! Behave yourself!" she teased, breaking away and running into the middle room, taking refuge behind the table in the centre and watching to see which way he'd move. He put his hands flat on the table and leaned towards her.

"I'm going to get you, gel!"

He jerked his shoulders as if to move to the left, stopped, then jerked to the right. Ivy squealed in mock horror. She slipped off her shoes so she could run faster, waited her chance and ran into the passage and up the stairs, Jim running close behind her.

"You can't get away!"

She squealed louder and ran into their bedroom. Jim caught her and fell with her onto the bed.

"Gotcha!" he whispered as he found her lips.

She turned her head to the side, struggling, not quite ready to give in, but he had her wrists above her head. Serious for a moment, she warned: "Now, calm down Jim, you use your head, mind. Be careful. You jump off the train before it reaches the station or there'll be hell to pay, mind!"

She couldn't help giggling at the look on his face but she

had meant it. She didn't want any more children. She had done once, but not now. She couldn't go through what she knew her parents were going through now when she reached their age – sick with worry from one day to the next about their sons, her brothers. You could grab a bit of happiness in the midst of it all while you were still young, maybe, but you still had to be responsible, think of the consequences.

Jim was waving a little packet before her eyes. "I'm not jumping off any train, gel, not tonight!"

"Where did you get those?" she said, smiling but with a touch of concern in her voice. He had come home empty-handed from his last trip to the docks. She hoped he hadn't bought them locally. She would never be able to hold her head up again passing Crawley's the chemist!

"Aha!" He wiggled the packet. "The Yanks don't only carry gum and silk stockings, Ive!"

He had five more packets stashed away. Two for Tom, so poor Elsie-May could get off that conveyor belt producing offspring for a while and two for Billy, to bring the sparkle back to his eyes and the colour to his cheeks. What were mates for, eh?

Jim and Ivy made mad, passionate love, with total abandonment, climaxing simultaneously, holding each other in a vice-like grip then slowly relaxing as they came back down to earth, loosening their hold on each other, their upper bodies parting and rolling back onto the pillows.

"Mm," said Ivy, like a cat that's had a belly-full of cream.

"Ahhh," said Jim, like a treble-chance football pools winner.

Fully sated, they both fell asleep in seconds.

CHAPTER 60

A Visitor Calls to Duke Street

THERE WAS A short, sharp rat-tat-a-tat at Carrie's front door that somehow sounded vaguely familiar. Albert, just home from his dayshift, was about to step into the zinc bath in front of the fire and she was picking up his discarded pit clothes to put them to soak in the bosh. She tutted. She wasn't in the mood for visitors. Perhaps they would go away.

The knocker banged again. Damn! She had to answer it. She marched to the passage and flung the door open. Her eyes met the chest of an American soldier. In the split second it took her eyes to reach his face, she thought: nice uniform, some kind of officer by the look of it. What the hell does he want? Then she stepped back, her hand flying to her throat as she screamed out: "Albert!"

Hearing her, Albert jumped out of the bath again with coal dust still adhered to his body. He grabbed a snow-white towel from the fire-guard, slung it round his waist and ran. Seeing the man's face, he stopped dead in his tracks – and dropped the towel.

"Hi Mam, hi Dad!" said Glyn.

Carrie, squealing with joy, reached out and clung to her son as if she would never let him go. Glyn, grinning and winking at Albert over her shoulder, extended his hand to his father who gripped it tightly in both of his. His eyes shining, his chin trembling and with a catch in his voice, he said, "God, it's good to see you, son!"

Laughing, Glyn replied: "Yes, same here! But I didn't expect to see quite so much of you, Dad!"

Albert, flummoxed and shocked, had completely forgotten about his nudity. Embarrassed, he quickly picked up the towel, covered himself and turned back towards the kitchen, saying over his shoulder, "Sorry, son. Er, just give us a few minutes, eh? I won't be long."

With mixed emotions that were now threatening to overwhelm him, Albert stepped back into the tub and started vigorously soaping himself, trying to concentrate on getting the pit grime off. His head was spinning; he fought to keep it in control. He was overjoyed to see his eldest son again after all these years, and what a fine example of manhood he had turned out to be. His chest filled with pride. His son, his first-born, home with them. But his happiness and gratitude were marred by the reason for his presence here: to train for war, to fight the enemy. Albert couldn't bear to imagine what the future held. Flashbacks were threatening on the perimeter of his mind, the past pressing in on the present. Panic rose with his pulse rate, his heart thumping against his ribs. He got to his haunches in the bath, ready to stand and step out but failed to find the strength. He sat back on his heels, desperately willing the thoughts and pictures and screams within him to go away. He could do it. He could master it. He would. He'd had enough practise, God knows. And he had gained ground in controlling it since Doris's death. He wouldn't lose that now. It had been hard earned. Pressing his knuckles hard into his cheeks, squeezing his eyelids together until they hurt, he focussed on breathing deeply and slowly.

Carrie, still holding on to her son with happiness and sadness fighting for supremacy inside her, leaned back to look at his face, murmuring quietly to herself, "Oh my boy, my lovely boy!"

He hugged her back, relishing her closeness again, realising just how much he had missed them both. "Mam, I am so sorry I couldn't be here with you for our Dor…"

"Sh, sh," said Carrie, her finger on his lips, "I know, I know. You are here now and that's all that matters."

Carrie couldn't bear to talk about that yet. She gave him another hug and kiss. "Come and sit down. I'll go and make us a nice cup of tea," and off she went, to get the dishes from the pantry.

"Are you OK there, Dad? Can I wash your back for you?"

Glyn had come into the kitchen, the sound of concern in his voice breaking through Albert's torment and shocking him back to the present, sorting his thoughts. Glyn mustn't see, he mustn't know, he mustn't transmit his dread and fear to his son. Today was what mattered. He realised that now. He would concentrate on that and extract all the pleasure he could from it, for all their sakes.

"Aye-aye boy, I'm fine. Just got some bloody soap in my eyes, that's all!"

Glyn wasn't deceived; he knew well enough what was on his father's mind. He knew all about the First World War and what he had been through. He had read all he could about it and covered and studied campaigns during his army training. But for his father's sake, he would play along, if that was what he wanted. He soaped the flannel and gave his back a good rub down, handed him the towel and helped him out of the bath, then busied himself emptying it and replacing it on the nail in the wall outside in the backyard while his father got dressed.

Carrie came out from the pantry with a loaded tray of cups, saucers, teapot, sugar basin, milk jug and a plate of Welsh cakes, plonked it down on the table and wet the tea from the kettle whistling on the hob, all the while firing salvos of questions at Glyn.

"How long can you stay?"

"We're here for a couple of months, I think, maybe more. I don't know for sure. Then it's off to the south coast for some further training before we're posted. Best keep it to yourself though."

"Can you stay here with us? We've got a spare bed." She didn't suppose for a minute, that he could. "Oh, wouldn't that be lovely!"

"Yes, Mam, I can. It's all sorted. I explained my position to my colonel and he says it's OK."

Carrie clapped her hands, dancing a little jig. "Albert! Did you hear that? Glyn's going to stay here, with us!"

"If you can put up with me for that long!"

There was nothing in the whole wide world that she would rather put up with, right now.

The questions kept coming as they all sat down at the table. Was Danny here as well, in Wales? No? Was he coming later then? Glyn didn't know. He was in a different division. Glyn hadn't heard from him for a while now. They had both been on the move and letters took a while to catch up, if they ever did. It dawned on Carrie that this was why she hadn't heard for so long from either of them. She had kept writing but getting nothing in return. She and Albert had been so worried, jumping to conclusions here, there and everywhere.

So far, the letters had been to America and back.

Had he seen the twins yet? They were a year old now, weren't they? Were they walking yet? How many teeth did they have each? And what was Miriam like? Yes, he'd seen them. They were such sweet kids, he couldn't believe he was an uncle. He loved them to bits. Miriam was a really nice girl and a great mother. No, it wasn't a spur of the moment thing. They had been living together for a year or more before they got mar…

Carrie, shocked, blurted out: "Living together?"

Glyn couldn't help chuckling at his mother's reaction. Nothing had changed here, then. "That's not frowned on in the States, Mam. It's quite common these days, especially since 1941."

"And what about you? Are you 'living' with someone?" She couldn't help the slight emphasis on the word.

"No, I'm footloose and fancy-free as the saying goes. Miss Right hasn't come into my life as yet."

He didn't know what qualifications his Miss Right required, all he knew was he wanted a girl who would love him as he would love her, who would stay with him through thick and thin and be content to make a life with him. And, of course, have his children. He'd had girlfriends, lots of them, but he'd never got passed that initial stage of infatuation. Those relationships had waned and died within months. No depth had developed. American girls weren't like the ones back home, he felt. There wasn't that commitment, that feeling of gradually building up into something tangible and lasting. It always seemed so temporary, somehow. He couldn't settle for that. Danny had been lucky. Miriam seemed the right one for him. He envied him a little. She had what it took and good luck to them. One day he would find the right girl and he'd know when he did.

"Hey, enough questions now," he said. "It's my turn to catch up. I want to hear all about our Ivy and her family. She's moved here now, hasn't she? Is it close by?"

All this time, Albert had sat quietly, sipping his tea, smoking his pipe, adding just a word or two now and again. Not that he'd had much chance, even if he had wanted to join in the conversation proper. Carrie had hardly paused for breath. His mother hadn't changed much in that department, thought Glyn. He had been watching his father, though. He couldn't get over how old and shrunken he looked. His eyes, always deep-set, were now sunk into his skull, the pale skin of his face stretched tight over the bones. Doris's death had taken its toll on both of them, obviously. His mother's shoulders slumped with the weight of her grief. He sensed how deeply it went, in her reluctance to talk about it. He wouldn't mention it again. He'd leave it to her to broach the subject when she was ready. They had weeks, maybe months, ahead of them.

But his father's suffering had begun years ago, before the loss of his daughter. Glyn knew that now. It broke his heart to look at him. And all these years he had kept on working in the pits. Those bloody pits! What a way to have spent his life, year after year, down in the bowels of Hell, slogging his guts out in the labyrinths of coal seams where you couldn't even stand up. He should have been out in the fresh air, surrounded by the things he loved: the birds, the trees, the mountains, the whole of nature and its yearly progress through the seasons. He had spent his childhood growing up on a farm, working hard but loving it – roaming the hills on horseback, mending fences, building walls, tending sheep and cattle. His spirits didn't stand a chance of lifting down in that hard, harsh, hopeless environment. Glyn couldn't do it, not for 'all the tea in China' as Mam would say. But he admired his father's stoicism and his reasons. Working in the pits was practically all that was available and he had a family to support. And the money was just that bit more than, as an otherwise unskilled man, he could earn elsewhere. How much longer, though, could he go on doing it? Maybe when all this was over, and it shouldn't be much longer now, he could persuade them to come back to the States with him. Plenty of sunshine and open spaces there for them. He may even be able to get his father on a horse again. But that was in the future. They had to live through the here and now first and for now, it was just damn good to be home with them.

The three of them made their way over to Ivy's, Carrie as excited as a child on Christmas Eve anticipating the surprise in store for her daughter and the rest of them. She was also very conscious of all the curious looks she was getting from the neighbours as they walked past, and relished in them. She had her arm linked proudly in Glyn's, held her head up, her bosom out and floated along like a galleon in full sail.

The whole of the Edwards family were in for once when they called. So was Vera. Ivy, gathering her composure after practically jumping on her brother and screeching like a young teenager, turned to introduce him to Jim and the children. Jim responded with the firmest of handshakes and the girls stared wide-eyed and stunned at this tall, tanned, well-dressed, good-looking new uncle of theirs – their very own Yank. Wow!

Glyn was looking at Vera. In fact, he had been looking at her since he entered the room.

"Oh, I'm sorry, Glyn," Ivy said, moving now to introduce her. "This is my very best friend and neighbour, Vera Roberts."

He put out his hand and took hers, holding on to it, as he still held her gaze. "Lieutenant Glyn Thomas, United States Army, ma'am, at your service."

His smile threatening to split his face, he still held her hand. It was only for seconds but to Ivy it seemed much longer. She glanced quickly round the room to see if anyone else was aware of the electricity that seemed to be passing between these two but they were all chatting away normally. Perhaps she was imagining it. Perhaps it was even wishful thinking on her part. Looking closer now, she thought she saw Vera's hand trembling as she gently withdrew it and a slight flush rise in her cheeks as she lowered her eyes.

"Um, and these are our two evacuees," Ivy jumped in, pushing them forward a little to save Vera any further embarrassment. "They're from Cardiff."

All introductions over, news of the years they had been apart caught up with and several cups of tea either drunk or left to go cold, the three men decided the Navigation was the best place to finish the evening off. Typical, thought Carrie, whatever the occasion, it always called for a drink. Back in her own house, she had the table laid for supper, a big saucepan of mutton broth on the hob and the spare bed freshly made ready for Glyn's first night back home.

CHAPTER 61

The Long Walks

IT WAS PAULINE'S first day at grammar school.

"Turn round," said Ivy, standing to look at her daughter in her new uniform, such as it was, coupons and money allowing. The gymslip was good quality, cheaper in the long run and had a good two-inch hem, invisibly stitched up by Vera, to allow for growth. The pleats below the yoke would allow for growth in other directions! There was a gold girdle for the waist, two white blouses, a bit long in the sleeve but Vera had put a neat tuck in those, too, a gold and navy tie, a hand-knitted navy cardigan, a navy beret with a gold and navy badge, navy knickers, compulsory for PT, black woollen stockings held up by a length of elastic tied in a knot for garters and a stout pair of black lace-up shoes. Her old navy burberry still fitted, so with the hem let down that would see her through the winter, come rain or shine. Then there was a white canvas overall and a wicker basket for cookery lessons sitting ready on the stone in the pantry. Hanging from her left shoulder was the *pièce de résistance* – Jim's contribution – a real leather school satchel. Not many of the kids would have one of those! Goodness knows where he had managed to get that from, thought Ivy. Him and his 'contacts'!

Michael Richards was at the door. Liz and the evacuees kissed Pauline and wished her good luck, then Ivy did the same, smiling at her proudly and asking, "Have you got everything now? Your season tickets for the train and the bus? Your dinner money safe?"

"Yes Mam, don't fuss!" she said quietly, embarrassed with Michael standing right there.

They were off. Ivy gave her another kiss and watched and waved as they walked down the street and out of sight by the shop on the bend. They were walking all the way down to the railway station to catch a train to take them up the valley to the next village. Liz and Mary had wanted to run up to the stile and down onto the railway bridge to watch the train go past and wave to her. Pity the station wasn't up there, thought Ivy. It would have saved her a mile's unnecessary walk every morning.

The transport home by bus in the afternoons was just as bad, if not worse. A double-decker bus picked them up at the school gates and dropped them off at the nearest stop to Crymceynon, which was nearly half a mile further up the road from St Mark's Church. Pauline would get off the bus by the Cross Keys Hotel, cross the road to a gap in the railings, walk down a bank, past a small youth club called the Wendy (little more than a shed but well patronised), along the path by the riverside with St Mark's up above, and the rest of the way home familiar from Sunday school. Another mile's walk.

Pauline would have these two long treks facing her every school day, come rain, hail, wind, snow or sun, in pitch dark for most of the year either going or coming, with a satchel to carry that weighed a ton even when empty but which got heavier by the day as text books and exercise books were allocated to her. Once a week, she would also have to carry her cookery overall, her basket, a tea towel, ingredients and an appropriate dish for cookery class. Never once did it enter her head to complain or moan about this. What difference would it make? There was nothing anyone could do about it and what couldn't be altered had to be accepted. That was that.

CHAPTER 62

Plans for a Picnic

THE SEPTEMBER NIGHTS were drawing in but the weather was lasting. It was Pauline's eleventh birthday and she was allowed to invite one friend, making five including the evacuees. Margaret Pierce had been her choice and Ivy was perfectly content with that. She was a nice girl, a proper little mother to the younger Pierces and a hard worker too, always trying to keep that house of theirs clean. "She will make somebody a good wife, one day," Ivy told Glyn as the two of them sat chatting in the kitchen while the party progressed in the middle room.

Glyn nodded in agreement but was thinking village life was just the same as when he left; it hadn't moved forward one inch. Outlook and opportunity was stagnant here, with hard industrial toil in the pits, the steelworks or the railways for the boys to look forward to, and a life spent looking after others for the girls. But change would come. The younger generation would want more out of life – better pay and conditions for a start. Girls wouldn't want to give up working since it gave them independence, and with the advent of cars and aeroplanes, boys would want to spread their wings a little and travel to different areas to see what else was on offer. Glyn didn't voice these thoughts to Ivy.

Margaret came to the kitchen door and said, "Thank you for our tea, Mrs Edwards, it was lovely."

"You're welcome, Margaret."

"We've finished now. Can I clear away for you?"

"Oh, there's kind. Isn't that kind, Glyn? My brother has to go in half an hour. Sure you don't mind?"

Margaret shook her head.

"If you could just bring the dirty dishes out and put them on this table, then I can wash them up later. Thanks." That would save her a few trips to and fro. She settled back to enjoy her brother's company for just that little bit longer.

In no time, Margaret was back carrying the dishes – all of them apart from two cups – stacked up in one big wobbly pile. A green glass cup handle was around each thumb, each hand holding the sides of the bread and butter plate, six tea plates and six saucers sitting on that, then the empty sugar basin and finally two more cups. It was nearly the whole of Ivy's green glass tea-service (minus the jug) and Ivy leapt from her chair, her heart in her mouth.

"Oh, thank you Margaret," she said, removing the top half of the pile. "You really shouldn't have carried them all. They are far too heavy for you."

She could have lost the lot in one go! But it was nobody's fault but her own. She did like to see the set all laid out on a nice white embroidered cloth but a children's party wasn't really the best time or place to display them. She quickly fetched the remaining two cups left on the table – Carrie had joined them for the first few minutes to sneak a sandwich and have a chat before going home to see to Albert's food.

"You can all go out to play now, girls," Ivy said. "I'll see to the rest. Don't forget to call in on your way home, Margaret, for some birthday cake for your young brother and sisters."

Glyn was often to be found at his sister's house now, much

to the delight of the four girls, as he never came empty-handed. Vera's name seemed to crop up quite frequently, Ivy noticed.

"Do you know what I'm longing to do, Ive?" he said now, when the shock of the dishes pile had passed and the house had emptied. "Walk up to the top of a mountain with some culfs and a jack of cold tea, just like we used to do with our mam," – he was already slipping back into the vernacular, Ivy noticed – "while Dad was away." He didn't add 'in the war'. They had already gone over and over all that in previous private moments, both of them getting so upset that it was best avoided for a while. But they would go over things again, he knew.

"Oo, that's a great idea! If it's fine this weekend we'll do it."

"Do you think Vera and the boys would like to come?"

His enquiry was said very casually. Ah, there she is again, thought his sister, reinforcing her suspicions.

"Well, I can ask her," she said, equally casually but with eyebrows raised.

It was fine and Vera and the boys did join them. They all set off mid-morning, apart from Jim and Albert, who had just come home off night shift and had gone straight to bed. Glyn had brought a huge tin of ham for their sandwiches, cutting off a thick slice for Mr Merryman's 'dinner' so he couldn't raise any objections to Vera's absence. The youngsters all raced on ahead, carrying two loaded baskets between them and taking the quicker direct route while the adults followed the path, taking their time and stopping and chatting now and then.

Suddenly, Glyn shouted to someone away to their left: "Hi Quince!"

A coloured soldier in the company of a young woman leapt to his feet and gave a smart salute. "Sir!"

Glyn casually returned the courtesy. "Isn't it beautiful up here?"

"Yes, Sir, it sure is."

"You settling in OK?"

"Yes, Sir, thank you, Sir."

"Good. Well enjoy yourselves!" He waved and they all walked on.

"I know him," said Ivy, "he's the one that was on the bus with me who was told to give up his seat. Remember me saying?"

"What, Quince? He's a great guy! If you ever spot the other one, Ive, you let me know!" He nodded back in their direction. "Looks like he's made one friend here, anyhow. All I can say is, she's a lucky girl, whoever she is. Quince is a real gentleman. I guarantee it!"

Carrie was saying nothing but thinking a lot. She knew who the young woman was and if anyone needed a bit of happiness coming her way, she did. She was married to a right bully of a man who treated her worse than a dog. There had been a big change in her since her husband had been 'called up'. She had really blossomed. Good. There were cases where Carrie could fully understand the need for divorce. Who could stick what that poor girl had for nearly six years now? Her father had been no better. Perhaps that was why she had stuck it, thinking all men were the same. Besides, where could she go? Divorce wasn't that easy to come by. Poor girl. Carrie didn't mention any of this to the others.

They reached the top. The youngsters had already found a suitable spot, grassy and level and free from sheep's 'currants' (manure) and had started in on the food and drink. Carrie sank down with a sigh of pleasure, her children one on either side.

"Oh, this is nice. Pity Albert and Jim couldn't come." Flashes of all she'd heard from Martha and Joe about Albert's walk up here flickered through her mind and despite herself her eyes filled. She busied herself pouring some pop into an enamel mug, before anyone noticed. "Never mind, there'll be other days, God willing."

"I'll drink to that!" said Glyn, noticing her watery eyes and clinking his mug with hers.

CHAPTER 63

Let's Make Chips

LIFE FOR THE three families was beginning to develop a pattern of sorts since Glyn's arrival. Once the girls were in bed on the weekends Ivy, or more often Glyn, would slip down to fetch Vera to make up a foursome at cards, playing sometimes until the early hours when Glyn would walk Vera home again before returning to Duke Street. Both his parents were always in bed by then and had no idea what time he actually got home. Neither did Ivy or Jim.

Christmas was drawing nearer. Ivy thought Pauline and Dorothy, who were eleven and nearing twelve respectively, were old and responsible enough to look after the two younger ones while the four adults slipped out to the Navigation – just for an hour or two. The girls would have their supper and be in bed with their comics and books before they left. They would be alright.

No sooner had the front door closed than Dorothy jumped out of bed and went to fetch Pauline.

"I'm still starving," she said. "Let's go down and make some chips!"

"No! My mother wouldn't be willing. She'd have a fit!"

"She'll never know, will she? Who's going to tell her? Come on, it will be fun, a midnight feast! Well, a ten o'clock one, anyway."

They all laughed. Pauline was wavering and Dorothy saw her chance.

"I have made them before. In the Girl Guides. It's easy," she said.

Pauline wasn't sure if that was the truth. You never knew with Dorothy, she had discovered. But now that chips had been mentioned, her mouth was beginning to water. Besides, what could go wrong?

So the four of them went downstairs, with the younger ones banished from the pantry until the deed was done. Pauline peeled two big potatoes and Dorothy set the chip pan on the stove and lit the gas to melt the lard. All went well. The chips were dished up onto four plates, salted and vinegared and were just about to be tasted when they smelled the smoke. Dorothy had put the pan back on the stove and replaced its lid but had forgotten to turn off the gas tap. Showing no outward signs of panic, she dished out the orders.

"You two," she said to the younger ones, "into the parlour with you and stay there!"

They scuttled off, but not without their plates of chips. Dorothy cautiously approached the pantry door and opened it slowly. The air inside was thick and black. Carefully, she felt her way to the stove and turned off the gas, at the same time telling Pauline to open the small pantry window as wide as it could go. With a towel wrapped around her hand as the air cleared a little, she located the pan handle, lifted it, backed to the window and tossed it out, wholesale, onto the garden. As the hot fat hit the air, a sheet of flames shot up from the ground taking their breath away.

"Put that bloody light out!" came a yell from the distance.

CHAPTER 64

Shall We Dance?

THE WHOLE FAMILY had a wonderful time at Ivy's house over the festive season, all nine of them. Albert, Carrie, Glyn, the evacuees and Ivy's lot all squeezed round the middle-room table for a feast, the likes of which they hadn't seen for years. Glyn had been quietly stocking both larders for weeks now with tins of fruit, fish and meat, dried fruit, tea, sugar, 'proper' coffee and 'real' butter! The main course of their Christmas dinner had been steaks, great big ones, each weighing more than a month's ration. They even had two bottles of red wine! The *crachach* had never dined better.

Carrie had shed some tears – she couldn't help it – but had managed to keep it under control until she reached the *ty-bach*, so no-one was any the wiser as far as she knew. She couldn't spoil that happy atmosphere emanating from No. 26. She and Albert stayed until the children had been sent to bed and then walked slowly home, silent but content. They left Glyn behind. They wouldn't expect him home for hours yet but she and Albert were tired. But oh, it had been a wonderful day.

Glyn, strolling around with a cigarette and a glass of wine, wandered into Ivy's parlour to see if the fire needed stoking up, when he spotted for the first time their pride and joy – a gramophone in a walnut cabinet with a stack of records. He glanced through them quickly; there was quite a lot of Glen Miller, some Gracie Fields, Bing Crosby, The Inkspots,

George Formby… Forgetting about the fire, he quickly returned to the middle room. "Hey, how about some music and dancing to finish the night off? You're not working tomorrow, are you Jim?"

"Aye, but afternoons, so it's fine with me. Go and ask Vera if she can join us."

Glyn was hoping he'd say that. "Yeah, that's a good idea. The boys wouldn't mind, would they Ive?"

"No, of course not. They'll be in bed, I expect. I'll pop and ask her."

"No, it's OK, I'll go. You and Jim get things sorted here. I don't mind."

I bet you don't, thought Ivy. She wasn't born yesterday! Our Glyn is smitten, I'll bet my last penny on it, she told herself, delighted at the prospect.

By now, Glyn knew all of Vera's circumstances, which only increased his liking for her. He'd got to know the boys, who he thought were two likeable, well-balanced kids, but hadn't had the 'pleasure' of meeting her father yet. He had already retired for the night whenever Glyn had called there. Not that he wanted to meet him; he might say or do something he would regret.

Glyn had asked Vera several times to come dancing with him or to the movies over-the-other-side but she had always declined. He understood by that faint flush in her cheeks what she was thinking. It was because she was a married woman, even though a widowed one, and what would people say? Damn the people and their narrow-mindedness. Life was for living for God's sake and too short to miss out on, especially now. Still, he respected her for it, frustrating though it was. But here was a chance to get to know her better, to get closer to her; he desperately wanted that. He was itching to hold her in his arms. He realised he had never felt quite like this about a woman before and he couldn't analyse what it was exactly that attracted him so strongly. All he knew was that she occupied most of his thoughts and dreams.

They are taking their time, mused Ivy. Nearly three quarters of an hour passed before they returned.

"She took a lot of persuading," said Glyn sheepishly.

Ivy could read him like a book. Aye-aye, Glyn *bach*, I'll believe you, though thousands wouldn't, her look said.

"I haven't danced for years," said Vera nervously as the music started and Glyn took her in his arms.

"Just relax," he told her, trying to restore her confidence. "It's just like riding a bike – you never forget once you've learned."

There was a slow foxtrot playing on the turntable, a Bing Crosby record which Ivy had chosen. Glyn tightened his arm around her, drawing her closer. Vera closed her eyes, the top of her head resting on his chin, their steps following each other in perfect harmony. Now and again, Glyn moved his head down to whisper something in her ear, his lips brushing her cheek in the process, and Vera lifted her head to smile at him.

"Look at those two," whispered Ivy to Jim as the two couples circled the floor in a clockwise direction around the room. "Our Glyn's a bit besotted there, I think."

"Mm? Naw, he's only here for five minutes, gel, they're just friendly, that's all. Enjoying each other's company and why not, eh?"

Men! They never could see what was staring them in the face.

"Vera's a nice girl, she deserves a bit of fun," he continued. "She doesn't get much, shut up with that old bastard day in and day out does she? No, I think you're barking up the wrong tree there, gel."

Was she? Ivy relished the thought of a budding romance between her brother and her best friend and was positive she wasn't reading too much into it. And given a chance once this war was over, who knew what might become of it. Glyn said it wouldn't be long now, what with the sheer numbers involved. Perhaps he would come back to live in Wales again. Our mam would be over the moon if that happened. Wouldn't she though! Her thoughts were running away with her. Well, we will just have to wait and see, that's all. But there was something there – she just knew it.

The gramophone was pulled out and wound up on a regular basis from then on, the four girls falling asleep to the music wafting up the stairs.

CHAPTER 65

The House to Themselves Again

EARLY IN THE New Year, Mr and Mrs Barksted turned up unexpectedly at Ivy's. Mrs Barksted looked very agitated and excited about something.

"I'm so sorry to arrive like this without warning," she said. "A letter would have taken too long and it wouldn't have been enough, you see, and we must know, a decision must be made as soon as possible. I need to know what the girls think about it all, I need to talk to them, to get their reaction, their opinion. We've brought all the details to show them."

She paused for breath and to rummage in her handbag, before carrying on again at a pace that Ivy was finding difficult to follow. Eventually, with a cup of tea in her hand and a slice of Cherry-Genoa to keep her mouth occupied, Ivy turned her attention to Mr Barksted who was about to take over, but before he could utter a word, his wife was off again. This time it was about the cake.

"Mm, this cake really is delicious. Wherever did you get it?"

Ivy, taken off guard, was suddenly very embarrassed. She hadn't expected such a question and was suffused with guilt. One of the consequences of having dealings with the black market, she told herself crossly. She had no ready answer. What could she say? Oh, my husband has friends 'in the know'? She needed time to think, quickly, so she said, "Uh, excuse me just a minute. I think I left the gas on when I wet the tea!"

Once in the privacy of the pantry, she could think. Glyn! Of course. With her dignity restored, she returned to the middle-room carrying some more of the cake and explained about her brother – a lieutenant in the United States Army – she loved saying that! Mrs Barksted was most impressed, not only about her brother but also the standard of nourishment her girls had been receiving.

"Er, would you care for another slice?" asked Ivy gratuitously, offering the plate.

At last her husband could get a word in. Apparently, his father had died recently and they had inherited his big, rambling house situated down the vale and quite near the sea. Mrs Barksted, her plate empty once more, butted in again.

"Our girls have been so happy here and we were so worried initially, weren't we dear?" she said. "But they have really loved it. All their letters are always full of enthusiasm about the place. And the people. And to return to city life now would be a very poor comparison, claustrophobic even, after all the freedom they have enjoyed here."

Ivy nodded, fully understanding, and admitting to herself with surprise that it was just the way she looked on the place now.

"Anyway," Mrs Barksted continued, "it will take years to sort Cardiff out and rebuild it and it's not a nice place to live in the meantime."

Her voice was sad. She obviously felt some reluctance at the thought of moving. Goodness knows what they had endured down there on those terrible nights. Mrs Barksted was looking quite upset and Ivy felt very sorry for her. She could only imagine what was going through Mrs Barksted's mind when she said quietly, "Cardiff will never be the same to us again."

Her husband put his arm around her. "Come, come, dear," he said. "We're all safe and well. That is all that matters. We are very lucky, mm? How many do we know whose lives have been ruined? Count our blessings, eh?" He looked at Ivy and told her, "She's overtired. She's been overdoing it I'm afraid, out every single night with the WVS, doing what they can."

Before they left, Ivy put what was left of the cake into a brown paper bag and handed it to them. "It might come in handy down there," she said. "Their need is greater than ours."

By the beginning of February the evacuees had gone, full of tears and promises to write and eagerly looking forward to the time when the war had ended and they could all meet up again.

CHAPTER 66

Their Final Meal

AT THE END of April the American soldiers were getting ready to move again. Rumour had it they were heading for the south coast but no-one knew for sure. Carrie and Albert were at their wits' end now that the time had come and they still hadn't heard from Danny. Miriam had written to say he was somewhere in Europe but she didn't know where and she hadn't heard from him for nearly a month.

Carrie sat with Albert and Glyn in the kitchen, the three of them quiet and thoughtful, all of them wanting to talk but none of them feeling able to. Carrie got up.

"Would you like another cup of tea, love?" she asked her son, then collapsed into tears as she caught his eyes.

Glyn stood up immediately and held her, trying to comfort her. "Mam, Mam, don't! Please!"

He looked over his shoulder at his father. His eyes were wet, too, his mouth opening for quick gulps of air then closing tight.

"Dad, tell her! It won't be like the last lot, will it! Not with all the men and weapons we've got now. It will be over soon, Mam. Please. Don't worry. I need to know you're not worrying."

That shook her. He couldn't afford to worry over them, of course he couldn't – he had to keep his wits about him. She had to reassure him. She looked up, nodding her head, patting his shoulders, swallowing hard. She managed a watery smile.

"You promise me you won't take risks, that you'll look after yourself. And our Danny when you see him. You tell him how much we love you both, how much you mean to us. We want to see you both home and safe. You hear me? Home and safe!"

Albert had stood up and clung to them both.

"We'll finish the bastards this time, Dad. They won't come back to haunt us any more, eh? You look after yourself and Mam. I've got plans for both of you. And some unfinished business here. I'll be back, OK? We'll both be back." His grip tightened a little on his frail father, trying to pass his own strength and confidence through to him.

Meanwhile, Ivy was preparing a sumptuous meal for them all at her house for seven o'clock. Vera and the boys had been invited, Mr Merryman hadn't. Vera had told him she would be straight back down after the meal to get his supper and put him to bed with his nightly cup of cocoa.

At a quarter to seven, Ivy stood back to look at the results of all her hard work. She had thoroughly enjoyed doing it – it was just like being back in service, she thought, only this time she would be recipient as well as cook. She had done four courses, with the help of tins, of course, but still… There was liver pate on Melba toast for starters, ham with parsley sauce for the main course, then fruit crumble (made with the blackberries and apples she'd preserved last summer thanks to Glyn's extra sugar) served with custard. Finally, there would be cheese and biscuits, washed down with the last of her precious coffee.

The meal had helped considerably with the atmosphere. Glyn had slipped out with Vera for a little while afterwards, under the pretence of checking if Mr Merryman was alright. They had gone the back way. Carrie, not one to miss much, saw the special attention Glyn paid to her, the way his hands lingered as he draped her cardigan over her shoulders, the little whispers and smiles that passed between them. Something's going on there, she concluded. Well now, isn't that good! She is a lovely girl and they look just right together somehow. Wouldn't it be wonderful if… maybe move back to Wales after… was this his unfinished business? Carrie stopped her ramblings. They all had to live through the here and now first. It was never any good making plans. Something always spoiled them.

Albert and Carrie returned to their house after all the clearing up had been done. The 'youngsters', as Carrie called the four adults, needed a few hours to themselves now. They didn't want their barely disguised sadness putting a damper on these last few days. They took their leave, thanking Ivy and Jim for all they had done, kissing them all and telling Glyn, "Come home when you're ready, there's no hurry."

Vera's sons had gone home, Ivy's daughters had said their goodbyes to their wonderful uncle and gone to bed, and now Ivy and Glyn were pouring drinks for the four of them while Vera and Jim sorted through records to listen or dance to.

"What will you do when it's all over, Glyn?" asked his sister. There was no room in her mind for any doubt about his survival. "Will you be coming back here or returning to America?"

"I don't know, Ive, it depends."

"On what?"

"Oh, Mam, Dad, Vera."

"Vera?"

"Yes, Vera. Do you think I stand a chance there, Ive? You know her well."

"I know she likes you. Likes you a lot, in fact. Do you mean marriage or what, our Glyn? Are you serious about her?"

"Aye, very serious. I love her. I do want to marry her."

"So you might settle here then?"

"America is such a great country, Ivy. Nowadays it is anyway. Don't tell our mam and dad, but it was hellish in the beginning!"

"But you and Danny said it was wonderful!"

"What would you have said in those circumstances after committing yourself? That it was every bit as bad as Britain, that you had fallen out of the frying pan into the fire? It was in the grip of its own depression. People were throwing themselves from high buildings, unable to cope any longer. Businesses collapsed, fortunes were lost overnight. We had a hell of a job just keeping our heads above water, lucky to get any sort of job labouring on farms or in factories for next to nothing. But things are much better there now. You wouldn't believe it. People like us with their own cars, telephones, fridges, all sorts of things. Britain will follow suit once this lot is over, you wait and see!"

"You still haven't answered my question, Glyn. Here or there?"

"I honestly don't know, Ive, I honestly don't know. We'll see, eh? A lot depends on how Mam and Dad are by then."

Ivy and Glyn had had long discussions over the months about Doris' death and funeral and they had cried in each other's arms at the effect it had had on their parents. If only they had known more, understood more from the very beginning, they could have shared their turmoil and broken the isolation they had both endured for so long.

"I tried to talk to our mam about everything but by the time she was beginning to accept Doris' death, Pearl Harbour happened. How could I say anything about war, past or present, then?" Ivy asked Glyn. "She's worried enough about you and our Danny as it is. I know she's not sleeping properly and you haven't even gone yet."

Glyn stroked her back, trying to calm her. "Don't take everything on your own shoulders, Sis. Don't you start keeping things in. Learn from this and share your concerns when I'm gone. Talk to Jim. And Joe and Martha. They're always there when you need them aren't they? Martha knows how to handle Mam. I've had a few good chats with her on her visits. And Joe. The two of them are worth the world. They've got right to the root of things and things are much better than they used to be. Dad and Mam talk about things much more now. They can help and support each other." He lifted her chin and smiled at her, saying, "Our mam's beginning to follow her own advice – 'a worry shared is a worry halved'. See that you follow it, too!"

There would be no talk of war in these last few days as far as Ivy was concerned. She wanted happy things to look forward to and focus on.

"Can I tell Mam about Vera and you? She'd love that bit of news. She's very fond of Vera."

Glyn pointed his finger at her. "You can hint at it, no more! And not until after I'm gone."

Ivy grudgingly acquiesced, nodding but saying nothing. She would hint in such a way that Carrie would catch on immediately. That would give her something to puzzle over and wonder about during the next few months – Glyn thinking of marrying a local girl and one that met with her full approval, too!

CHAPTER 67

The Last Night at the Hall

SATURDAY NIGHT HAD been a great night at the Workmen's Hall. The American bands had played non-stop until the early hours, the musicians taking it in turns to play so that everyone had a turn on the floor. Couples sat and talked between dances or strolled out into the night air, heading for the quiet and dark of the canal bank to say personal 'goodbyes' or maybe to get to know each other a little better before having to part. Some progressed as far as the Navigation, popped in for a drink or two, then crossed the stile and walked down the path past the allotments, looking for a more secluded spot. Some stood on the bridge over the railway, waiting to be engulfed by the steam as the frequent trains passed below, then shrieking and laughing like children. Excitement was in the air. You could feel it, taste it.

Some girls drew back from the edge of total indulgence though, knowing they would never live it down. If the likes of Madge Lloyd, that paragon of rectitude, got to know they had been in a pub, let alone discovered in a compromising situation, it would be all over the village like wildfire; and reputations once broken, like Humpty Dumpty, could never be put back together again.

CHAPTER 68

The Last Glimpse

IT WAS A beautiful spring day in early May, with sunshine and blue sky. The last convoy was due to leave around mid-morning, the vehicles going by road to the coast and the rest of the men by train. Most of the Yanks were as loath to go as some of the locals were to see them going. Living in and getting to know the village and its people during these last months had been as much of a culture shock for them as it had been for the villagers having them in their midst. On the whole, the majority on both sides would not have missed it for the world and had memories to last them all their lives – mostly happy ones.

Vera had not seen Glyn since the get-together at Ivy's two nights ago, nor had any of his family. He had been unable to leave camp and they had all said their 'goodbyes' then. Now his parents, his sister and her husband and his two nieces waited patiently by Martin's for a last glimpse of him as his jeep went passed.

The long march began, the jeeps and lorries driving slowly, the men marching behind carrying their kitbags and the weight of the world on their shoulders. Who knew what tomorrow would bring? Down the main street of houses they came, with the pavements on both sides lined with locals. Subdued, but wishing to show them how they felt, there were shouts of "Good luck, boys!" and "Give 'em Hell for us!" with sporadic cheers here and there.

Glyn's jeep was one of the first to pass. He was looking out for them. The women and the girls blew kisses from hands that were wet with their tears. Jim held up both his thumbs and shouted, "All the very best, mate!" Albert stood straight and with his face expressing all the love, pride and respect he had for his son; he held Glyn's gaze and saluted him. Glyn stood up in the back of his jeep and with equal sincerity, returned his salute. When he had passed, his father whispered to himself, "God bless you, son, and your brother."

Carrie heard him, caught her breath and squeezed his hand. "Amen to that," she said.

The convoy continued down the street of shops, turning the corner by Morelli's – who stood in his white apron by the door, his rosary moving in his fingers – then over the bridge and down the road which ran alongside the river. All the windows of the pop factory were thrown wide open, each one jammed with girls vying for a view. Several were sobbing their hearts out, while others cheered or whistled. Some of the soldiers had tears sliding silently down their cheeks too, maybe over what they were leaving behind or facing ahead. Now and again a hand would creep up surreptitiously and flick them away. One of the girls started singing, others quickly joining in, till the sound of their voices matched that of the marching feet:

"We'll meet again, don't know where, don't know when,

But we know we'll meet again, some sunny day..."

What were the chances of that happening? One in hundreds, one in thousands? Someone began a Gracie Fields song, altering the words to suit the occasion:

"We wish you luck as we wave you goodbye,

Cheerio, here you go, on your way..."

CHAPTER 69

Seeds of Doubt

VERA SAT SILENTLY in her kitchen, her mind running riot. She hadn't dared to join the crowd of well-wishers, giving Mr Merryman and his requirements as her excuse in response to Ivy's invitation. Ivy didn't believe her for a second, but accepted it without question. Vera was afraid her face would give her away to all and sundry, after what had happened between her and Glyn on their last night. That was when he had told her that he loved her, that he would be coming back for her, that he was going to marry her. It was then that she had admitted, to herself and to him, that she loved him too – more than she had ever loved anyone, except her two boys. She had totally abandoned all the restraint of recent months and let loose all her pent-up passion, submitting herself to him willingly, eagerly even.

Vera had loved her first husband. He was a good man, one of the best, liked and respected by everyone. She had enjoyed their marriage; they had been happy and content during their few years together and had been blessed with two lovely boys. But this had been different from the very start. Her feelings for Glyn had invaded and taken over her whole body and she was forced to succumb. She had no control over them, no willpower; there was nothing she could do. Every bone in her body was aching for his presence as she sat alone by the kitchen fire, waiting for her father to wake and tap the bedroom floor with his stick to summon her.

She folded her arms across her breasts, reliving the new, excruciating, thrilling peak of emotion she had experienced. Would she ever know that feeling again in Glyn's arms? Seeds of doubt began to grow in her mind. Her common sense told her she had been foolish to fall in love and ignore the consequences. Would he come back for her? Maybe she was just another conquest. What did she really know about him, about his life? There must have been other women. What if he just forgot about her, met someone else and returned to America? Perhaps there was someone there already, waiting for him to return. She rocked herself to and fro in the chair, nursing the pain these thoughts brought.

Then came the taps on the ceiling above. She glanced at the clock. It was half-past nine. She'd have to get him up, get his breakfast and carry on as normal as she had done with the boys earlier. They had gone to school, ignorant of her mental turmoil. She was good at that – keeping her thoughts to herself, hiding her feelings, putting on a brave face – except when she was with Glyn.

CHAPTER 70

Waiting for the Post

THE POSTMAN APPROACHED the bottom of Duke Street. There she was again: Mrs Thomas, looking out for him. He smiled to himself. He had three for her today, making a total of five since Glyn had left. He knew what she was going through, especially since D-Day. His son was also in the army.

Carrie sat with the letters, ready to drink in their contents with her usual cup of tea. There were two from Glyn – and one from Danny! She opened Danny's first. She assumed he was in Europe, like Glyn, but there was no mention of them meeting up. But then she remembered seeing in the atlas she had borrowed from the doctor that Europe was a big place, making it unlikely that they would meet.

Danny's letter contained no details about the war – at least none that she could read, since several sentences were blacked out. She hated this censorship of 'her' letters and the thought that someone else had read them first. She didn't see the necessity for it; she was their mother, not a German spy for goodness sake! Who would she give any 'secrets' to? Not knowing what her boys were up against was worse than knowing, in her opinion. It let loose all kinds of speculative thoughts to set her worrying.

Most of Danny's letter was about his twins. Miriam kept her regularly informed about them as well, and much as she loved them, it was him she wanted to know about. Was he getting enough sleep and enough to eat? Was he anywhere near the danger zones and the bombs the allies were dropping? Was there any sign or hope of it ending? She was just as wise on these counts as she had been before opening the letter. Having read it, she felt frustrated, but comforted nonetheless. She folded it carefully and put it in her pocket so it would be to hand as soon as Albert came home, then opened Glyn's two.

Glyn mentioned Vera and the boys in both of them, saying what a nice family they were, what a good woman she was, what a cantankerous old curmudgeon her father was and how she deserved better. Well, she knew all that too, and she could read between the lines: his intentions were to give her a better life! Carrie wouldn't, of course, show the letters to Vera; she wouldn't interfere. But she knew damn well that by showing them to Ivy, they would be relayed to her friend in detail. A bit of encouragement wasn't the same as meddling. Besides, Ivy had mentioned Vera was receiving letters from Glyn herself!

In the rest of his letter, Glyn asked how his mother and father were getting on, advising them to get out and about as much as possible to help pass the time more quickly. And, of course, there were more crossed out sentences. Bloody infuriating. She stamped off to the dresser to get her pen, ink and paper.

CHAPTER 71

Vera's Secret

VERA WAS ABOUT four months pregnant. She had told no-one and so far no-one had guessed. She was 'carrying' quite neatly, like she had done during her first two pregnancies. No-one had known then, apart from her husband, until she had gone six months. She always wore one of her smocks when doing the housework. She had made them when she had been pregnant with David, and there was plenty of wear left in them. The one and only coat she possessed hung loose from her shoulders. But she wouldn't be able to hide it from those close to her much longer.

It had been a shock to find herself in this condition. Not that she regretted it, now that she'd had time to get used to it. In fact, she was actually looking forward to having the new baby. But she knew her circumstances would prove to be a problem. She would have to run of the gauntlet of people finding out, then see their reactions. And what would her boys think? They had liked Glyn very much, but how would they react on learning what they had 'been up to'? What opinion would Ivy and, worse still, Carrie and Albert have of her? Would they think that she had seen an opportunity to try and trap him?

She hadn't even told Glyn yet and had no intention of doing so. She wanted him to come back for her because he loved her, not because he felt obligated. Besides, he had enough on his plate looking after himself without worrying about her. But would he still want her when he found out? He may not want to be tied down with a wife and baby and another man's two sons. He could easily escape back to America and leave her to it. It was generally looked on as the woman's fault if she 'fell' pregnant. Men just sowed their wild oats, but it was the women who reaped the harvest of years of shame and misery. Thinking of his loving letters to her, she immediately dismissed that thought. No, Glyn wasn't like some men she had heard stories about – her father for instance.

Then there were the gossips that would delight in her predicament. She knew well enough what they would say: like mother, like daughter; the apple never falls far from the tree; she couldn't have known him more than a few months; she's no better than she should be! Vera had heard it said about others.

Finally, there was the whole situation with her father and two stepsisters. It was a great chance for them to come down on her like a ton of bricks. Oh, if only Glyn was here, if only he could come home. She had no idea how to resolve all these questions she was asking herself. She tried to focus on Glyn's return and dismiss all other problems as the old man entered the kitchen.

CHAPTER 72

The Worst Nightmare

CARRIE FELT THAT hope was in the air and that things were definitely changing for the better. She was living from day to day, her usual routine back in full swing and the wireless continually on to hear the latest bulletins. It was coming up to dinner-time and Albert was moving about upstairs getting ready for work. She was about to rearrange the dust in the parlour when she noticed a letter on the front door mat. She had been so busy that she hadn't noticed it earlier. It was pale blue and light as a feather, just like the ones the boys had sent her from America. Since they were always upper-most in her mind, her first thought was, 'but they're not there any more'. Then it dawned on her: of course, it would be from Miriam.

Excitedly, she tore it open. She read it and re-read it, then dropped it in her lap and stared ahead in shock. Miriam, now being next-of-kin, had been notified first. She had tried to break the news as gently as she could, leading up to it gradually, but the words leapt out at Carrie from the page: Danny was missing, believed killed.

Meanwhile, Albert, on his way downstairs, heard a knock on the front door and opened it. A young boy stood on the step before him, a buff envelope in his hand. He said nothing and avoided eye contact as he handed it over, but put his hand gently on Albert's arm. God, he hated this bloody job!

Albert never noticed him getting on his bike and riding

off. Slowly, he turned and walked to the kitchen, opening the envelope as he went. Glyn had been killed in action. He looked down at Carrie, saw the pallor of her face and the airmail letter in her lap, and knew. Carrie looked up as Albert's face crumpled and saw the buff envelope in his hand, and she knew. She sucked in her breath until her lungs could hold no more, then let it out in the most terrible, animal-sounding, tormented wail. "No-o-o!" Albert, losing all his strength, dropped to his knees before her, wrapped his arms round her and wept like a child with his head in her lap. Carrie stared straight ahead, unmoving.

All who were affected by this terrible double blow dealt with it in their own way. Ivy's immediate concern was her parents. Again, she pushed her agonising grief to the back of her mind. She was their only surviving child now and she would have to look after them both. She needed them to be there.

The first thing she did was send for Martha and Joe, and again they came at once. Her father couldn't be allowed to slip back into that dreadful state – she couldn't bear it. And for her mother to lose her own children after giving them life – no-one should have to endure that. Worst of all was not knowing how or where it had happened; the family couldn't even to have them home to see it through to the end, like they had with Doris. There was just this terrible void, this emptiness, with no resolution or closure.

Vera couldn't allow herself to grieve, either. She had to keep her feelings to herself. She couldn't risk breaking down in their presence – she might well let slip about his baby and that would only add to their grief. What would they think of her if it got round the village that she was soon to bring his illegitimate child into the world? It would give people the opportunity to gossip about their son, to sully and vilify his name. She couldn't do that to them.

And so life went on for them all – slowly, painfully and full of anguish.

CHAPTER 73

More to Come

VERA WAS NOW five and a half months pregnant. History was repeating itself: she was in exactly the same position when her first husband died. She still had no idea what to do about anything; she couldn't concentrate enough to think things through. She had decided one thing, however: she couldn't stay here. She would have to leave Crymceynon and find rooms somewhere else before the birth. She had about fifty pounds saved and her mother's wedding and engagement rings to pawn. Just a week or two more of scrimping, saving and finishing her sewing orders and she could make her savings last a little longer. If she stayed, she would only be adding to Glyn's family's misery and they didn't deserve that. Better if she left without telling them anything. She had started to pack a few little things and store them under her bed, but finding rooms would be difficult.

She had very little time to fully assimilate the predicament she was in and the dreadful fact that Glyn had gone out of her life forever, before more bad news came her way. Her life was about to unravel completely, but for the sake of her boys and the baby she was carrying, she would have to concentrate and stay in control. Her sorrow, like Ivy's, had to be tucked away every day until, awake and alone in her bed at night, she could let go.

CHAPTER 74

Mr Merryman's Demise

VERA HAD GONE up to Ivy's late in the evening for a break from Mr Merryman's demands. He wasn't feeling well, he said, he must have a cold coming on or something. She had been run off her feet all day at his beck and call. Finally, after a cup of hot cocoa and a hot water bottle to warm his bed, she had persuaded him to retire. Putting her coat on and leaving strict instructions with her sons to come and fetch her if he was any worse, she had left.

She still called to Ivy's as regularly as before, deriving some comfort from being in Glyn's sister's company in that house with all its happy memories. Besides, they would all wonder what was wrong if she didn't call. She had barely sat down when David came rushing in to fetch her.

Gareth had been summoned by the old man knocking on the bedroom floor and had gone to see what he wanted. From the doorway he could see that something was seriously wrong. Gingerly, he approached the bed. The old man's eyes were glaring at him, his mouth twisted and drivelling black liquid from the corner of his lips onto the pillow. He looked like he was trying hard to say something. Gareth tentatively moved closer. Suddenly, a bony arm shot out and gripped his forearm like a vice. Terrified, Gareth snatched his arm free and ran down the stairs and out through the door. David heard the door slam and ran after him, thinking he was going to fetch his mother, but Gareth was running down the street to fetch the doctor, knowing instinctively that the old man had had another stroke.

Mr Merryman died in the early hours of the morning, just as it was getting light. Dr Treadwell had been and left, saying he would notify the undertaker, being one of the very few in the village to own a telephone. He left Bessy-Ann to wash the body, dress it in a clean night-shirt and make the necessary arrangements to have it brought downstairs to the parlour where a trestle table stood waiting. This had to be done before rigor mortis set in, because the sharp bend near the top of the stairs made it very difficult, if not downright dangerous, to manoeuvre a coffin down them.

Gareth and David had been dispatched to bed at Ivy's after having something to eat. After checking on all four children and leaving them a note to say they would be back as soon as possible, Ivy and Vera returned to No. 22 Stephen's Street.

"Is everything alright up there Bessy?" asked Ivy quietly from the foot of the stairs. "Can I give you a hand?"

"No thank you, Mrs Edwards, we're nearly finished. You go with Mrs Roberts and keep her company."

Vera was slumped in her father's chair, staring at the grate. Ivy made up the fire – the kitchen was cold and Vera looked perished. She filled the kettle and put it on the gas stove. She'd make a nice cup of tea for them all when it boiled. She glanced again, concerned, at Vera.

"You alright Vee?"

Vera shook her head. Ivy crouched before her.

"Is there anything I can do?"

Again she shook her head. Over the last ten hours, her head had been spinning with the fact that her time had run out. As soon as her half-sisters got her message, she would be gone. At least she now had an excuse to leave the place. She latched on to that. Now all she had to do was find somewhere – and within days!

Ivy thought she sensed what Vera was thinking about.

"Don't worry about the future, Vee. You can always move in with us, you know."

"Thanks, Ive. You're a good friend. But I've got a cousin who lives on her own further up the valley. She'll take us in, I know. I daresay she'd be glad of a little company."

It was a lie but said with such conviction that Ivy believed her.

Upstairs, Bessy-Ann was giving instructions to Tom and Jim: "We'll need another one to carry him downstairs, boys, two for the shoulders and one for the legs. Who else can we ask?"

"Well, Billy's on the right shift, I'll go and get him!" said Jim.

Tom shook his head. "He's not a good choice, wuss. I told you, him and death don't mix!"

"Well, they will this morning," said Jim. He wanted things sorted quickly for Vera's sake. "I'll go and get him."

Billy was far from keen but felt he had no option, so over he came.

"Right," said Bessy-Ann, in charge on the landing. "You two take the shoulders, and Billy, you have the legs. You will be going down first – and backwards, so take care on that bend – we don't want any mishaps. Count the steps and stop on the fourth, ready? One, two, three, four. Stop. Drop the legs a bit now, Bill, and you two lift the shoulders a bit. Careful now!"

The jolting and shifting of Mr Merryman's body disturbed

accumulated, trapped gases. They found an escape route via the anal orifice with a loud 'brrrp'.

"Cripes!" shrieked Billy, dropping the legs, turning and running down the stairs two at a time. Tom and Jim, hanging onto the shoulders for dear life, called after him in hushed voices.

"Bill! You daft bugger! Come back, mun! It's only wind!"

Billy, opening the front door, called back over his shoulder, "Well if he's still got that much left, he can walk down the bloody stairs himself!"

Ivy heard the commotion, got up and walked to the passage to see what was wrong, by which time the indefatigable Bessy-Ann had managed to squeeze past and pick up the legs and both men had regained control of their hysterics.

"Is everything alright?" asked Ivy.

"Yes, don't worry Mrs Edwards. We had a bit of a hitch, but everything's fine now. You go back to the kitchen."

Comedy and tragedy often bump violently into each other in the most unexpected circumstances. That's life.

CHAPTER 75

The Secret's Out

MR MERRYMAN'S WILL was to be read. Vera had received a letter from his solicitor stating that he had been instructed by Mr Merryman to carry this out at his home, in the presence of Miss Merryman, Mrs Rhys-Jones and herself, as early as possible after the funeral. He planned to do so on the following Friday at 2pm, if that was convenient, and enclosed a telephone number for confirmation. He had already been in touch with Miss Merryman and Mrs Rhys-Jones, and intended arriving on the same train as them.

This is it then, thought Vera. As soon as he's gone they will give me my marching orders, making it plain that I no longer have any right to live here. The postal orders had stopped with her father's last breath. She would be left to fend for herself with two young boys, a baby well on the way, and no roof over their heads. Any slim chance of renting the house from her half-sisters was well out of the window. They would want to sell it and divide the spoils. Anyway, she wouldn't be able to afford the rent of a whole house with only her small Lloyd George pension and her sewing money. Besides, it would be best for all concerned if she could make a clean break and get rooms away from the village altogether, as she had originally decided. She hoped they would at least have the decency to give her a few days grace to get things sorted, make some enquiries and pack.

Vera had cleaned the whole house from top to bottom for

this visit, hardly noticing the effort as her mind raced over all that had recently happened. Her life was falling apart before her eyes. Her only consolation was knowing that when you're at your very lowest, things couldn't get any worse. One thing was for certain: she would keep her dignity until she was safe in her bed that night.

It was half-past twelve. She took a final look around the parlour before putting the polish and dusters back in their box. Now all she had to do was make herself presentable. Her clothes were laid out ready on her bed: clean underclothes, a tweed skirt that just fitted (now that she had let out the side seams and moved the button at the waist), a knitted jumper that had stretched slightly in the wash and an old corset that she had last worn after David's birth to support her tummy muscles. She hoped it would camouflage her ever-increasing bump.

She washed and dressed and stood sideways to look in the dressing-table mirror. She might just get away with it. But the corset was tighter than she had hoped it would be and was very uncomfortable. Still, it wouldn't be on for long and she wasn't going to give them the satisfaction of looking at her, or the house, with disdain. She still had her pride and hopefully, after today, their paths would never have to cross again.

They were here. She put a smile on her face and opened the door, welcoming them in, automatically shaking hands and exchanging pleasantries. The four of them sat in the parlour with the sisters on the couch, the solicitor in an armchair alongside a small table to hold his briefcase and papers, and Vera on a high-backed chair. She straightened her back, held in her corseted tummy and folded her hands in her lap for extra coverage. Staring blankly in front of her, she switched off her thoughts and waited for it all to be over.

The solicitor's slow, soft voice droned on, Vera not registering one word of what he was saying, until Audrey and Marjory suddenly shrieked in unison: "WHAT?"

There was stunned silence for a few seconds before Vera's half-sisters continued:

"That can't be right!"

"When was this will made?"

"There must be some mistake!"

"He can't do that!"

The solicitor answered in his professional voice, "The will, properly signed and witnessed, was handed to me personally by Mr Merryman himself in the summer of forty-one. His instructions were that I should set up this meeting to deliver its contents. I can assure you, ladies, that it is perfectly legal and correct." He handed it to them. "See for yourselves."

The shout had jerked Vera out of her trance. What was happening?

"Mrs Roberts," said the solicitor, turning to her, "have you any comments or queries on the matter?"

"Me? No. Why?"

"Ahem! Perhaps you didn't quite take in all I said."

He had become, over the years, quite intuitive at times like these and had noticed the absent, vacant look in her eyes from the start. He had seen it before in families, when the least expectant of the beneficiaries had walked away with the lot. Power from the grave. He did a quick resume for her benefit: "Mr Merryman has left everything that he possessed, that is, this house and all its contents and money to the value of one thousand, three hundred pounds, plus savings certificates to the value of fifty pounds, to his daughter, Vera Alice Roberts."

Vera promptly passed out.

She recovered quite quickly, much to the solicitor's relief, as the two sisters had left in a huff before her body hit the floor.

"Are you alright now, Mrs Roberts?" he asked, holding a glass of water to her lips. "No, don't try to get up. Is there anyone nearby I can fetch to stay with you? You see, I must catch this next train."

His solicitor's mind was telling him this could be a compromising situation, should anyone passing look through the parlour window and find him on the floor with a woman alone in the house! So Ivy was quickly collected and he took his leave.

Knowing about the will reading, Ivy rushed to her side and said, "Whatever's the matter, Vee? What have those two bitches been saying to you?"

Vera waved her arm dismissively and shook her head. Then, with Ivy's help, she got to her feet and started unbuttoning her skirt, worried about the baby.

"I'll tell you all about it in a minute," she said, "but help me to get out of this damn corset first."

Corset? Why was Vera wearing a corset, for goodness sake? She wasn't fat – she wasn't even what you would call 'well-covered'. With its removal came the answer. Vera watched her face closely for any sign of disapproval. Their whole friendship would depend on how she took this news. Ivy rose slowly from picking up the skirt, her eyes glued to Vera's stomach.

"You're pregnant!" she said, her mouth and eyes opening wide with the shock.

Vera nodded, anxious and wary. Their eyes met and suddenly Ivy's face lit up.

"Our Glyn's baby!" Her voice was ecstatic as she reached out to hug her. "Why the hell didn't you tell us? Oh! Wait till our mam hears about this, Vee!"

"No! Oh no, Ivy, please. Not yet. She's had enough. I don't want to upset her."

"Upset her? This is the absolute best thing that could happen right now. It will do her the world of good. I know it will. Besides, there's no hiding it from here on, is there? What if someone else should tell her first? Now, that would upset her!"

Vera wasn't convinced.

"Tell you what," said Ivy, "I'm going over to fetch her later, when it gets dark. She can't face meeting people yet in daylight. She's afraid of anyone's sympathy, it always starts her off again, but Dad is back in work and on night shift and she can't bear being in that house on her own for long, so I said for her to come and sleep at ours. You call up and we'll just let things take their course. You won't have to say a word. She'll catch on, I know she will. And she'll be pleased about it, you'll see. You don't know her like I do."

Vera sighed. Ivy was right, of course. She couldn't hide it now and Carrie should be the first to know, so she nodded her assent.

"Right," said Ivy, "you go and have a rest now before the boys come home and I'll see you at seven. OK?"

It wasn't until she got home again that Ivy realised she hadn't asked about the will business.

CHAPTER 76

Carrie's Reaction

CARRIE WAS THERE when Vera arrived. She looked dreadful – quiet, lifeless and withdrawn. She began to seriously doubt Ivy's plan. She received only a cursory, half-hearted response to her greeting – one glance, one word.

Ivy and her mother were sitting at the kitchen table with two cups of tea before them, both untouched and going cold. Vera pulled out a chair at Ivy's bidding and sat and joined them. They chatted for a while, with Carrie saying very little unless asked a direct question. Try as they might to engage her, she was not interested; nothing mattered to her anymore.

Trying desperately to hold her attention, Ivy broached the subject of the will. "Well, tell us then, Vee. What happened this afternoon? Is there any chance of you staying in the house? Surely they couldn't want you out? Even they couldn't be that spiteful and cruel."

Vera beamed, she couldn't help herself. "On the contrary, I'm going nowhere! It's all been left to me: house, furniture and money!"

Spontaneously, Ivy let out a whoop of joy at Vera's good fortune and the two ugly sisters' come-uppance. Carrie hadn't been listening. She looked up at them both – confused, puzzled and very angry. They were laughing! Why were they laughing? What were they laughing at? How could they laugh? She knew she would never laugh again.

Ivy, aware of her reaction, took both her hands in hers and

smoothed them gently. "It's alright, Mam," she said quietly, "don't worry. It's good news for Vera. About the house."

Carrie tried to concentrate.

"Ol' man Merryman finally turned up trumps. He's left it to her."

This time it registered.

Ivy continued: "Not only that, but his money as well! To his daughter Vera Alice Roberts. His 'daughter' Mam! He finally admitted it!"

Carrie lifted her head and with an "Oh," of comprehension, turned to Vera. "Oh good. Yes, that is good news." Her hand reached out and gave Vera's elbow a squeeze.

Now that Ivy had her attention, she saw her opportunity. Winking at Vera, she said: "Let's have a fresh cup of tea, eh? Vee, there are some pikelets on the stone in the pantry, put some on a plate for me and bring them in, while I wet a fresh pot."

As Vera got up to do Ivy's bidding, she was conscious of Carrie's eyes following her. When she returned with the plate of pikelets, she found Carrie had turned her chair around and was facing her, her eyes locked onto her stomach which was protruding unrestrained under her skirt. The penny had dropped.

Sucking in her breath, Carrie almost shouted at her, "You're pregnant!" There was accusation in her voice. It halted Vera in her tracks. This was it then, there was no going back. In her nervousness the plate in her hand tilted and the pikelets slowly slid off onto the floor. Carrie was on her feet, her expression still accusing, and flying towards her. The plate dropped as well, smashing to bits, as Vera raised her hands in momentary fear, only to find herself wrapped tightly in Carrie's arms.

"Our Glyn's baby! Ivy! Our Glyn's baby!" Carrie was hysterical now and Vera was hardly able to breathe in her vice-like grip. Her hands moved to Vera's cheeks, pulling her face down towards her and smothering it with kisses, then to her stomach to gently caress the 'bump', at the same time repeating over and over, "Oh, thank you, thank you, Vera."

Ivy caught Vera's eye over her mother's shoulders and mouthed the words 'told you so' with a self-satisfied nod of her head.

When Albert came home off night shift, he was amazed to find the fire lit, the water boiling for his bath and Carrie back home, sitting serenely in the armchair crocheting with white wool. She looked up at him and smiled and a weight fell from his shoulders. Carrie was his mainstay, his strength. If she was alright, if she could cope and come to terms with life, then he could hope to as well.

She held up the nearly-finished matinee coat and with her eyes brimming, whispered, "For our Glyn's baby. Vera's having our Glyn's baby!" Albert held out his arms and Carrie rose into them. For a long while they stood like that, neither of them speaking.

When Ivy had come downstairs, she found Carrie had left a note on the kitchen table to say she had gone home to see Albert and that she had borrowed two ounces of the white wool she had found in a bag by the teapot. Ivy breathed a huge sigh of relief. With the courage of her convictions, she had scrounged some coupons from Elsie-May, then made a hurried visit to Wright's wool shop just before closing time. She deliberately left the bag wide open, revealing its contents.

Not a one for organised religion, Ivy nevertheless had a strong faith of her own making, interpreting parts of the

Bible to suit her beliefs. This, she decided, was what the Bible meant when it referred to life after death. The new life in Vera's stomach had definitely put new life back into Carrie. And thank God for it!

CHAPTER 77

The Only Way Out

AS A DIRECT result of the war, deep sorrow and adversity were to hit the village once again before October was out. This time they were civilian deaths – two young women made pregnant by departing American soldiers committed suicide.

The first girl, Sian Pritchard, was married to a beast of a man, well known for being free with his fists. Sian was his punch bag. She had always done her best to hide her injuries by saying that she had fallen or bumped into something, convinced the fault must be hers. It must be, because her father had been the same: hit first, shout after. It was the way men were. As head of the household their way was law, and if they thought you had broken it then you had to be punished. She had never known any different. But others had. Sian's friends and neighbours had voiced their concerns to their own husbands who were on the verge of teaching him a lesson one dark night. Jack Pritchard's call-up papers had come in the nick of time.

Sian, being childless (for which she again blamed herself, because Jack told her she was to blame), was given a job in the munitions factory. After the first few weeks, she began to enjoy herself for the first time in her entire life. She went shopping and to the pictures with her new friends. Having her own money (quite a lot of it, since the wages were very good) set her free. With her friends' support and encouragement, she began to take an interest in her appearance, her confidence increasing by the day. She discovered to her surprise that people liked her, sought her company and valued her friendship. Her opinions mattered. She blossomed and became a person in her own right, and the revelation that she wasn't to blame for her former lifestyle increased her self-esteem.

By the time the Americans arrived at Crymceynon, she was completely transformed into a very attractive young woman. Coaxed and cajoled into going dancing with her friends, it wasn't long before the inevitable happened. A tall, smart, very handsome, young coloured soldier fell head-over-heels in love with her – and she with him. Never had she known such tender feelings from or for another person. The plans they made during those few months! Quince, for that's who he was – the soldier who had saluted Glyn the day of the picnic – would come back for her as soon as the war was over and they would make a good life for themselves in America. She had woken with excitement every morning, thinking of this wonderful future that awaited them.

She soon discovered she was pregnant and hugged the fact to her like a comfort blanket. She could have children, she would have children – it was Jack who was deficient. When she had written to tell her love about the baby, his letters back had been full of his enduring feelings for her and reassurance. He began sending her money to save, so that when she could no longer work she could still support herself and find a place to live, away from the village. Then, should her husband come home on leave, he wouldn't be able to find her. She hadn't thought of that!

The girls in the factory received many letters from the soldiers and word soon got around if any they had known were wounded, captured or killed. Sian heard of Quince's death in late September and was sinking deeper and deeper into depression and hopelessness by the day. What would happen to her now?

By the end of October she was desperate. She wouldn't be able to work soon, and having no money coming in meant she wouldn't be able to afford to get away. But she couldn't afford to stay either. She knew in her bones that her husband would survive and return home. Whether or not she left him, he would always be a threat. She had no fight left in her.

Walking along the river bank with all these thoughts flooding her mind, and with rising panic drowning her in despair, she climbed the steps of the viaduct. Her mind made up, she walked above the black, silty river to where it was deep and fast flowing, and jumped. Her body was found half a mile downstream two days later, caught by tree roots in the river bank.

The second suicide was an unmarried girl in her late teens, Josephine Morris. She was her parents' only daughter and was their youngest by ten years. She was idolised by her parents and three brothers. A combination of youth, excitement, daring and rising hormones had led to just one fleeting moment of utter madness after the last dance, before the Yanks had left. She had regretted it immediately. She hadn't heard a word from him since and had no idea how to get in touch with him – not that it would have solved anything. All she knew about him was his first name, Ed. She was three months into her pregnancy before she realised the predicament she was in. Her first thought was to get rid of it – for someone, somehow to take it away so she could be her old self again. But she was far from street-wise and had no idea whatsoever as to how to go about achieving this.

Josephine's future held nothing but dread for her. She had

to have time to think and had to act normally so that no-one suspected anything. At five months her tummy was quite round – huge in her eyes. She couldn't afford to put on any more weight, but her mother showed concern if she didn't eat her meals. So she ate them, then painfully vomited them up again in the *ty-bach* at the first opportunity. Her health began to fail with the worry and lack of nourishment, and her whole family began to think that something was wrong. The last Saturday of October brought things to a head.

"Josephine, I think we had better take you to the doctor's on Monday, first thing," her mother said. "You don't look at all well these days."

She feared her daughter had tuberculosis – her own sister had died from it five years before.

"I'm fine, Mam, really."

"No. To please me. First thing Monday."

"Alright." What else could she say? "But I'm going out now, with my friends. I promised them. Only for an hour or two. I won't be late."

She had made no such arrangements. She went into town and sat in the park for three hours. Then she got up, walked to the main street, waited for a bus to come along and deliberately stepped out in front of it.

CHAPTER 78

Carrie Sets Madge Straight

CARRIE WAS SPENDING more and more time over at Vera's as her time grew nearer, calling there whenever she was over at Ivy's. These visits didn't go unnoticed by Carrie's neighbour and arch enemy, Madge Lloyd. Judging by her disapproving looks, Carrie knew Madge had guessed the situation.

"Just let her say one word to me about Vera's condition," Carrie said to her daughter, "and she'll get more than she bargains for!"

In the eyes of the chapel, and hence Mrs Lloyd, illegitimacy was the ultimate sin and the woman always the sinner. Over the years, several female chapel members had had to ask permission from the 'big seat' to rejoin the flock if they had 'indulged' and become pregnant before marriage. Carrie knew of more than one instance being down to the deacon himself! The dissemblance of it astounded her.

"Take no notice, Mam," said Ivy, "put it down to where it comes from."

She knew Carrie's capability in a verbal battle, especially if it concerned her or her family. Anyone tangling with her, she could tie in knots and finish off with a bow on top. Madge wouldn't stand a chance, she would floor her in the first round.

Some girls certainly had to shoulder a large portion of blame for their pregnancies. The colliers had a crude term for that sort, adapted from the term used to describe hens which followed the cockerel around: 'cock(erel)-happy'. Madge Lloyd, Carrie knew, fitted snugly into that category when she was young. She had been no angel – far from it. Her veneer of saintliness had only developed since her marriage, thirty-odd years ago, to a county councillor twelve years her senior. Give the Devil his due mind, people sometimes changed. But relishing in other people's misfortunes whilst polishing one's own halo didn't wash with Carrie.

Carrie could tell by Madge's hovering whenever they met that she was itching to engage her in conversation, especially since the suicides. So far, she had managed to avoid her, knowing full well that Madge would take the opportunity to hint – if not comment openly – about Vera, while mentioning the suicides in the same breath. Just let her dare!

Carrie was coming out of Martin's the grocer's as Madge went in. The bloody woman was following her now! They had met at the post office only yesterday.

"Going my way Carrie?" Madge had asked.

"And which way would that be, Madge?"

"Well, home now. I'll wait for you." Madge had picked the wrong option. But she would have, whatever reply she gave. Carrie was prepared.

"Ah," she said, with a twinkle in her eye, "I've got to go all the way over-the-other-side!" She knew that however desperate Madge was to crow, a long walk like that was too big a price to pay. Not that Carrie intended walking there, either. She was just going to pop down to the paper shop and then home again when the coast was clear.

This time though, she had no excuse. She had to get back to cook dinner for Albert. Walking slowly up the little steep hill by the Workmen's Hall, it wasn't long before the subject was broached.

"Wasn't it terrible about those suicides?" Madge began.

Here we go then, thought Carrie. "Yes. Sad. Very sad," she said.

"I could see that sort of thing coming, as soon as the Yanks arrived."

Well, you would do, wouldn't you, thought Carrie.

"Did you know the two girls?" Madge asked.

"Oh yes," said Carrie, "and their families."

Madge put on her sympathetic face. "What they must be going through, poor things. Shocking for them. Shameful."

She paused, waiting for a reaction. She didn't get one.

"And the worst thing is, two quieter girls you never met." She looked sideways at Carrie. "It's always the quiet ones though, isn't it? The ones who get up to mischief."

Carrie let her rant on, admiring her skill at leading up to what she wanted to say. Well, just wait. Two can play at that game.

Madge carried on: "The ones you wouldn't think could say 'boo' to a goose. Deep. Sly. Little trollops."

Carrie bit her tongue. They walked on a little further, Madge feeling more and more frustrated at Carrie's lack of response. Just one word of agreement from her would satisfy her. Then she could pounce!

"There's a few more in the village that have gone down that road and been up to no good, from what I can gather," Madge continued.

Do your gathering while ye may, thought Carrie, warming up.

"There's two over lower Crymceynon. Have you heard about them? Both married, both well into their thirties."

Carrie shook her head, smiling faintly to herself, biding her time.

Madge continued, relating all the details. "They lost no time chasing and trapping some Yank, and them only here for five minutes! I mean, you can't blame the soldiers, can you. If it's on offer, they are not going to say 'no', are they? The brazen slatterns. They must have been desperate."

Yes and forty years ago Madge, you would have been foremost in the field, thought Carrie, biting her tongue again and giving her no feedback whatsoever on this piece of gossip. It was obviously infuriating Madge, who cast another sideways glance at her, before moving in for the kill.

"Then there's that Vera Roberts, living by your Ivy. Have you heard about her?"

Right! Enough's enough, thought Carrie. She stopped and turned to face Madge, looking her straight in the eye.

"I'm surprised at you, Madge. I would have thought a big chapel-goer like you would have had more compassion and understanding about these tragedies. You know: 'Forgive us our trespasses as we forgive those...' and 'Let the one without sin cast the first stone...' and so on. Those two poor girls who took their own lives, for instance. I've known both of them and their backgrounds since they were babies. I can see what drove them both to do it and I must say, I admire their courage. My heart bleeds for them and for those who loved them. Two nicer, more decent girls never lived. They are far more to be pitied than blamed, don't you think? They weren't promiscuous girls, were they, after any old Tom, Dick or Harry? Not like some we know, or knew when we were girls, eh Madge?"

Carrie's eyebrows lifted into a querying expression and Madge's face was a picture of alarm. She let all that sink in before continuing. She was beginning to enjoy herself now.

"And in my opinion, Madge, it's the ones that make the most noise about other people's mistakes that have the most to hide. Have you found that to be true?"

Madge nodded, warily but automatically and feeling an implication there.

"Er, well, ye..." Carrie had her scared now. Madge didn't know just how much Carrie knew!

"And I've always found that they are the ones who always manage to get off Scot free. Haven't you?"

Again, Madge was forced to nod in agreement.

"And why? Because they know all the 'tricks of the trade', so to speak, isn't it?"

She paused again, while she watched it hit home. Relishing her discomfort, Carrie carried on. She had a lot more to say yet.

"It's always the innocent ones who get caught, poor things. You think back to when we were young, Madge."

But Madge didn't want to. She had put the past behind her years ago. She was feeling distinctly uncomfortable as Carrie turned the screw.

"We both know the ones who carried on playing 'doctors and nurses' long after they were old enough to know better, don't we?" Carrie could feel the corners of her mouth twitch and sucked in her cheeks in an effort to control them. She hadn't finished yet. "And the ones who suddenly had to go to stay with relatives down the country because they weren't well, eh?"

Madge shuffled her carrier bags and quickened her step,

wanting to get home as quickly as possible. But Carrie had stopped and put her shopping bags down. She raised her voice a little to fire her final salvo.

"Oh, and by the way, Madge, about our Vera," – she emphasised 'our' – "yes, she is pregnant with our Glyn's baby, and to be honest, we all couldn't be happier about it!" She let the smile loose now. "Grandchildren are the ultimate pleasure, aren't they? Oh, but there, you wouldn't know would you, never having reared any children of your own."

She had had them alright but never reared them.

"Aw, now that is a shame!" Carrie said with a sympathetic smile and a pat on her arm. Take that whichever way you choose, she thought.

They were nearly home now. Carrie reached her gate, unlatched it, turned to Madge and said sweetly, "Well, so long Madge. It's been nice having a chat with you."

There would be no more bother from that direction.

CHAPTER 79

The Budding Entrepreneur

LIZ HAD LEARNED to knit during the months following the fateful news of her uncles. She needed something to fill the awful void their deaths left. When Auntie Doris had died, both her mother and her grandparents had gradually 'come back' to her. There was no sign of that happening now.

She had tried to coax her gran to teach her to crochet, longing to sit snuggled up in that warm comfy lap again and watch the hook going in and out to make the lace grow. Gran never crocheted now. She had kept asking but the reply was always, "Not now, sweetheart. Later on, eh?" But 'later on' never seemed to come.

The same thing happened when she nagged her mother to teach her how to knit, only her mother's refusal was more abrupt: "Can't you see I'm busy? Ask Margaret Pierce or someone!" So she had.

Margaret was at more of a loose end now Pauline was at grammar school, with new friends taking up most of her time. Pauline spent most Saturdays in the other village now, visiting one or other of them, and went to the Wendy Youth Club with Michael Richards every Wednesday night. Though Pauline had been equally traumatised by what had happened, with so much that was new going on in her life, she had got over it easier and quicker and hadn't missed any attention from the adults around her. She was growing up and spreading her wings.

Margaret and Liz both missed her. So, over many hours and days, they had sat on the doorstep, teacher and pupil enjoying each other's company. In no time, Liz could cast on, do backstitch, plain, purl and cable stitch, decrease and increase and cast off. It was her salvation. She soon became totally absorbed as this new craze took hold and the void started to shrink.

She started with egg cosies and kettle holders, quickly progressing to mittens and gloves, everything knitted in stripes from oddments of wool she had scrounged and cadged. Lately, she had been trying her hand at knitting a small doll. Its trunk and head were knitted in one, with a tight rubber band forming the neck. The arms and legs were knitted individually and sewn on. All of its body, apart from the hands, feet and face, which were in plain fawn, were the usual striped pattern, as was the detachable skirt and bonnet. The hair was a plait of yellow wool stitched around the face, the eyes were blue wool stitches, the mouth and nose red ones.

Lucy, the little girl from Lowe's shop, sat by Liz as she put the finishing touches to the skirt, reaching over to pick up the doll from her lap and cuddling it to her face and kissing it, which pleased Liz no end. Somebody else liked what she had created.

She took the doll to the shop when it was finished and proudly handed it over to Mrs Lowe to give to Lucy. Mrs Lowe admired it and thanked her and said what a clever girl she was – and gave her half a crown! She didn't want to take it; it was enough that the woman thought it was worth that much. But Mrs Lowe insisted, and gave her a bag full of wool oddments into the bargain. Liz put the money in the top drawer of her half of the tallboy in her bedroom, together with the egg cosies and other things. She had plans: it would be dolls from now on. Her mother and her gran would be pleased – and proud of her. By the end of November there were three more dolls in the drawer.

Ivy, excited and happy about Vera's pregnancy, had more *hwyl* these days. She decided to do some 'spring cleaning' before Christmas, so that early in the New Year she could have her full share of nursing Glyn's baby. She started on the girls' bedroom, deciding that now was the time for Pauline to have a room of her own. Jim had put up some shelves in the small front bedroom after the evacuees had gone and made a very nice wardrobe to fit in the alcove behind the door. Well, he thought, it would be a pity to waste all that wood that still found its way to the shed!

Emptying the tallboy drawers, Ivy soon found the hoard – and the money. Where had she got that? When questioned, Liz had to confess her intentions: to sell the dolls around the doors, like whinberries. She said she had wanted to keep it as a nice surprise.

Oh my God! thought her mother, I'll have to nip this in the bud somehow! First off, she would have to see Mrs Lowe and explain that she knew nothing about this business venture of Liz's. She didn't want everyone thinking they were so short of a bob or two that they had to resort to child labour! Stop now, Ivy, she thought. Don't get carried away, don't exaggerate this. The child has done nothing wrong. She didn't ask Mrs Lowe to pay for the doll, for goodness sake. And what was wrong with showing a bit of initiative anyway? It would be wrong to destroy that. And the dolls did have a certain appeal – they were soft, cuddly and colourful, (definitely colourful).

God, it was difficult on times, being a parent. You had to keep stepping into a child's shoes to see things from their point of view, to remember your own childhood and your own failures, successes and feelings. One consolation was that no-one had got full marks in this job yet, and a full time job it was, too. Everyone made mistakes. All you can do is try your best. Here goes, then.

"Wasn't it nice of Mrs Lowe to give you all that money? She wasn't buying the doll from you, of course, she wouldn't have wanted to offend your kind thought. She obviously appreciated it and your cleverness."

Liz liked that. So far, so good, thought Ivy.

"That's much nicer, isn't it, to be appreciated rather than paid? Much nicer to give them away, to a new-born baby perhaps, or as Christmas or birthday presents." A picture of Elsie-May, the matinee coat and the glass of port flashed through her mind. "People often like to reciprocate, and that's nice, too." She swallowed, reliving the memory.

Liz butted in. "What's 'reciprocate'?"

"Give something back or exchange," said Ivy, momentarily losing her train of thought.

A bell rang in Liz's head, something Mr Pomfrey had said – "Give and you shall receive," and "Cast your bread upon the waters," – though she didn't get the last bit at all.

"Um," said Ivy, getting back on track, "and they haven't cost you anything, have they? You've had all the wool given to you."

True, thought Liz. She realised she would get more pleasure from… er… reciprocating than from a whole stack of half crowns. There were lovely colours in the bag Lucy's mam had given her, that she'd never had before: turquoise, emerald and lime green, orange, purple and scarlet. She couldn't wait to use them. She rummaged quite contentedly, wondering which one to pick for the next stripe and thinking about what her mother had said. Reciprocate. That sounded much more interesting than selling.

Watching her, Ivy breathed a sigh of relief, shaking her head from side to side, but smiling. Sometimes Liz could be the bane of her life. She just never knew what she would get up to next!

CHAPTER 80

All Together

CHRISTMAS WAS DRAWING nearer and so was Vera's confinement. She asked Ivy, "Could you and your parents possibly spend Christmas Day with me and the boys this year? I'm so grateful to you all and thankful for the kindness and support you have all shown me."

"Nonsense! It's you we are all grateful to," Ivy replied. "Just look at the difference you've made to my mam and dad! Yes, of course we'll come Vee, we'd would love to. I think it's a great idea."

And it was. Though it was a quiet Christmas, with everyone occupied with their own thoughts, being altogether meant they made an effort to put on a face and make it as happy a time as possible, if only for the sake of the four children. They had all mucked in, decorating the room and making newspaper hats, and the three women had shared in the preparations and cooking of the dinner between them. After the meal, the men had done all the washing up, even putting everything away. Then they had all sat round the big table playing cards, doing jigsaws and playing word games with the children. They even managed a few laughs now and then. Nevertheless, it was a relief when bedtime came and everyone went home. The effort had wearied them all.

CHAPTER 81

The New Life

ON THE LAST Saturday in January, Vera's waters broke with the dawn. The midwife was sent for, and Ivy and Carrie waited on pins downstairs. Bessy-Ann was on hand as usual, to do all the fetching and carrying and cleaning up afterwards. She marched, business-like, to and fro from the kitchen to the bedroom, delivering progress bulletins to the two waiting women as she passed. Whatever the midwife said was noted, digested and regurgitated, with confidence and authority.

"She's doing fine. She won't be long now. She's fully diluted!" said Bessy-Ann, passing through with her arms full of aired nappies and baby clothes. Oh, that's good news, then!

The two boys had been sent to Ivy's house, on the assurance that they would be sent for as soon as anything happened. By eleven o'clock, it had. A beautiful, bouncing, baby boy was born, weighing eight and a half pounds. The bed was remade and all the blood-stained sheets and towels were put to soak in a zinc bath full of cold water. This was left in the yard and covered with a board, away from prying young eyes. Once mother and child had been made presentable, Carrie was the first in line by the bedroom door. Ivy hovered close behind, itching for her turn.

Vera sat upright, dressed in a pretty floral nightie she had made for the occasion, her head framed by lace-edged pillows, her precious bundle in her arms. Carrie rapidly approached, her hands against her cheeks, her mouth open in awe and her eyes spilling tears. She aimed straight for the baby as Vera lifted it and held it out to her. Bessy-Ann quickly brought her a chair and put her hand on her shoulder to make her sit down. With the baby safely in her lap and her eyes still fast on his face, Carrie reached out a hand and took Vera's, squeezing it tightly.

"He's beautiful. Beautiful." was all she could say.

Ivy tapped the door. "Alright if I come in, too?"

Grudgingly, Carrie handed the baby over to her daughter but still couldn't take her eyes off him. She fidgeted with the wrap, moving it back from his face; commented on his eyes, his lips, his weight; stroked his hair back and inserted her little finger into his fist. Ivy, smiling at Vera, said, "Oh, go on, our Mam, you have him while we have a little chat. I'll have my share later." Carrie, needing no second bidding, took the child and wandered with it out onto the landing, billing and cooing and dropping gentle kisses on top of the little fair-haired head.

"Well done, Vee. He's gorgeous!" said Ivy, plonking a kiss on her cheek.

"Yes he is, isn't he!" She lay back against the pillows, very pleased with herself, happy but exhausted.

"How are you feeling? Shall I go and let you sleep?"

"No, stay for a little while. I'm alright. It was a lot easier then I expected it to be."

Funny that, thought Ivy, thinking back to her own confinements. Giving birth was no picnic, not by any stretch of the imagination, but once over, all memory of the pain quickly receded.

"Have you thought of a name for him yet?" Ivy asked.

Vera sighed. "Oh, he is so like his father, Ive, I would love to call him Glyn. But perhaps your mother wouldn't like it. She might be offended. I mean, Glyn was her baby. I wouldn't want to upset her."

"Well, I think that is a lovely idea. You leave it to me. I'll find out, carefully, how she feels about it. You have a sleep now. I'll be back later."

She shut the bedroom door behind her and walked over to Carrie, who was still strolling up and down the landing and talking baby-talk to the bundle in her arms.

"Hey, come on Mam, it's my turn now. You go and fetch the boys and I'll carry him downstairs to introduce him to his big brothers. Vera is going to have a little nap."

As Carrie reluctantly handed him over to her, she said, "He's the spitting image of our Glyn, isn't he Ivy?"

This was going to be easy!

"Mm, he is. I wonder what Vera will call him, Mam?" She looked at her mother's face. "He's little Glyn to you already, isn't he?"

Carrie nodded, smiling at the baby, her eyes flooding again. "Yes. But it's Vera's choice. It wouldn't be fair to influence her. It's her baby not mine."

Funny you should say that, thought her daughter, grinning to herself.

So, Glyn Thomas Roberts he became, making all three families perfectly pleased and satisfied.

CHAPTER 82

The Best Of News

A MONTH HAD passed. The snow that had fallen in January still hung around, slushy and grubby on the black earth, while the sky was grey with drizzle, making everything even more drab.

Carrie hated drizzle, she found it unshakeably depressing. She would rather have a good downpour and finish with it, any day. She had a bit of a cold coming on. Albert was in work and she had no *hwyl* whatsoever to do anything about the house. But there was no escape in weather like this. Ivy would think she was mad if she traipsed over to her house in it. Besides, she'd had strict instructions off Albert to stay in the warm to nip the cold in the bud. He didn't want her getting flu or worse. She had to look after herself for a change, he had said, how would they all manage if she was taken ill?

She stood by the parlour window, looking up at the sky for any sign of it clearing. There wasn't any. The postman was coming up the street. There would be nothing for her. Her spirits sank even lower and she turned away, going to the kitchen to make yet another cup of tea.

Then, since the house was quiet as the grave, she heard the letter box rattle. There was post! Maybe from Miriam, at last. She didn't write that often. Well, they didn't have much in common really, never having met. But, fair play, her letters were regular if infrequent – she sent one about every three months – and she kept her up to date with news of her grandchildren's progress.

She rushed to the passage. A pale blue envelope lay on the mat. It was from Miriam. She picked it up and scooted back to her chair with her cup of tea, easing it open as she went. You had to be careful with airmail letters, the paper was so thin, though this one seemed thicker than usual.

As she finally got it open, a photograph fell into her lap – a coloured one! She picked it up and stared at it, taking in every detail. A pretty, small, dark-haired woman looked back at her, her hands resting on the shoulders of the children standing on either side of her: a fair-haired little boy, the image of Danny; and a dark-haired little girl, a smaller version of Miriam. Carrie kissed both their images. They were nearly two and a half years old now! Time was flying by.

Both children were wearing little navy-blue crocheted jackets. Carrie had made them and sent them out weeks before Christmas, hoping they would arrive in time. Oh, wasn't that nice of Miriam to send this photo of them, wearing them. They fitted perfectly.

Carrie leaned back and said, "Well!" For a full five minutes she scrutinised the snap. If only this damn drizzle would ease up, she could go over to Ivy's to show her. And to Vera's. She glanced up at the window. No, there was no sign of it slackening. It was worse, if anything. Resigned to her imprisonment, she put down the photo, picked up the letter and started to read.

She had only got as far as the end of the first sentence when she shrieked out loud, leaped out of her chair and ran out of the house, leaving the door wide open behind her. She had the letter and the photo firmly in her hand as she headed straight for Stephen's Street. With no coat on her back and bedroom slippers on her feet, she slithered and sloshed at a record pace to Ivy's front door, yelling her name as she got there.

"Mam! What on earth is the matter? Come in, for goodness sake! Sit there, by that fire!" She grabbed a towel from the fire guard and started rubbing her soaking hair.

Carrie, breathless and lost for words, waved her away with one hand and waved the photo and letter with the other. Mystified and worried, Ivy took them from her but before she could look at them, Carrie got her breath back.

"Danny! It's our Danny! He's alive!"

"What?" Her mother must be mistaken. She had misread something and jumped to conclusions. Dazed, she opened the letter. "Calm down Mam, let me see."

Carrie couldn't calm down. She needed affirmation, someone to tell her she wasn't dreaming or imagining things. "Read it! Read it! See? I told you!"

The Red Cross had informed Miriam that Danny had been captured and was now a prisoner of war and would remain in Germany until the war ended. There was an address that they could write to and even send parcels. Socks on four needles, thought Carrie, long ones to keep him warm – if your feet were kept warm, the rest of your body stood a better chance. She would start them tonight. She had coupons!

Fruit cake, thought Ivy, Danny's favourite. She still had dried fruit left in the pantry and they'd all forfeit their butter ration for the week. She wouldn't use margarine for this cake! Elsie-May would spare her two eggs, she was sure, when she explained why she needed them.

These were their first thoughts that came with the rush of energy this good news brought. Carrie's cold seemed to have disappeared. Every day now would be one day nearer. Surely the war couldn't go on much longer?

By two o'clock, both Carrie and Ivy were waiting

impatiently by the colliery gates, bobbing their heads as they searched for a sign of Albert. He spotted them from a distance, his heart in his mouth. Oh God! What now? He started to run. As he got nearer he saw it was good news of some sort. The women were waving and laughing and yelling his name and Carrie had something in her hand, a letter by the looks of things. What was it? With a smile cracking his face, he rushed towards them to find out.

CHAPTER 83

A Finger of Guidance

NOW IT WAS Liz's turn to come home with a letter from Mr Hughes. Surely not about the eleven plus, thought Ivy, she wouldn't be ten until next month! "But she will be ten and a half by the time she starts grammar school," Mr Hughes had written, "and I'm sure she is perfectly capable of it."

Ivy wasn't so sure. Pauline had a system, but Liz seemed to work in organised chaos. No, disorganised chaos. Pauline always did her homework before going out to play, sitting quietly and tidily by the rosewood table in the front room with all her books to hand. Whereas whenever Liz had any to do, it was either last thing at night while she listened to the wireless, with her books and herself stretched out on the floor in front of the fire, or first thing in the morning while standing by the table munching her toast, fidgeting and jigging, rushing to finish so she could dash up the garden for a pee. She never had enough time for anything! Oh, she was quick in most things, Ivy had to admit that, but she was also slipshod. Jim said to let her have a go, she could have another shot at it again next year, anyway, and Mr Hughes had been right about Pauline. If he thinks she can do it…

So she began with the maths exam. Problems – Liz liked doing those. She glanced at the first one: 'If one pound of apples costs tuppence three-farthings, how much do seven pounds cost?' She remembered her mother's last words to her: "Concentrate now, Liz. You can do it. And check your work! That is important, mind! Mistakes cost marks."

"Yes Mam," said Liz, in the type of voice that meant 'So you keep saying' and 'I heard you the first time'.

She's totally unconcerned, unruffled by it all, thought Ivy. I'm in a worse state than she is. Today is just another day to her. Perhaps that is the best way to be, then if she fails, that won't bother her either.

The invigilator who, Liz thought, looked exactly like Moonface from the *Sunny Stories*, strolled quietly up and down the tiered rows of desks. Liz sailed through her work and was the first to finish, so she sat back with her arms folded.

Moonface approached her row. Liz was in the last seat, at the back. She was watching him, imagining him in *The Magic Far Away Tree*. He caught her eye and smiled. She smiled back. He wasn't allowed to speak, of course. As he turned, he paused behind her, then, on his way back down, he quietly leaned forward and put his finger on a sum at the bottom of the page. What did he do that for? There weren't any blots or crossings-out there. She puzzled over it for a few seconds, then saw what was wrong. She would have lost marks for a simple, slipshod mistake. She spent the rest of the exam time checking over the whole paper, finding two more silly slip-ups. That would teach her. And it did. In the days following, she checked and re-checked all her work. As Gran was always telling her: "Learn from your mistakes, Miss!"

CHAPTER 84

The Age-Old Lullaby

CARRIE WAS OUT more than in these days, over at Ivy's or Vera's. She had to have her daily ration of baby Glyn. Vera was quite content to let her do so, knowing he was in the safest of hands. Besides, she had quite a lot of sewing to catch up on. So Carrie had dug out the family shawl, and with Glyn 'cwtched' into it Welsh fashion, warm and comfy on her bosom, she had spent many happy hours strolling up and down the canal bank, singing a lullaby to the baby that her own mother had sung to her:

"'Ah me,' sighed the red breast, 'Ah me, I could weep.
The wind is so cold and the snow is so deep.
My nest it is ruined, no crumbs can I find.
Ah me,' sighed the red breast, 'the world is unkind!'
He flew to a farmyard, to find a snug spot,
Where the cold, icy blast would trouble him not.
The barn door stood open, that cold winter's day,
But there, on the threshold, were kittens at play.
'Ah me,' sighed the red breast, 'I dare not go near.
Those kittens would eat me, I very much fear.
But if I stay here, I shall die in the night.
Ah me,' sighed the red breast, poor shivering mite.
At last he took courage, flew in at the door,
And sang his best song to those kittens on the floor.
They did him no harm, dear, but let him remain,

In comfort and warmth, till the sun shone again!"

Carrie was making the most of it while she had the chance. Glyn was growing so quickly. Three and a half months already. A few more and he would be too heavy for her to carry.

Glyn moved in the shawl. Carrie realised it was because she had stopped singing. She had always found it amazing how quickly babies could let you know what they wanted. She gave his bottom a few little scolding pats, pretending to be cross.

"Oo, you're a little glutton for punishment aren't you, my boy? Wanting more of Gran's old foghorn of a voice? Alright then, one more time.

"'Ah me,' sighed the red breast..."

CHAPTER 85

Home at Last

A FEW WEEKS after Hitler and his entourage had committed suicide in his bunker, the war in Europe was officially declared over. The Germans had been beaten. Euphoria swept the country and spirits soared. It could only be a matter of time now, surely, before Japan capitulated.

Having listened to the news on the wireless, Carrie switched it off and went to see if the post had come yet. She was in regular contact with Miriam now, exchanging letters every ten days or so.

Ah, there was the postman, his hand was on the gate. Oh no! He had passed. Damn and blast. She was so disappointed. She was sure she would have one today. There must be some news soon about Danny. She was on pins waiting for it. God forbid anything should go wrong now, she couldn't bear it. Her nerves were on edge. Ah well, maybe second post they'd have one.

She went back to the kitchen to wash up the breakfast things. The front door had opened, she felt the draught. It would be Albert back with the baby. He was on afternoons and spent every spare minute he had in Glyn's company. What a difference his arrival had made to her husband. He was like a new man these days. And then that news about Danny – that miraculous news! She would never forget that day down by the colliery gates as long as she lived. He had shouted it out to all his mates as they'd walked home together, beaming with happiness. Now he was shouting again, wanting help over the step with that big pram, probably. He could never manage it on his own like she could.

"Carrie, Carrie, where are you? Come quick, quick!"

"Alright, alright, I'm coming, I'm coming! Hold your horses, man!"

She scuttled to the passage, wiping her hands on her pinny as she went. The postman, seeing Albert with the baby, had stopped for a chat and handed him the letter.

"Look, love, look!" said Albert, waving the letter. "He's home. Our Danny's home safe and well!"

Oh! She snatched it from him and leaned back against the passage walls for support as her legs began to tremble. Her fingers shaking, she opened it and ran her eyes rapidly through the sentences. He was very thin, wrote Miriam, but not to worry, he was already gaining ground. He was still the handsome man she had married and he was going to be the best father that ever lived. The twins and he idolised each other already – she didn't get a look in these days!

"Albert, look! He's written as well!" She put the letter to her lips and kissed his handwriting.

The best tonic he could possibly have right now, he wrote, was being home with his beloved wife and beautiful children – and having a nice long letter back from both of them. "OK Dad?" he had written. "I'm expecting you to put pen to paper, too!" He was overwhelmed with happiness and plans for the future, grateful that he had one. As soon as the world settled down, his intentions were to fly to Britain with his family, for them all to meet up and get to know each other. Hopefully, in the not-too-distant future. He was longing to see "our Glyn's young son and the woman he loved so much. We'll talk about everything when we meet. Give Ivy, Jim and the girls our love. Look after yourselves Mam and Dad. You're both so precious to me. My love to you both, Danny."

Carrie and Albert looked at each other across the pram blocking the doorway, the combination of happiness and pain evident in both their faces.

CHAPTER 86

Celebrations and Gorse Wine

NO SOONER WAS victory in Europe announced, than people began preparing to celebrate. First, there had to be the biggest and best bonfire of the century. Children of all ages started gathering anything combustible without being asked – or without asking. If it wasn't to be burned, then best nail it down! The residents of Duke Street and Stephen's Street would have their bonfire at the edge of the big field nearest the top of the two streets, where the ground levelled out. Over the coming days it grew like Topsy, the men helping and overseeing its construction to ensure its stability and safety. Trestles and tables were made or borrowed and lists drawn up of what was where in readiness for the 'teas' that were planned. Sewing machines hummed with the making of streamer flags – triangles of red, white and blue – which were strung together to stretch across the streets from bedroom window to bedroom window. Union Jacks and Welsh Dragons of all sizes and conditions were hunted down and draped from upstairs windowsills. Magazine and newspaper pictures of the King and Queen and Winston Churchill were taped to parlour windows.

The big day dawned, planned down to the last detail. Well, almost. The celebrations began mid-morning with a carnival parade going twice through the streets. As many adults as children had dressed up, relishing the excuse to enjoy some silliness and indulge themselves in a second childhood, just for the day. They had been busy thinking up and cobbling together all sorts of fancy dress costumes since the day they had heard of Hitler's demise. Excitement was rife and tangible amongst both the young and the old, as they all lined up for the 'off'. There were John Bulls, cowboys, Indians, Charlie Chaplins, Zulus with grass skirts (and long johns!), ballet dancers (mostly men with hairy chests), Shirley Temples, nurses, scarecrows, Nazis doing the goose-step and, of course, Hitlers with ridiculous moustaches that kept trickling away with sweat. Some costumes were unidentifiable and some totally bizarre. But who cared? 'Off' then, to a good start.

While the judging of the fancy dress took place up on the big field, non-participants brought out the trestles, lined them up in the street and draped them in tablecloths ranging from house proud white to 'degrairn' grey. Jam jars crammed with flowers scrounged from gardens, allotments and the farmer's field, were placed at intervals along them.

Then out came the food. There were mountains of sandwiches, delicate or doorstep, depending on who wielded the bread knife; jellies in a variety of colours; blancmanges made from arrowroot and cakes of all description and quality. Tins of fruit were brought out of hiding and all poured together into a bread pan to be rationed out at three pieces per head till everyone had a taste. Crates of pop, courtesy of the local factory, completed the requirements. Nearly everyone tucked in like there was no tomorrow – very little was left for the birds. The doors of every house were wide open and remained so for the duration of the celebrations for the making of pots of tea, replenishing of empty plates or washing of dirty dishes.

When everyone had eaten their fill, it was up to the big

field again for the games. First came the races, with most of the participants still in fancy dress: men's, women's and children's hundred-yard dashes, egg and spoon, sack, three-legged and wheelbarrow. All were highly enjoyable and entertaining. Tug-of-war teams, with men against women or adults against children followed, then someone brought out a long rope for communal skipping. Two strong men wielded the heavy length at the top of Stephen's Street as a crowd gathered, eagerly waiting to jump in and out, once the rhythm of the rope got going. Skipping, like riding a bike, once learned is never forgotten. Children were amazed and impressed by their parents' agility. Some were a bit embarrassed to see their father 'acting the goat' or their mother's wobbly bits bouncing up and down between her waist and her chin – sights never before seen and difficult to erase once they had been. Everyone's energy seemed boundless and endless. The children will sleep tonight, thought the parents, but not until the early hours!

With the blackouts torn down and front doors still standing wide open, light shone out from every house as it gradually grew darker. It was time to light the fire. The flames slowly took hold, cracking and sparking the wood. People began singing, which brought a gradual change of mood. Reflection, gratitude and calm settled like a comfort blanket over the raucous excitement. Jim and Ivy brought out their gramophone and records and dancing began on the hard black earth by the pine-end of Stephen's Street. Some, feeling hungry again, buried large potatoes in the outer embers of the bonfire and more plates of sandwiches were cut and handed round. The very young were now 'cwtched' in Welsh shawls to their mother's or grandmother's bosoms and the older ones, still with energy to spare, played chasing and hide-and-seek in and out of the groups of standing, chatting adults.

Now was the time, thought Bessy-Ann, to bring out her contribution to the festivities: twenty flagons of gorse wine, made just before the war had broken out and specifically kept for this occasion. It tasted and smelled, faintly, of coconut, and was absolutely delicious. It was also dynamite! There was enough for all the adults to sample it; some did so more than others. Even Billy Griffiths indulged. Though he hadn't drunk since the card-playing episode outside the cemetery walls, tonight was exceptional. You had to drink a toast to peace, didn't you? Besides, wine was a woman's drink, not like beer or whisky – more like pop. Boy, it warmed you up. He managed a second helping and, at Tom and Jim's insistence, a third. Bessy-Ann liked those two, they were always laughing at something or other. She had given them a flagon to themselves. Well, they had both been good to her and she could always rely on them to help.

Billy lifted his glass for the third time and proposed the same toast, more or less, as he had for the other two: "Cheers, mates. Here's to peace! Rong may she leign!"

"Aye, we'll drink to that!" said his two mates, chinking glasses and shaking with laughter. Nights like this only came once in a lifetime, please God, and they would make sure Billy had a night to remember.

Carrie and Albert had gone home not long after the teas. They could only take so much of this happiness and rejoicing. There were too many painful memories associated with the war years. But at eleven o'clock they returned to the crowd around the bonfire for a little while, before baby-sitting Ivy's girls and little Glyn, so that Ivy, Jim and Vera could relax with their friends and neighbours until the early hours.

Vera's boys were big enough to look after themselves now.

Tom, Jim and Billy were on the edge of the crowd and saw them approaching. Jim went to meet them and bring them over, telling them on the way about Billy, thinking it would amuse them to see him tiddly and talkative and full of the joys of spring. It might cheer them up a little.

Billy was in fine fettle by now, the drink was certainly taking effect and had unlocked his tongue, letting it run amok. There was no shutting him up. He was holding forth as they approached: "Evnin' Mrs Thomas, evnin' Mr Thomas. And what a wunerful evnin' it is. An' what a wunerful whole day! Eh? Eh? Peace at last! We got peace at last! A's good, in' it!"

Jim poured some of his wine into his cup for Albert and went to fetch a clean one from the house for Carrie. In his absence, Tom had topped up Billy's glass a little. Jim came back with the cup, took the bottle and poured a little for Carrie. Billy chinked containers with them all again, repeating the toast and amazingly getting it right.

"Here's to peace, long may she reign! Mind, we were lucky here, wern' we? Up in these mountains. The bastards didn't get to us, did they? Lucky, aye. Tha's what we were. It don't bear thinking about what some poor buggers went through, does it? Ow!"

Halfway through these ramblings, Albert and Carrie had turned to go, unable to bear it and realising just how vulnerable they still were. They didn't for one moment blame Billy but Jim, feeling responsible for bringing this on them, had given him a sharp kick on the shin for his part in renewing their pain. The silly sod! Billy bent to grab his injured leg and brought it up beneath him, hopping about on the other one.

"Cripes, Jim! Wha' you do tha' for wuss? Tha' bloody hurt tha' did!"

"Bill, you haven't got the bloody brains you were born with!" said Jim.

"Carrie and Albert, of all people," said Tom. "One son a prisoner of war, the other son killed in action and their daughter killed by a bloody bomb. Where's your bloody sense, mun? Come here for me to kick your other bloody leg!"

"Naw, I didn't! Did I? Oh hell, I'm sorry, Jim!" He limped off, saying he was going for a walk to clear his head. He had to make amends for this somehow or he wouldn't sleep tonight, worrying about how he had hurt them. He saw them go to Ivy's house. He would call round the back way, that's what he would do.

Meanwhile, Carrie, after sending Vera out to join the throng, settled comfortably in the chair by the fire to give Glyn his bottle, while Albert banked up the fire with some damp, small coal. The front door opened and closed with a bang and Liz burst in clutching her crutch and aiming for the back door. Last minute as always! The grandparents looked at each other. They had to smile.

"Don't go all the way up to the top of the garden, pickle, you might fall on the path in the dark. Have a quick wee in the drain in the back yard. We won't tell anybody, will we Albert?"

"Oh, you speak for yourself!" he teased.

"Oh, Grampa!"

Liz was grateful. She wouldn't have made it all the way to the toilet anyway. By the light of the bonfire and the light from their middle-room and kitchen windows, she located the drain and was in mid-stream, when she noticed a hand and arm attached to the garden door latch. The door opened slowly and a trilby peeped round. Liz screamed, grabbed her now wet knickers to her knees and ran in to bury her head in Carrie's lap. "There's a bogey-man out there! He's coming in to our garden!" she exclaimed.

Carrie, ever ready to console or defend her family, passed the baby to Albert, reached for the frying pan and with a wink at her husband, said, "Don't you worry lamb, Gran will soon sort him out!"

After a minute or two, she returned to reassure Liz that it had only been one of the neighbours wanting to use the toilet. This was feasible and Liz believed her. She was content enough, after changing her knickers, to rejoin her friends.

It was illegal and a punishable offence to urinate anywhere out in the open, whatever the circumstances, so 'ty-bachs' were often used by passers-by in emergencies and most people left their garden doors unlocked to allow for this. The local bobby, William Price, was a vigilant watcher of those likely to offend and had been known to follow drunks home from the pub, quickly earning himself the nickname of 'Willie Pee'.

The 'bogey-man', Billy Griffiths, intent on apologising to Jim's in-laws, panicked at Liz's piercing scream and beetled back to the crowd around the bonfire as fast as his limp would let him. Everything he said or did seemed to go wrong and he desperately needed a drink to calm his nerves.

CHAPTER 87

Ivy Meets Annabelle

THE DAY AFTER the celebrations, the women spent most of the day sorting out dishes and cutlery as to who's was what. They were in and out of each other's houses like busy bees. Ivy discovered that she had two bread and butter plates that weren't hers and set about hunting down the owners. Wendy's mother recognised one of them.

"Oh, that's mine Ivy, the one with the roses on," she said. "And I think the other one is Bessy-Ann's. Did it have scones on it yesterday? She made the scones we had, I know. That's her speciality. She brought me some when I had bronchitis last year and they were on a plate just like that. Ask her."

So Ivy set off to find out. Reaching Lowe's shop, she spotted Bessy-Ann at the bottom of the street about to climb Annabelle's front steps. She shouted and Bessy-Ann turned, waved and beckoned to her and waited for her to come down.

"Oh yes, that's mine. Thanks Ivy. I think I've got a big enamel jug belonging to you, haven't I? Can you wait till I take this in for Miss Jackson? Then you can pick it up on the way back." She lifted the basket she was carrying to show Ivy its contents. "It's her dinner and some wine I saved for her to taste, from last night. It's like carrying coals to Newcastle, I know, but it will do her more good than that ol' gin." She lowered her voice. "She's got stacks of it in that cellar of hers but don't you tell anyone I said so! Listen, come in with me.

She won't mind. She doesn't get to see many people. It will do her good."

Well, Ivy did need the jug – she used it a lot when she did the washing, to add cold water to the bathful of boiled whites. It was lighter and easier to carry than a bucketful. Hesitatingly, she followed Bessy into the house. Better to wait inside than out, decorating the pavement, she supposed.

"You're in for a shock mind," warned Bessy, "if she's been on the pop all night. She does that sometimes. You'll just have to shut your ears to it. Her language can be terrible!"

Ivy grinned to herself at the irony in those words.

"Morning Miss Jackson!" said Bessy, blithely.

Annabelle was standing by her grand piano, a half-empty glass of gin in her hand, muttering expletives at a silver framed photo of herself and a dark-haired man, taken when she was about twenty years younger and on board a ship by the look of it, Ivy thought. Annabelle didn't turn round.

"Bugger off, Bessy! What's bloody good about it?"

"Ahem. I've brought a friend with me – hope you don't mind. I met her outside."

Annabelle turned round. Ivy made to step forward, her hand half outstretched to greet her, but Annabelle wasn't interested. Without spilling a drop, she waved the hand containing her glass towards Dudley, the recipient of her venom.

"See him?" she slurred at Ivy. "That bastard? I hope he rots in hell!" She rolled a clove around her mouth, muttering to herself.

Ivy knew the reason for her hatred. She had heard what had happened to Annabelle all those years ago from different people, mostly Bessy. Annabelle had known better days –

much better. Then she had met this tall, dark and handsome man on a winter cruise whom she had fallen for hook, line and sinker. He had courted her, flattered her, taken her to all the big events, bought her expensive presents – and then embezzled her of most of her money.

"The swine!" she continued. "The swindling, sodding swine!"

"She gets these black moods now and again," whispered Bessy. "Take no notice."

Easier said than done, thought Ivy. She was fascinated by the woman, her history and her resulting behaviour.

Bessy took her dinner out of the basket. It was covered by a saucepan lid and wrapped in a spotless tea towel.

"What is it?" asked Annabelle.

"A nice bit of belly pork and apple sauce."

"Put it in the pantry, I'll have it later." She shoo'ed it away with her hand, adding to herself, but audible to the others, "At a more civilised time!"

There's gratitude for you, thought Ivy. Bessy needed her head read, pandering to her.

"What's that?" Annabelle demanded now, pointing to the bottle.

"Oh, some of my home-made gorse wine for you to try," said Bessy, not at all put out by the woman's ignorance. "It's seven years old now. I kept it specially for the celebrations and saved some for you, since you weren't there."

"Celebrations? What celebrations?"

Bessy looked at Ivy and let her breath out slowly in disbelief. This woman lived on cloud nine, she had no idea of what went on around her! Bessy raised her voice and said slowly and clearly: "VE Day! The end of the war in Europe!"

"Oh, that!" said Annabelle, dismissively, taking out the bottle and pulling the cork.

"Yes, that!" said Bessy, reaching out to take the bottle back from her, intending to pour her just a little sample. But Annabelle moved it out of reach.

"I can manage, thank you!" She filled the glass to the brim and lifted it to her lips, not losing a drop of it. She took a good swig, then chewed on her clove and bottom lip appreciatively. "Mm, very nice Bessy!" she said. She took another swig, and another. She turned her back on them and walked to the piano again, bottle in one hand, glass in the other, helping herself to a refill when she got there and putting the bottle down.

Bessy was worried now. The woman was three sheets to the wind already. She nudged Ivy. "She'll be legless! I shouldn't have brought it. I'll keep her talking, you get the bottle, quick!"

Raising her voice a little, Bessy addressed Annabelle again. "Yes, we all had a great time, all day long, at the carnival. You really should have come, you would have enjoyed yourself."

Annabelle grunted over her glass.

"We had a carnival first," Bessy continued. "Nearly everyone dressed up. Oh, you should have seen some of them!"

Ivy was having great difficulty in retrieving the bottle. If she came in on the right, Annabelle moved it to the left, and vice versa. Drunk as she was, there were no flies on her.

"Then we had the teas. Ivy's mother, Carrie Thomas, made loads of Welsh cakes. That's Ivy there." Bessy pointed at Ivy, who had just managed to get her hands on the bottle and had put it quickly behind her back. "I should have saved you some of those, too. She always makes lovely Welsh cakes, Carrie, and yesterday she expelled herself!"

Ivy nearly dropped the bottle with the jerk of air that hit her diaphragm, bounced to her throat and burst out, quickly disguised as a cough. She deposited the re-corked bottle in the bottom of the basket. Annabelle, searching for the wine, moved to the settee, where a half bottle of gin was peeping out from behind a cushion, and Bessy brought her narrative to a rapid close to make a quick getaway.

"Then, after it got dark, we lit this huge bonfire and we all conjugated round it," she said.

Ivy gasped. Annabelle fell back on the settee, her head back, her arms waving and her legs in the air.

"Whaw!" she shrieked. "That must have been a sight! Whaw! I'd have loved to have been there to see that! Everyone having a f★★★ing good time around the bonfire! Whaw!"

Bessy turned puce with embarrassment and quickly ushered Ivy to the door. "Well!" she said, as they reached the gate. "Well, really!" Her face still looked shocked.

Ivy had a very serious look on her face, too. How she managed it, she didn't know. It took every ounce of her will power. She dare not open her mouth. "Mm," was all she could manage – her stomach muscles were going into convulsions.

"There was no call for language like that, was there Ivy?"

Ivy shook her head.

"Even though she's abbreviated! That's no excuse."

Ivy nodded, several times.

"A fine example of the articrocity, she is! I'm glad I'm not one of them, if that's how they behave."

When Ivy finally reached home, jug in tow, she related it

all to Jim. Laughter can be quite painful at times. They both had to hold their aching sides for quite a while.

CHAPTER 88

A Terrible Accident

AT THE BEGINNING of the summer holidays, Wendy Williams' cousin from Scotland came to stay with her – for good. Alec Mcgrath had been orphaned, aged just eleven. His father, a bomber pilot, had been shot down a year previously and recently, his mother, a sister to Wendy's mother, had died of cancer. Mrs Williams, being his only living relative, had immediately insisted on bringing him home with her after the funeral. "*Chwarae-teg,*" (fair play) said the villagers when word got around, their estimation of her going up overnight.

Within a few days of his arrival at Wendy's, most of the children were aware of his circumstances and it wasn't long before they sought him out and included him in their games – partly due to compassion, but mainly out of curiosity. They had a subconscious need to find out how anyone could cope with this, their ultimate fear, and maybe learn from it. Just in case.

Alec was well used to mountains and could climb, run and leap with the rest of them. His accent was a bit difficult to understand at first, but they soon got used to it and his new-found friends enjoyed mimicking it. Alec, taking it all in good part, returned the teasing by mimicking the Welsh accent.

The last days of the summer holidays found all the boys, as usual, up the mountain. The short grass, regularly trimmed by the sheep, had dried in the sun and was now quite slippery.

So, with sections of cardboard boxes under their armpits, they climbed to the top and looked for a boulder-free run to slide down. Finding a suitable one, they sat on their cardboard with feet tucked in or held aloft, hands gripping tightly to the front edge, and they were off, careering down the hill at a speed which increased with each consecutive run as the polished grass flattened.

A few hours at this game and they had tired of the long haul back to the top. Too much climb, not enough slide, they decided. Time to move on and find another adventure, another thrill. They wandered along the sheep paths discussing and arguing over what to do next, not noticing where they were going, till they found themselves near an old, disused quarry, overlooking lower Crymceynon. This whole area was considered out of bounds to the younger boys and Heaven help you if your father found you had been playing there! Just being there was a daring adventure in itself.

A huge rowan tree grew a few yards in from the quarry edge and at the beginning of the summer, while the youngsters were still at school, some of the older youths had attached a long, strong, colliery rope to one of its thicker branches. Pulling the rope backwards up the slope behind them, they had run down towards the quarry and leapt off, swinging outwards in an arc over the abyss. The exhilaration of this highly dangerous game was more-ish and had become increasingly addictive with each perilous leap. They had spent a large part of the hot, dry summer up there until they had worked it out of their systems. Their parents knew nothing of the rope's existence and none of the boys had thought to remove it when they left. Now, the younger boys had found it.

It didn't take them long to find out its purpose. Timid at

first to actually fly off the edge, they gradually became more confident, daring each other, trying to beat each other – boys being boys.

Alec's first attempts weren't very impressive, but watching and learning and being encouraged by the others, he soon got the knack and flew like a bird. This time would be his best so far. Walking back as far as the rope would allow, he held it in one hand while he rubbed his free hand down his trousers, then swapped hands and did the same to get rid of any trace of sweat and get a better grip. All eyes were on him. A big breath and he was off, running like the wind down the slope and mentally preparing for this huge leap into space. Just as his feet left the ground, the branch snapped and the sudden jarring loosened his grip on the rope. To the horror of the rest of the group, he teetered and fell over the edge, bouncing on the jutting-out rocks to the bottom, where he lay bloodied and motionless, like a rag doll.

Petrified, the gang stood frozen, peering over the edge, then turned and ran like stampeding animals back to their houses. Brian Pierce and David Roberts shouted to each other as they ran. They would bring back towels or pillow slips or something that they could use for bandages, to stop the blood, to make him better. At that moment, they had complete blind faith in their ability to do that. It was practical thinking for a ten and a fourteen year old, but it was also wishful thinking over-riding the reality.

They ran into Vera's and went straight up the stairs, crashed through a few drawers, then ran down again and away. Vera ran after them and shouted for a while, but to no avail. They were deaf to her screeches. They ran down the canal bank to Lower Crymceynon to get to the bottom of the quarry.

By the time they got there, Alec was being lifted into an

ambulance on a stretcher, the whole of his body covered by a red blanket. A crowd had gathered. The boys dropped the linen and stared. They knew he was dead.

That night, the huge rowan tree was mysteriously chopped down. No-one seemed to know who had done it.

Chapter 89

Getting Things Ready Again

Liz had passed her exams and was out shopping with her mother, getting the last items of her uniform. For hours now, it seemed, they had been searching everywhere for a cookery overall. Ivy was worn out.

"Oh come on, Liz," she said, "we can get that again. There's no hurry for it."

Liz's face started to crumple. "But what if we can't get it next week? I'll be the only one without it!"

"Oh alright!" said Ivy, through clenched teeth. "We'll try another two shops but then it's definitely home!"

She had housework to catch up with on Saturdays. She was at her wits' end getting Liz sorted. She didn't remember having all this bother with Pauline. The gymslip was picky and made her itch, the elastic in her navy knickers wasn't tight enough and those long, black stockings... well, she would just have to get used to them, that's all. Just wait till she was old enough to wear a brassiere! Shopping for those would be a whole barrel of laughs – Ivy didn't think!

The very last shop in town, thank goodness, had an overall. A bit on the big side, but if Ivy offered to have Glyn for an hour or two, Vera would work wonders on it for her. Phew! Time to go home.

Coming out of the shop, Liz spotted a girl about her own age with her hair done in a page-boy style. She liked that. That was what she would do to her hair for her first day at her new school. Gran had some Dinkie curlers – little metal slats that held the hair in place while you rolled it up, then fastened it securely with a tiny metal band that slid over the open ends. She would ask Gran for some on the way home.

On Sunday evening, bathed and in pyjamas and dressing gown, Liz sat on the bed in her mother's bedroom in front of the dressing-table mirror to put in her curlers. She had borrowed three. That would be enough – one for each side and one for the back. Half an hour later, when they were in place, her mother called her. Brian Pierce was at the door.

"Hiya, Liz! All ready for tomorrow?" he asked.

"Yeah. I've just been doing my hair."

"I can see that!" Brian laughed.

Liz hit him.

"I, er, I just came over to wish you good luck. I hope you're going to like it there."

"Thanks. So do I. I hope you like Central School, too."

"Aye, mm, ta."

Brian didn't sound very enthusiastic at the prospect. He wasn't fussed with school and couldn't wait to be old enough to leave. Another four to five years or so till he would be free of it; free to work underground with his father.

"I won't be calling for you for school anymore, now then," he said. "You'll be off early. No-one else going from up here, is there?"

"No, only Pauline and Michael. Oh, and Sylvia Mitchell from the Catholic school. She's passed. You know, she lives in the big house up by the farm. So I'll meet her on the train tomorrow, I expect."

"Ooo! The colliery manager's daughter, eh? Going up in the world, now then! You won't want to be friends with the likes of us anymore!"

"Don't be daft," said Liz. "There's still the weekends. Who else am I going to play marbles with? And beat!"

"Beat? How come I won your best taw off you last time, then?"

"You cheated!"

Brian scowled.

"No I didn't!" he exclaimed, with hurt pride.

"Only joking," Liz consoled him.

"You better be!" he grinned. "Right, then. Better go. All the best for tomorrow!"

He stepped up on the doorstep and plonked a kiss on her cheek before running into the road and shouting, "You missed three hairs in that curler at the back, Liz!"

CHAPTER 90

A Bath of Sweat

LIZ WAS UP and dressed and fidgeting. The shoulders of her gymslip kept slipping out of place. She had tied and re-tied the girdle tightly to try to prevent this and it now looked more like a piece of old rope than a girdle. Ivy, watching her, gave up in despair. At least her hair looked quite nice, she thought; it was combed out and formed a tight, neat and even roll.

Every few minutes, Liz stood before the oval dresser-mirror to see the back of her head reflected in the oak-framed one over the mantelpiece. As she moved her head from side to side, her hair swung slightly but fell neatly back into place. Oh yes, she was very pleased with the result. Very satisfactory. And no clips, slides or ribbons to bother about. One small snag though: she had tried her beret on several times but had only to move her head the slightest bit for it to slip sideways. It will spend more time in her satchel, thought Ivy, than on her head.

Now it was the long black stockings that were again worrying Ivy. They will want darning tonight; you can guarantee it, the way she keeps tugging at them. Liz then put the new leather satchel that Jim had somehow managed to get, onto her shoulder and walked about a bit. Ivy watched. She was going to start whingeing, she knew it.

"It's too long, Mammy."

There, she was right!

"Well. There's nothing I can do about that, Liz, the strap is in the last hole. I can't shorten it any more."

"But it's banging my knees when I walk."

Ivy's blood pressure was mounting.

"Daddy will fix it for you tonight. Don't worry."

Jim was on days – never the right shift in a crisis. And she could feel one developing. Liz's face was crumpling.

"Oh, give it here!" said her mother, shortly.

It took nearly quarter of an hour of precious time to find a sharp nail and a hammer to make another hole in the strap by placing it between two flag-stones in the yard, standing on it to hold it taut and hammering the nail through the leather into the earthy gap between them. Why did Liz have to leave every damn thing till the very last minute? By the time Michael Richards called for them and she had kissed her two daughters 'so-long', watching with pride till they were out of sight round the corner of the street, Ivy was a bath of sweat.

The three children got to the station, meeting Sylvia on the way, just in time for the train. From then on, Liz's first day turned out to be a complete and utter disaster.

CHAPTER 91

Birdy Catches Liz

ON THE LONG walk down to the railway station, Pauline and Michael reminisced about the time they had turned the bluebells pink, trying to keep Liz's mind off her nervous fidgeting. It seemed to work.

"Vincent Griffis said the ants had pee-ed all over them, when I showed them to him. That's how they'd gone pink," Liz said.

"Ha, he would!" said Michael. Trust Vincent to have hit the nail on the head through pure guess work, he thought. He wasn't having that. Trying to impress Liz (and Pauline) with his superior knowledge, he explained: "Bluebells are plant indicators, like litmus, which is made from lichen. You've seen that growing on rocks and boulders and trees and things. The ants spray the flower heads with formic, or um, urea acid," – I think, he thought to himself, not enlightening Liz to the fact that urea acid was in fact, pee. He wasn't going to give Vincent Griffiths any credibility, if he could help it. Continuing to baffle Liz with science, Michael went on: "You see, blue turns pink when exposed to acid and pink turns blue when exposed to alkali."

Liz was very impressed. "How do you know all that?" she asked.

"I do chemistry," said Michael, smugly. Tell that to Vincent Griffiths! It was during a lesson about chemical reactions that Michael had mentioned the bluebell phenomena to his teacher and had found out, at last, what had caused it.

"Do you do chemistry, Pauline?" Liz asked. She hadn't heard her sister mention it.

"No, cookery. There's a choice with some of the subjects."

Liz liked the sound of chemistry. It seemed very interesting.

The train pulled in and they all got on. Two minutes later, Liz was standing by the open window. She was excited by the whole prospect of this first day. To begin with, she hadn't been on a train that many times – never without her mother telling her to sit down, and never up this way. Holding her beret on with her hand, she stuck her head out of the window, trying to see the engine as it went round a bend, her hair blowing straight again in the damp, September air. As the train turned, with clouds of steam blowing back and engulfing her, a piece of grit got lodged in her eye. Instinctively taking her hand away from the beret in order to rub the instant pain, it slid off onto the track.

"Liz!" yelled Pauline, "I told you, didn't I? Serves you right! You'll cop it now if Birdy spots you!"

Liz, still rubbing her eye and starting to cry, asked apprehensively, "Who's Birdy?"

"The headmistress, Miss Finch. She's a stickler for correct uniform at all times. 'We are the representatives of the school and our behaviour reflects on its reputation'," Pauline quoted in a high and squeaky voice. "You'd better be very careful going up the drive, her window overlooks it and she's always there as we go in and out. If she spots you without your beret, you've had it!"

Liz sat down dejectedly, her hair limp and wispy, her eye

smarting and her stomach churning. She wished she was in Central School with Brian and Wendy.

They reached the school gates and Pauline gave some last instructions to Liz before parting. "Don't hang around when the bell for home time goes, Liz. Our bus is the first to come in. It will be there waiting at the bottom of the drive."

"Alright."

Her eye was feeling worse, but she had to concentrate now, to get her bearings in these new surroundings. She and Sylvia went to assembly together, each one knowing no-one else, and then to their form room to get their time-tables sorted out.

"Art or music?" asked their form mistress, Miss Morrison. "Hands up those who wish to take art, first."

Liz put her hand up. She liked drawing but had no experience whatsoever with musical instruments.

"Chemistry or cookery? Hands up for chemistry, first."

Before she realised it, Liz's hand had gone up. Then she remembered the cookery overall. Her mother would not be best pleased about that! But there was no going back now – she would look an idiot that didn't know her own mind in front of this classroom of strangers. Her eye suddenly felt much worse.

By break time, she was in agony and Sylvia took it upon herself to report it to the teacher, Liz being in tears by now and the eye red and swollen with the constant rubbing. The teacher examined it but could find nothing. "It's trapped beneath the eyelid, I expect. How did it happen?"

Liz, praying that Sylvia would keep her mouth shut (she was in enough trouble as it was), said, "I don't know, Miss."

"Mm. I think the best thing for you to do, would be to

take her to the optician's, down in the main street," she said to Sylvia, "and for you, Liz, to refrain from looking out of train windows, when the trains are in motion!" She had guessed but she had smiled. Liz liked Miss Morrison.

The optician rolled back the eyelid and removed the grit before Liz had time to get scared. The relief was wonderful, the pain all gone, and the rest of the day passed surprisingly pleasantly. That is, until the bell went for home time.

Liz, remembering Pauline's words about their bus home being the first to arrive, grabbed her burberry and satchel and ran down the drive. Sylvia's father was picking her up in the car and she had offered Liz a lift. But she had refused, saying her sister would be worried as to where she was. If only she had accepted! She had totally forgotten the rest of Pauline's advice – that Birdy would be watching, like a hawk, as they all went in and out. She was spotted.

Miss Finch rapped rapidly on her window with her bony knuckles and, when heads turned in her direction, motioned that she wanted 'that girl, there, to report to her office, immediately!' Liz didn't know whether to obey or make a run for it. She decided the former to be the lesser of the two evils and reluctantly turned back.

"Young ladies do not run like young colts down the school drive," Miss Finch stated, when Liz stood forlornly in front of her.

"No, Miss."

"They walk, with dignity and decorum."

"Yes, Miss."

"This is your first day, isn't it? And this is not a good beginning, is it?"

"No, Miss."

"We begin here as we mean to go on. See that you remember that in future."

Looking suitably contrite, Liz replied: "Yes, Miss. Sorry, Miss."

"Very well. You may go."

"Thank you, Miss."

Liz reached the door, very worried now about her bus.

"Just a minute, young lady!"

Oh heck, no!

"Where is your beret?"

"I lost it, Miss."

"You lost it. How, might I ask?"

Liz sighed. "On the train, Miss."

"And how did that happen?"

Liz couldn't think of an excuse. Her thoughts were totally wrapped up in thinking about how and if she would get home today. She had to get out from here as quickly as possible. She blurted out, to get it over and done with: "I was looking out of the window, Miss, and it blew off on the track."

There. Now kill me!

"Are you a budding hooligan?"

"No, Miss!" Liz was shocked. Of course she wasn't!

"Only hooligans hang out of train windows."

She wasn't 'hanging out', she was looking out, but she dutifully hung her head in shame.

"Yes, Miss."

"And what will your mother have to say about this?"

Plenty, thought Liz.

"Berets cost money, you know, and coupons. Or didn't you realise that?"

"No, Miss, um, yes, Miss." Three bags full, Miss. She'd be here for hours!

Miss Finch got up from her chair and turned to a large cupboard behind her. Opening it, she took out a Deanna Durbin style school hat, the type that had been worn in pre-war years.

"You will wear this until such time as your mother can replace your beret. Then you will return it to me in this condition. Do you understand?"

"Yes, Miss."

Liz's face fell. She would be the only one in the whole school with a hat like that, you could bet on it. She would stick out like a sore thumb. Oh joys!

Five minutes later, Liz walked slowly and sedately down the drive, desperate to run but afraid of being called back again. Once out of view of the window, she risked it. There was the bus, at the bottom of the drive. She ran and jumped on.

When the conductor came to check her season ticket, he said, "You're on the wrong bus, love. You want the one that goes down the valley. This one goes up."

She had no idea where she was or where she was going and she had no money to get back. Panic set in. She was on the verge of tears.

"I'll put you off here, love," said the conductor. "You need a twenty three bus. It should be along in about ten minutes. The bus stop is there look, on the other side of the road."

She was totally lost and disorientated. There was nothing anywhere that she could recognise. She had never been in this area before. The tears began to fall.

Another girl, who had got off the bus at the same time,

came up to her and asked, "Are you alright?"

Liz shook her head. The girl had the same uniform on and Liz had seen her in school, in her form.

"No. I got on the wrong bus," she said between sobs, "and I'm lost. I don't know where I am."

"Where are you from?" asked the girl.

"Crymceynon."

"Oh, I know where that is! My auntie lives there, over-the-other-side. Your bus won't be long. I'll stay with you till it comes, if you like."

"But I haven't got any money," said Liz, frantically searching her pockets for her hanky, to wipe her eyes and her running nose.

"Don't worry. I can lend you some." The girl handed her a shilling piece. "You can give it back to me tomorrow. I'm in your form. My name's Ann Jones."

"Thanks. I won't forget. I'm Liz Edwards."

"Look! Here's your bus. See you tomorrow then, Liz. Bye!"

Liz got on board, turned and waved, smiling again.

"Bye, Ann!"

When Pauline arrived home with no Liz, Ivy was beside herself with worry. Jim was up the allotments, never there when she needed him.

"Where is she? Why didn't you wait for her?" she demanded of Pauline. "You know it's her first day. She doesn't know her way around yet or anything!"

"Mam, I didn't even know she wasn't on the bus till I got off," said Pauline defensively. She didn't see it fair that she should be getting the blame. "She lost her beret and…"

"What? How did she do that?"

"Looking out of the window on the train. She's probably got detention and will be on the next bus."

"And where were you, to let her do that?"

"Mam, you know she won't listen to me!"

Ivy looked at the clock. The next bus was due around now and it was getting dark.

"Go and fetch your father!" she said. He would have to go and meet the bus. Liz wouldn't know the way from there, either.

Liz sat in the bus by the window, so that she could keep a look-out for the Cross Keys pub, the place where Pauline had said to get off, worrying all the time that perhaps they had passed it.

"Cross Keys!" shouted the conductor, pressing the bell.

At last! She got off and looked around for the Wendy Youth Club that her sister and Michael had joined in the summer holidays of their first year. It was a little wooden building, not much bigger than a hut, perched on the slope down to the river and not very far from the pub, Pauline had said. Where was it? She crossed the main road and looked over the railings. Yes! There was the river on her right, way below her, and on the left, a path leading down to it. By the side of the path was the Wendy. And there, up on the main road at the bottom of the mountain, St Mark's. She had her bearings at last. Relief swept over her and she quickened her pace. It was getting dark and she had a long way to go yet.

When she was halfway down the path, it began to rain. Now she had that damned hat to worry about. If the felt got wet, it would go out of shape. She stopped, opened her satchel and put it carefully inside. The rain came down faster and she ran faster, mud from the path splashing up over her shoes and stockings, her satchel bumping her hip at every step. In no time, she had passed 'Gilbert's Ducks', crossed the river, climbed the hillside and trotted over the railway bridge.

As she reached the slope up to the stile, she slowed her pace, not through tiredness but apprehension. She was running from trouble into trouble, heading for another row, she knew. Both her parents would be worried, and therefore cross, at her being so late. Then, after that was over, there was the small matter of the missing beret – not to mention the now redundant cookery overall. She didn't know which row she dreaded the most. She bet that Brian and Wendy had enjoyed their first day at the Central. When she came to think about it, Moonface hadn't done her any favours!

As Liz was crossing the stile, Jim was crossing the field. Though it was dark now, she recognised him instantly and ran, clutching her satchel in her arms. Her wails reached him before she did and he held out his arms and scooped her up.

"Ah, there she is, our little cockleorum!" said Carrie, who had come over to hear all about her first day. Liz, dripping like a drowned rat, made a bee-line for the safe haven of her lap. From that vantage point, she could safely relate all that had happened. Gran took off her wet Burberry and Ivy got her hot meal out of the top oven. Liz, in her account of the day's events, conveniently forgot to mention the cookery overall. Sufficient unto the day…

As she scoffed her food, her mother combed and stroked her hair. The reception she had expected hadn't materialised. She relaxed, and with her tummy full and her mother smiling at her, she left the table and climbed again into Carrie's lap.

"You're home safe now, pickle," said Carrie, soothingly, "and you coped with it all, didn't you? All's well that ends well, eh? The way I look at it is this: things couldn't have got much worse for you, could they, on your first day? So, they can only get better! You'll see. And you've made a new friend already."

She fished in her pinny pocket and handed Liz a shilling.

"Put this safe in your pocket now, ready for tomorrow, in case you forget it. And I bought you this bar of chocolate as a treat, but I think it would be nice if you gave that to Ann too, as a thank you, don't you?"

"You can have half of mine," piped up Pauline, generously.

It was nice being back home, thought Liz, cwtching closer into Gran's comfy pillow of a bosom. Gran was wise. She knew what to do about everything. Liz was asleep in five minutes flat.

Grampa and Jack Jones came into Ivy's kitchen. Carrie put her finger to her lips and said, "Sh, don't wake her."

Grampa had a beret in his hand. A ganger 'walking the length' had found it on the track by the railway bridge and handed it to Jack, knowing his best mate's grandchildren went to that school. They put it on top of Liz's satchel on the table. When Liz woke up, it was the first thing she saw. Magic!

CHAPTER 92

The Job

WITH LIZ AND Pauline in grammar school and out for the best part of each day, Ivy found she had a lot more time on her hands. Taking baby Glyn for a long walk in his pram, she paused by Powell's the paper shop to read the cards in the window advertising things for sale. She had found a few bargains there, and it was nice to have time to browse. She had bought a lovely little dressing table and wash stand for Pauline's bedroom last year and a bike the year before that for the girls for Christmas. Jim had done it up like new. Oh, and another time she had bought a steel meat mincer, boiling it in a bucket before using it, to kill any germs. She had borrowed her mother's up until then but her mother 'got her hair off' if it wasn't returned promptly. Mm, there was nothing of interest there today. She entered the shop, bought a copy of the *Western Mail* and made her way home again. Glyn was sleeping fast. She would take him home when he woke for his feed.

She made herself a cup of Camp coffee, a poor substitute for the real thing she had been used to in service, and more suitable for flavouring cakes than drinking, but she'd got used to it now. She sat by the table and opened the paper. It was nice to have some space in the day to herself. She'd read most of it and was on her second cup of coffee and still Glyn slept. She turned the page. Job vacancies. One stood out: a cook wanted in the canteen for school dinners – locally, in the infant and junior schools. She wouldn't mind applying for that. The hours were from 8 am till 2 pm. That would fit in with all Jim's shifts. He wouldn't be keen, though. He was a firm believer in men being the bread winners and a woman's place being in the home.

Ivy took down the details. She would apply without telling him. She doubted very much if she would get it, anyway, so why start an argument unnecessarily? And if she did get it, well, she would cross that bridge when she came to it.

The following Monday, she walked to Lower Crymceynon, going over what she would say during her interview. As she was about to enter the door of the council offices, Madge's husband, County Councillor Lloyd, was coming out and almost collided with her.

"Oops! I'm so sorry!" he said. "Er, it's Ivy, isn't it? Carrie Thomas' daughter?"

Ivy nodded and he smiled.

"Ah, I thought it was! Your mother and my wife are neighbours and big pals!"

If that's what you think, then who am I to disillusion you, she thought.

"Er, what brings you here? Anything I can help you with?"

Ivy had a quick answer for most things in most circumstances but she was no good at lying. Her father had always told them when they were young that "a liar has to have a good memory. Speak the truth and shame the devil." Besides, why did people call to council offices? She couldn't think of any reason there and then, apart from the truth.

"I'm here for the interview for the post of cook in the infant and junior schools."

"Ah, yes. Nice little job, that. Have you got any experience?"

Ivy mentioned her years in service at the Goldberg's.

"That's very impressive. I shouldn't think you'd have much competition there." He turned to re-enter the building. "I'll see what I can do."

"Oh, thank you, Mr Lloyd."

Ivy got the job – on her own merit, she liked to think. She wouldn't mention her meeting with the county councillor to her mother and she hoped he would keep his mouth shut, too. He seemed a decent bloke. Carrie wouldn't like to think she was indebted to Madge in any way. All she had to do now was tell Jim she was starting work next Monday. She wasn't prepared for his response.

"Good for you, gel," he said. If Ivy was happy, he was happy and they might just settle here for quite a while, at least until the girls finished their education.. He'd like that. Besides, the extra money wouldn't go amiss and lots of married women worked these days. There was no shame in that.

CHAPTER 93

Two Choices

IT WAS FRIDAY and Jim was late coming home from work. He wasn't there when Ivy got home from her job. He usually was and had the table laid ready for them both. She hoped the rent man hadn't called while they were both out. She didn't like being in arrears with anything. Jim was probably standing talking to one of his mates about something. Ah, there was the rent man now. She knew his knock.

"Come in, the door's open," she shouted, taking the money and the rent book from the dresser drawer.

He put the money in a little draw-string bag and signed the book. Picking up the book and replacing it in the drawer, she said, "Thanks. See you next Friday, then," as she always did. But instead of making his way out, he waited.

"I'm afraid next week may be my last call here, Mrs Edwards," he said.

"Oh, I'm sorry to hear that. Why?"

"Your house is going up for sale."

"Up for sale? Why? We've always paid our rent on time, we've never kept him waiting!"

"No, no. It isn't that. The owner is selling up to move back to Ireland. His health is failing."

"Oh, dear!" She pulled out a kitchen chair and sat down, stunned by this bombshell of news.

"Selling up," she repeated quietly. "Where will we go

now? Are there any houses that you know of going for rent in this area?"

He shook his head.

"You won't have to move straight away, though. I should imagine you'll have a good few weeks to look around for one. What about going in for it yourself? You might get it a bit cheaper, being a sitting tenant. And he wants a quick sale, which would be another thing in your favour. Would you be interested?"

A few years down the line, maybe, thought Ivy, but at the moment they stood no chance.

"How much is he asking for it? Do you know?"

The rent man shrugged his shoulders.

"About three hundred, maybe a bit more, I should think, going by my experience."

The most Ivy and Jim could lay their hands on would be about a hundred pounds. And the bank wouldn't lend the rest to them – not without collateral.

The rent man left, leaving Ivy worried. Moving house – again. She suddenly realised that she really didn't want to go. She was happy in the village, really happy. Her girls were happy, Jim was happy. Why did this have to happen now?

Jim still hadn't come home. He was only about twenty minutes late but she needed to talk to someone now. She went down to Vera's to tell her about it.

"Moving? Oh, no! Oh, Ivy, you can't. Please don't go."

"We'll have to. We have no choice, Vee."

"But the girls are settled and everything. You can't uproot them now. And you and Jim love it here. I know you do, it's obvious."

Ivy shrugged, sad at the thought of it all.

"You buy it!" said Vera suddenly.

Ivy laughed derisively.

"With what? Monopoly money?"

"No, with my money! I'll lend it to you. It's just sitting there in the bank doing nothing."

"Oh, Vera, we couldn't, we couldn't do that, love, but thank you all the same. You never know what might happen when money is involved between friends. Your friendship is more important than that to us."

"Oh, for goodness sake, don't be so daft. We'll see a solicitor, the one who read my father's will, and get it all sorted on a legitimate, professional basis. I'll even charge you interest at the same rate as the bank. Oh Ivy, say yes, please!"

Ivy was tempted, very tempted.

"We'll have to see what Jim says."

"How much is the owner asking for it?"

"The rent man said about three hundred to three hundred and twenty-five, but we might get it a bit cheaper because we already live there and he wants it all sorted as soon as possible."

"Well, there you are then. Go for it, Ive!"

"We've got about a hundred saved, I think, for the proverbial rainy day, so we wouldn't have to borrow it all."

The more they talked the more they both saw it as a solution.

"Well, your rainy day is here now and you can pay me back with your wages every week. You won't miss them because, knowing you, you've been putting them away too for a rainy day, haven't you? Better for me and better for you. It will come down in no time, Ive. Two, maybe three years and the house will be yours. Go on, go and talk it over with

Jim. I'll call up this evening."

Ivy had forgotten all about Jim and his dinner. It would be spoiled.

He must have reached home just before she did. He was in the middle of taking his jacket off.

"Sorry I'm late, gel. I had to go over-the-other-side about something important. I've got some news for you." He winked and grinned.

"Jim, I've got news too, important news. Sit down, I'll get your dinner."

Damn, has she heard it already then, thought Jim? Well, she couldn't know where he had been. He'd get in first.

"Guess what I heard today, gel? The council is only going to build a new estate down by the park!"

There was no reaction. She must have heard.

"That's where I've been, that's why I'm late. I've been straight over there to put our names down. We are pretty near the top of the list. We should be one of the first to move in there. In about a year's time, I expect!"

She would be pleased about that. Ivy pulled out a chair and sat opposite him, her expression puzzling him.

"Well, you can take it off again," she said quietly.

"Take it off? I thought you would be pleased. I thought it was what you always wanted – a bathroom, constant hot water, no more black-leading…"

"Well, I don't want it. I want to stay here, in this house, in this street, in this part of the village, near my parents and Vera and the baby and my friends and neighbours. I want us to stay in this house, Jim and I don't want to pay any more rent."

He misunderstood what she had said.

"But the rent wouldn't be much more, gel. We managed

last time didn't we? And we can afford it easily with two wages coming in now."

"That's not what I meant. The rent man says this house is going up for sale next week and I want us to buy it."

She told him all that she had discussed with Vera and the solution they had come up with. He sat in his collier's dirt and listened and thought, his dinner going cold. Finally, he said, "Are you sure this is what you want, gel?"

She nodded. "I've never been more sure."

"We would have to do things properly, everything above board, sign papers and things. Money can cause trouble between people, mind, Ive."

"It's Vera we're dealing with Jim. Can you see us ever falling out with her?"

He shook his head. "Well, if that's what you want!"

"It is.

"Well in that case, gel," he said, clasping her round the waist and swinging her to her feet, "we'll become property owners! Us! Members of the *crachach*! Hey, we could be called on for jury service, have you thought about that?"

They both burst out laughing at the prospect. Suddenly, Jim was serious.

"I promise you gel, I will turn this into a little palace for us, eventually. I've got good mates and we'll all get stuck in. What I can't do, I will learn to do. You just wait!"

Ivy was fully prepared to wait this time. She definitely had no inclination to run.

CHAPTER 94

The Future

THE WEATHERWAS STILL lovely for the end of October. Albert, taking the baby in the pram for a long, slow walk up the canal bank, felt his senses waking to the environment as he drank in the clean, fresh air with sounds, sights and smells seeping into him. He knew he was as close to contentment as he would ever be, but worry and anxiety were still hidden away gnawing now and then on his gut. It would always be there but that terrible feeling of impotence and anger was gradually fading, with an immense sorrow taking its place. Life was, could be and should be good. It was people who ruined it. Why they did so was a question he had been continually asking himself since 1914. He had never found an answer. He knew he never would.

The trees were turning; it would soon be winter again. The years came and the years went. Did they have good years in front of them now, he wondered? The whole world had been through enough suffering, surely. Had humanity learned anything from it? Now that those awesome, horrific bombs had been dropped on Japan, would that be an end of man's inhumanity to man? Or would they be used again in the near future? Who could tell? Once a thing had been invented, it couldn't be un-invented. Pandora's Box had been opened now, right enough. It had taken the edge off the relief that everyone felt at the war ending. Or could it be the turning point? According to the legend, hope was left in the bottom of the box. His hope was that people would come to their senses and realise now that war must end throughout the world. They must find another way or the world itself would end.

Albert sighed deeply, looking at little Glyn. What sort of life lay in store for him, he wondered? His spirits rose a little – things would change. They would have to. Bit by bit, change would come. It would start slowly and gradually build up. He unbuckled Glyn from his pram and set him down on the dry grass on the edge of the big field, kneeling beside him and gently parting the grass to draw the baby's attention to the flowers and insects that lived there. It was foolish to waste precious times like these worrying about what might be, he concluded. Some things remain constant in life, don't they? The important things.

Life here in the valleys hadn't changed much over the years. It would be a long time probably – and hopefully, in some ways – before it did. It wasn't a bad life here in this little village taking everything into consideration, or a bad place to live. There were many worse, God knows.

Little did Albert know, as he played with his grandson, that change was already on the doorstep and knocking loudly at the door. Life in the village would never be the same again. It was going for good – or bad.

The end.

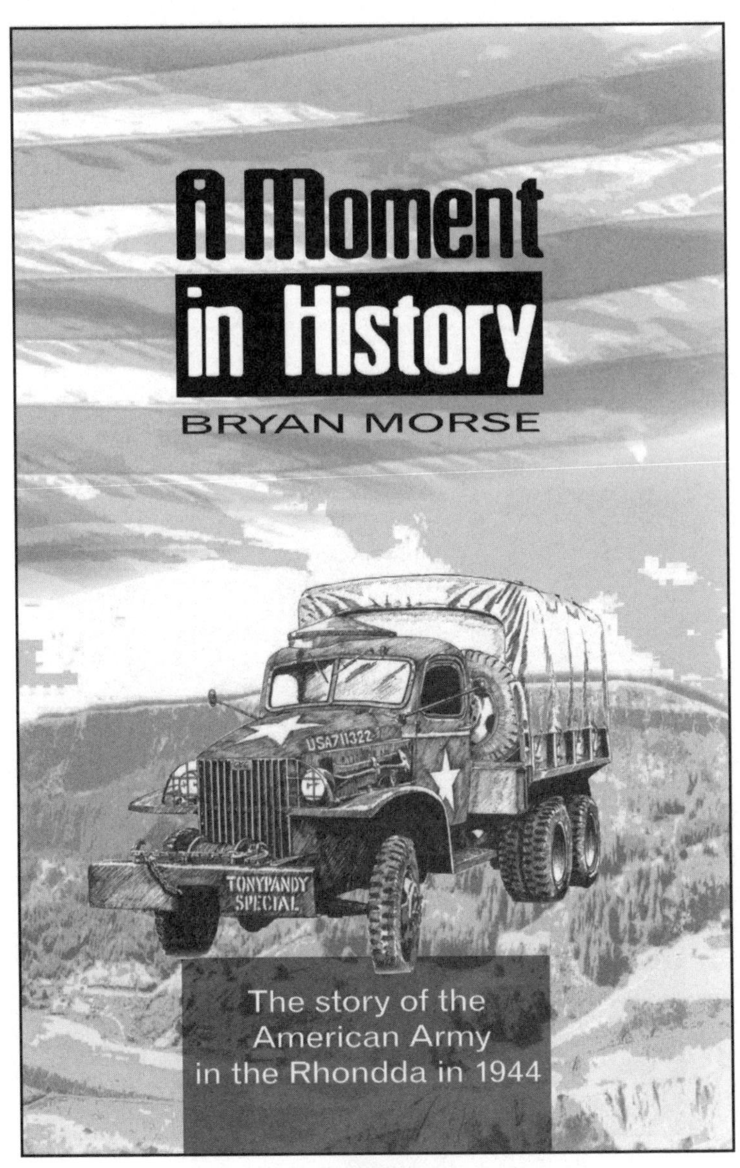
A Moment
in History
BRYAN MORSE
USA711322
TONYPANDY
SPECIAL
The story of the
American Army
in the Rhondda in 1944

£9.95